Simon Beckett

FINE LINES

A Novel

SIMON &

SCHUSTER

New York

London

Toronto

Sydney

Tokyo

Singapore

SIMON & SCHUSTER
ROCKEFELLER CENTER
1230 AVENUE OF THE AMERICAS
NEW YORK, NEW YORK 10020

SIMON & SCHUSTER AND COLOPHON ARE REGISTERED
TRADEMARKS OF SIMON & SCHUSTER INC.

DESIGNED BY PEI LOI KOAY
MANUFACTURED IN THE UNITED STATES OF AMERICA

1 2 3 4 5 6 7 8 9 10

LIBRARY OF CONGRESS CATALOGING-IN-PUBLICATION DATA
BECKETT, SIMON.
FINE LINES : A NOVEL / SIMON BECKETT.
P. CM.
I. TITLE.
PS3552.E276F56 1994
813'.54—DC20   94-13613
CIP

ISBN: 0-671-89206-1

To Hilary

And Mom and Dad

Chapter

1

Anna and Marty were very obviously in love, and when I decided to end their relationship I knew I would need help. I had neither the skill nor the experience necessary to attempt such a task on my own.

Fortunately, I knew someone much better qualified.

Zeppo did not remember me when I telephoned, which was not altogether surprising. We had met, but only twice, and I am not the sort of man who makes a lasting impression. Zeppo, however, was quite the opposite.

London was dismal and drizzly as I closed the gallery and drove to the West End restaurant where we had arranged to meet. He was late, and I had turned the waiter away for a second time before Zeppo finally arrived. I signaled to him and he strolled over, apparently unaware of the looks he received from the other diners. But he walked just a little too slowly and a little too deliberately to be entirely unconscious of them.

He greeted me pleasantly enough but made no apology for his lateness. I chose not to mention it.

"You're looking very tanned," I said. "Have you been away?"

"I've just got back from Italy." His eyes strayed around the room as he spoke. Checking his audience, I thought.

"Work or pleasure?"

"A bit of both. I was over there on a shoot, but I managed to slot some skiing in as well." He grinned. "You've got to, really, haven't you?"

"I take it the modeling's going well, then?"

"It pays the rent. And it beats working for a living. How's the art business?"

"Oh, hectic as ever."

The waiter appeared and handed him a menu. I ordered a wine I thought should be expensive enough to impress. "So. You said you'd got a business proposition," Zeppo said, once the waiter had gone.

I had hoped to wait a little longer before broaching it. "Why don't we discuss it over the meal? There's no rush, is there?"

He shrugged. "I'm just curious to know what it is, that's all."

I opened my menu. "Shall we at least order first?"

"I'd rather you tell me now, if you don't mind. Put me out of my suspense." He gave me a rather flat smile. Reluctantly, I closed the menu again.

"As you like." I made a minute adjustment to my cutlery. "The thing is, I . . . ah, want to hire your services." From the look on his face I realized he was jumping to the wrong conclusion. "It concerns a girl," I added hurriedly.

"A girl?" He seemed amused by my awkwardness.

"Yes." I felt a tickle in my throat and coughed to clear it. "My assistant. At the gallery. It's, ah . . . well, it's a rather difficult situation, actually." I cleared my throat again, conscious of Zeppo's faintly condescending smile. There was no easy way to say it. I plunged on.

"I want you to seduce her."

Whatever he had been expecting, it was not that. His amusement vanished. "You what?"

"I want you to seduce her." I felt my face burning. Although, from what I knew of Zeppo, I had no cause to be embarrassed.

He was about to speak when the waiter reappeared. I sampled the wine and pronounced it acceptable without tasting it. Zeppo waited until he left, then leaned forward.

"Is this a joke? Has someone put you up to this?"

"Oh no." I shook my head emphatically to convince him. "No, it's no joke."

He stared at me. "Let's get this straight. That's the 'business proposition' you said you'd got? You want to hire me to sleep with someone?"

I looked around to make sure no one could hear. "Ah . . . yes, that's right."

"Christ!"

"I'm prepared to pay well."

"How well?" I told him. He looked surprised. "You'd give all that, just for me to go to bed with this girl?" I nodded. "Why?"

I attempted a shrug. "Let's just say I disapprove of her current boyfriend."

"And that's it?"

"Well . . . yes."

He gave a stunned laugh. "I can't believe this. I hardly even *know* you, and now you're calmly asking me to sleep with somebody, because you don't like who she's going out with?"

"I realize it's an unusual request. That's why I'm offering such a large sum."

"This is . . ." He shook his head mutely. "Why are you bothered who she goes out with anyway?"

I tried to sound nonchalant. "Anna's a beautiful and intelligent girl. She can do better."

He snorted. "Oh, come on. You're not doing this out of the goodness of your heart. What's the real reason?"

I hesitated, feeling myself blush again. "I find Anna . . . very attractive. But I realize a young girl like her is hardly going to be interested in a middle-aged man like me. I accept that. What I can't accept is seeing her throw herself away on someone who doesn't deserve her. I find that intolerable."

Zeppo frowned. "But you're asking to me go to bed with her. If you fancy this girl yourself won't that bother you?"

"Not as much as the thought of her with him." Some skepticism still lingered on his face, so I added, "Apart from anything else, you would only be temporary. And it would split them up. That's the main thing."

That was not entirely true. But it was a motive Zeppo could easily believe. He appeared to accept it. "You've really got it in for the poor sod, haven't you? What have you got against him?"

"I haven't anything against him personally. He's just not the sort of person I think is suitable for Anna, that's all."

"Why? What's wrong with him?"

"He's . . ."—I searched for an explanation—"unexceptional."

"In what way? Socially? Intellectually? What?"

I fussed with my napkin. "Physically."

A look of understanding came onto Zeppo's face. "And if you've got to stand back while she goes off with anyone else, you'd rather it be someone good looking. Is that it?"

"I wouldn't have put it quite like that. But yes."

He smiled drily. I took a drink of wine and was surprised to find my glass nearly empty. I refilled it. "So how close is she to this boyfriend?" Zeppo asked.

"Very, I'm afraid. They haven't known each other long. Less than a year, at least. But they're living together, and as far as I can tell they're both infatuated." I paused. "How much of a problem do you think it'll be?"

He gave a shrug. "I don't know. I can't really say without meeting them, can I?" He looked at me. "And I haven't agreed to do it yet."

"No, no, of course," I said hastily.

He twirled the stem of his wineglass. "Why ask me, anyway? I've only spoken to you at a couple of parties. What made you think I'd be interested?" There was an edge of suspicion to his voice. But I had been prepared for that.

"You're a model. You're used to living off your looks. This isn't really so very different. Besides which, you were the only one who sprang to mind. I don't know many people who might be suitable for this sort of thing. I'm only an art dealer. I don't move in those sort of circles."

There was also another reason for choosing him. But I would keep that to myself. For now.

He watched the wine swirl in the glass. "Suppose I say no?"

"Then I'll have to find someone else, obviously." I hoped

I sounded unconcerned. "I've told you how much I'm prepared to pay. And it's hardly an unpleasant ordeal. I dare say I shouldn't have too much difficulty finding someone willing to do it. But it would save trouble if it was you."

Zeppo accepted this without comment. I tried to gauge his expression, without success. "How soon can you give me an answer?" I asked.

"Is there any rush?"

"Oh no," I lied. "But if you're not interested I'll have to make other arrangements. So the sooner I know where we stand, the better."

He contemplated his glass again. I noticed the waiter hovering and waved him away. "Where are the toilets?" Zeppo asked abruptly.

"Ah . . . I think they're through there."

He pushed back his chair and went out. I picked up the menu and went through the motions of reading it without seeing a single word. I put it down and took a drink of wine instead. Zeppo seemed to be gone a long time. I was glad when he reappeared in the doorway. This time he scanned the room openly as he crossed it.

"So how old is this girl anyway?" he asked as soon as he sat down. "Anna, is it?"

"Yes, Anna. She's in her early twenties."

"And you say she's good looking."

"Oh yes. Very. At least, *I* think so."

Zeppo nodded to himself. His right hand rested on the table, fingers drumming an erratic beat. There was a subtle change in his manner. He seemed more decisive than before. I tried not to raise my hopes.

"And you'll pay cash?"

"Cash, check. Whatever you like."

He was silent again. His fingers continued tapping out their uneven tattoo. I waited. Suddenly he grinned.

"Okay. Why not?"

"You mean you'll do it?"

"That was the general idea, wasn't it?"

I hoped he could not see how relieved I was. "Oh, good," I said, letting my breath out slowly. I smiled at him. "More wine?"

❦

Anna had worked at the gallery for nearly four months. For the first three of those I hardly noticed her. I had taken her on after her predecessor, whose name I forget, was stupid enough to be killed by a bus, of all things. Anna had simply been another assistant, the latest in a long line of young women I had hired to help out over the years. So long as she remained punctual and reasonably competent, nothing else concerned me. The fact that she was attractive was incidental and unimportant.

My attitude toward sex had always been one of indifference. Even as a young man I had no great interest in the subject, and what little curiosity I had went unanswered until my mid-twenties, when I misguidedly hired the services of a prostitute. The experience was distasteful and I felt no inclination to repeat it. Instead, putting the incident behind me, I concentrated on a more dignified outlet for my energies. Art.

For a time I had aspirations of becoming an artist myself. Unfortunately, my talent seemed to lie more in appreciation than application, a fact that mercifully led me to abandon my own attempts before they became too embarrassing. I was disappointed but realistic. I reasoned that if I could not make a career from my own work, I could at least do so from other people's. I already owned a modest collection of oils and watercolors. The next step seemed obvious. I became a dealer.

My interest in erotic art did not develop until I bought my first example of it, however. It was an eighteenth-century French snuffbox, unremarkable until it was opened. On the underside of the lid was a picture of a girl, coquettishly lifting her skirts to reveal that she wore nothing underneath. I was enthralled. I had to have it, and was mortified when the owner, an elderly man I went to see about another matter, repeatedly refused to sell. It was only when he died that I was able to con-

vince his widow that her husband had come to an agreement
with me, and managed to buy it for my original offer.

The snuffbox became the first piece in my private collection. I was, of course, aware of the irony of being fascinated by
erotica when sex itself held no appeal. But that piece, and subsequent ones, seemed to possess a subtlety and charm completely lacking in the physical act. It impressed me in a way
mere fornication never had.

I entered middle age content with my life. I had everything
I wanted: a flourishing business and a private, harmless passion that I could afford to satisfy. I neither wanted my situation
to change nor saw any reason why it should. And, had I not
been absentminded one evening, it might never have done so.

I had left Anna to close the gallery, while I went to an auction. It was by invitation only, and halfway there I realized I
had left mine in the office. Annoyed, I turned back for it.

I expected the gallery to be empty. It was past closing time
when I returned, and I assumed Anna would have already gone
home. I parked in the alleyway around the back and let myself
in. The building was in darkness. Two flights of stairs led up
to the office, one from the gallery at the front, the other from
the storeroom at the rear. At the foot of the latter, I switched
on the light. The bulb blinked and went out. Exasperated, I
began to climb the stairs in the dark, and was almost at the top
before I realized there was a light on in the office.

My first reaction was to go back to the car to telephone the
police. If it was a burglary I wanted no part of it. But the fear
of humiliating myself over a false alarm prevented me. I hesitated. Then, surprised at my own courage, I went up the rest
of the stairs and onto the landing.

The office door was partly open. Light spilled out from it
into the darkened corridor. I tiptoed slowly closer, more of the
room coming into view as I approached. Then, when I was
only a few feet away, I heard Anna cough.

I relaxed. Relieved and irritated, I took another step forward,
intending to announce my presence, and stopped.

Through the gap in the doorway I could now see the large

gilt-framed mirror that hung on the opposite wall. It showed part of the office that was still hidden behind the door. The bookshelf. My desk. The desk lamp, casting a golden illumination into the room. And Anna.

She was naked except for a white bra and pants. She stood poised with her weight on one leg, the other slightly crooked as she strained, reaching behind her back with both hands. For a moment she did not move. The mirror, set against the blank surrounding wall, framed the scene as perfectly as a painting. Then there was a sudden forward motion of her breasts as the bra came undone, and Anna bent her shoulders and slipped it off. Dropping it out of sight, she hooked her thumbs in the top of her pants and pushed them down. Her breasts swung heavily as she stooped, her hair sliding over one shoulder in a dark club. Then she turned to confront herself in the mirror. And me.

Instinctively, I flinched back. But the hallway was in darkness: I was invisible. Cautiously, I moved forward again. Now Anna's reflection directly faced me. Her hands went to her hair, tying it behind her head with a black band. Her head bowed slightly; her breasts stretched and quivered. Her stomach was smooth, slightly rounded at its base and deeply indented by a long, oval navel. Below this, the thick wedge of dark curls was still pressed flat from her underclothes.

She turned then and reached for something out of sight on the floor; the pose presented me with an angled view of her back. It gleamed where the light caught it, her spine a shadowed groove. She bent further, head and shoulders dipping out of sight until her buttocks became almost heart shaped. A small, dark diamond formed where they joined her thighs. Straightening, she stepped into another pair of pants, black this time, and pulled on a pair of tights. She drew them up her legs and over her stomach to her navel so that the lower half of her body was all black, the upper still white and naked.

Suddenly I lost sight of her as she moved out of view of the mirror. I felt a surge of panic. But her reflection returned almost immediately, holding a black dress. I watched, regretfully, as her body was concealed in it, cherishing one last glimpse of her breasts as she eased them inside. Then she was fastening the dress behind her, clothed and hidden once more.

I remained in the corridor, reluctant to accept it was over. It was only when Anna began to put on her lipstick that I remembered where I was and what I was doing. I crept away from the doorway and went back downstairs, trembling and light-headed. At the bottom I leaned against the cool wall and closed my eyes. An afterimage of Anna naked in the mirror instantly appeared, and I quickly opened them. I waited until the tightness in my chest and throat had subsided and then began to climb the stairs again.

"Anna? Is that you?" I shouted.

"Mr. Ramsey?" There were hurried sounds from the office. Then Anna appeared in the doorway. She looked embarrassed. "I'm sorry, I was just getting changed. I wasn't expecting you back."

"That's quite all right. I'm sorry if I startled you. I forgot some papers." I found I could not actually remember what I had gone back for.

"I hope you don't mind me using the office as a changing room."

"Not at all." I followed her into it. There were no signs of what I had witnessed. The ceiling light had been turned on and cast a bright, harsh light over the room. I tried not to look at the mirror. "Are you going anywhere nice?"

"I'm meeting my boyfriend for something to eat, then we're going to the theater. There's an Alan Ayckbourn play on."

"Ah." I could not help but think of the body under the dress. Concealed by a thin layer of fabric. I realized that she had taken a bra off but not replaced it. I wondered if she only wore one for work. In my presence. The thought disturbed me. "Well, I hope you enjoy yourselves."

She smiled. For the first time I found myself really looking at her, noticing her features. The dark eyebrows and straight, rather long nose. The large mouth with what I now saw to be sensuous lips. I envied her boyfriend. "We better. The tickets cost a fortune." She turned and picked up a shoulder bag from the floor. Her buttocks briefly molded themselves against the fabric of her dress. I remembered the smooth, pale heart shape they had formed.

"Do you like Ayckbourn?" I asked.

"I don't know. I've never seen anything of his before. But Marty—that's my boyfriend—thinks he's brilliant." She grinned. "It's pathetic. It takes an American to get me to see an English playwright."

"Your boyfriend's American?" I was suddenly aware how little I knew about her. It had never bothered me before.

"He's from New York. Well, Boston originally. He's at university here." She repositioned the bag on her shoulder, a signal that she was ready to leave. But I could not let her go just yet.

"Really? What subject?"

"Anthropology. He's a research student."

"What made him choose London? It's rather a long way to come, isn't it?"

"Well, I think a lot of it had to do with his wanting to see England. But he says the course here is quite a good one."

She glanced at her watch. I knew I was delaying her, but I felt compelled to make up for my ignorance. I tried to sound casual. "Have you been going out together very long?"

"Almost a year." A pleased smile spread over her face.

"You seem very fond of him." She blushed. "I'm sorry, I shouldn't pry."

"That's okay. It's not prying."

I could think of nothing else to say. There was a brief silence while we both stood there uncertainly.

"Well, I'd better be off," Anna said. "There's nothing else you need me for, is there?"

"No, no, I don't think so." I did not want her to go but could think of no excuse to keep her. I moved out of her way, and with a shock realized I had an erection. Flustered, I went behind the desk, thankful I still wore my coat.

"I'll see you tomorrow, then. 'Bye." Anna left the room, and

I heard her go downstairs. After a moment the door slammed.

I did not move. I felt confused, in turmoil. I looked across into the mirror. Now it held only the office and me, gray haired, middle aged and unprepossessing. I switched off the ceiling light so the room was lit only by the desk lamp, as before. I moved a chair until my view of the mirror was approximately as it had been from outside. I stared at it. It was still empty, but with only a little concentration I could picture Anna moving into it again. I closed my eyes. The image held. Once more I pictured her breasts, traced in my mind's eye their every curve and swell. I saw the plane of her stomach, her navel, the black wedge of curls. She bent over again in front of me, her haunches smooth and round, cleaved by modest yet provocative shadows. Eyes closed, I ran through it all in slow motion, lingering and reviewing at will. Almost without consent my hands moved, careful not to disturb the images.

For the first time since I was a teenager, I masturbated.

Chapter

2

From then on, I was a man obsessed. I could not look at Anna
in the same way again. Or, rather, for the first time I actually
began to look at her. I noticed things I had never been aware
of before, either in her or anyone else. Each morning I would
wait eagerly for her to arrive at the gallery, wondering what she
would be wearing, if her hair would be taken back or loose. I
noticed how her clothes touched and briefly clung to her body
when she moved, how she had a particular scent all her own.
Everything about her seemed perfect.

But if I was obsessed, it was a modest obsession. I knew my
limitations, I had no ambitions of making her my mistress.
Such a thing was so far beyond my experience as to be virtu-
ally unimaginable. The best I could ever hope for was to become her friend, and so to that end I began to try and break
down the reserve that existed between us. It was surprisingly
easy. The hardest part was not making my sudden interest appear too obvious. I could have spent hours watching her, cherishing each unconscious movement, storing it for later, private
perusal. The arch of her neck, a few bare inches of flesh, could
hold me mesmerized for hours. I was constantly aware of her
body underneath the clothes. They seemed only to emphasize
what they concealed. One day she was very obviously not
wearing a bra, and I could barely take my eyes from the judder

and swing of her breasts. I convinced myself that this was a sign she was beginning to feel more at ease. In fact, I had never noticed in the past if she wore a bra or not.

As she became more relaxed with me, I began to hear more about her private life. And in particular about Marty, her boyfriend. Her feelings for him were patently obvious, and the more I heard, the more I was filled with envy for this unknown man. And also curiosity. I tried to imagine what he looked like. I formed an image of him in my mind: tall and darkly good looking, a male equivalent of Anna. I admit to a slight disapproval that he was American, but I was prepared to admit that was probably my own prejudice. The object of Anna's affection surely could not be anything other than exceptional. I felt certain she would not give herself to less.

Then came the opportunity to meet him for myself. Anna approached me one afternoon. "Are you busy tonight?" she asked.

I tried to hide my rush of excitement. "No, not really. Why?"

"Well, if you aren't, you could do me an awfully big favor. But only if it's no trouble."

"I'm sure it won't be. What is it?"

"A friend of mine is an artist, and it's her first show tonight. I wondered, if you weren't doing anything, if you'd mind coming along to it? She's really nervous, so the more people who go, the better. And with you being quite influential, I know she'd like you to be there."

I felt a thrill of pleasure. "I'd be delighted."

"You're sure it's no problem? I know it's short notice."

"Really, I'd love to come."

Anna beamed at me. "Thanks, that's great! Marty said you wouldn't mind."

I was unsure whether or not I liked the implications of that. Then another thought struck me. "Will Marty be going tonight?"

"Yes. We'll be there around eight-ish. But you don't have to be there that early."

I reassured her that it was not too early for me and tried to be attentive when she gave me directions to where the exhibition was being held. But I was hardly listening. I was going to meet Anna's boyfriend. Her lover.

I was suddenly acutely nervous.

෨

The exhibition was in a small gallery near Camden. I arrived there just before eight. My stomach was coiling. I had not eaten anything since lunch, but I was too on edge to feel hungry. The gallery looked warm and bright, and I could see people milling about inside as I approached. I peered through the windows, trying to pick out Anna and settle my nerves before going in, but succeeded in doing neither. I took a deep breath and opened the door.

A glass of wine was immediately pushed into my hand by a cadaverous young man in a baggy sweater. The wine was obviously from a supermarket's bargain bin, but I accepted it gratefully and looked around for Anna. There was no sign of her. I looked at my watch. It was not quite eight o'clock yet, and feeling anticlimax mingle with relief, I turned my attention to the exhibition.

The daubs were even more amateurish than I had feared. I dislike abstract art at the best of times, and this was nowhere near the best. I recognized one of the critics there, and the look he gave me supported my own opinion. The majority of the crowd appeared to be more interested in the free wine than the paintings, and I could not blame them. I was considering accepting a second glass myself when Anna's voice came from behind me.

"Hello. Have you been here long?"

I turned, surprised and flustered. "No, no. I've only just got here."

I breathed in her perfume. She still wore her coat, and a scarf was draped around her neck. Her face looked pinched from the cold. "Sorry we're late. The tube was delayed again, and we couldn't get a taxi. We walked from the underground." She moved to one side. "You've not met Marty, have you?"

I had been aware of someone standing just behind her, but only peripherally. He was so unlike my idea of what Marty should look like that I had taken no notice of him. Now, as he stepped forward and held out his hand, I felt a shock so strong I could barely respond.

The tall, good-looking Marty of my imagination did not exist. The creature Anna introduced was small, slight and runtish. His clothes hung on his meager frame, and dark-framed glasses made his eyes seem disproportionately large in his thin face. His hair was unkempt and mousy, completing the image of a bookish schoolboy.

I managed to smile as I shook his hand. "I'm pleased to meet you. I've heard a lot about you."

"I don't know if that's good or bad." His American accent was relatively slight. But by then his nationality was the least of my complaints.

I was recovering now from the initial shock. "Oh, you needn't worry. It was all good."

"I only told him the good points," Anna said. They smiled at each other.

"Here, I'll find somewhere to put your coat," he said to her. "Would you like another glass of wine, Mr. Ramsey?"

I felt I needed one. "If it's no bother." I gritted my teeth. "And please, call me Donald."

Taking Anna's coat, Marty disappeared into the crowd. There was nothing about him to make him stand out from it.

"So what do you think?" Anna asked. I blinked.

"Pardon?"

"The exhibition. Have you had a chance to see much of it yet?"

For a moment I had thought she was asking my opinion of her boyfriend. "Well, I haven't seen it all," I hedged.

"Oh, there's Teresa," Anna said, looking beyond me. "She's the artist. I'd better go and have a word. Would you like me to introduce you?"

I could think of few things I would like less. But it would keep me close to Anna. "Yes, all right."

Teresa was a thin, intense young woman dressed completely in black. Her eye makeup was almost as alarming as her art. For Anna's sake I did my best to sound encouraging without committing myself. Marty joined us a few moments later, and the evening reached a nadir when the artist insisted on escorting us personally around a selection of pieces, explaining her intentions and methods in stultifying detail. But by then reaction to seeing Marty was beginning to set in, and I was glad the young woman loved the sound of her own voice enough for me to keep the exercise of mine to a minimum.

Eventually, she went in search of other victims. I stood with Anna and Marty in front of a huge canvas that looked as though a child had smeared crème caramel on it.

"I think Teresa must be nervous," Anna said, after a moment. "She's not normally as pushy as that."

"I suppose your first exhibition must be nerve-wracking," I said, for Anna's sake.

Marty studied the painting. "It's nerve-wracking enough having to look at it."

"Marty!" Anna tried to look severe.

He gave an apologetic shrug. "I'm sorry, but I might as well be honest. I hate to say it, but I just don't think this is any good, that's all." One hand went up to push back his glasses. "What do you think, Donald?"

I was annoyed at being put on the spot. "Well, this sort of thing's not really my cup of tea anyway. I've never been fond of the abstract movement."

"Would you say it's well done, though?" Anna asked. "I know you won't like it, but do you think there's . . . well, anything there?"

I struggled to be diplomatic. "Well, there's an obvious enthusiasm. And it is only her first exhibition, but . . ." I shied away from the criticism.

"But you don't think it's really any good," Anna finished for me.

I sighed. "No, not really. But that's only my opinion, of course."

"I know Teresa's an old friend and you don't want to hurt her feelings," Marty said, "but you've got to admit this is a mistake. She should have stuck to doing portraits at Covent Garden. It might not have got her any reviews, but at least it made her money. She's wasting her time with this."

Looking at the canvas in front of her, Anna reluctantly nodded. "Poor Teresa. She's put everything she's got into it, too."

"That doesn't say much for Teresa," Marty murmured. Anna gave him a little push and turned to me, smiling ruefully.

"I'm sorry for dragging you down here, Donald. I didn't realize it would be this bad."

It still sounded strange to hear her use my Christian name. "No need to apologize. I've enjoyed the experience, if not the art."

Marty looked at his watch. "Well, we've done our duty. I can't see any point in staying any longer, can you?"

I felt a sudden emptiness at the thought of them leaving. I remembered I had not eaten and wondered if I dared invite them out for dinner. But while I was trying to gather the courage to ask, the opportunity was lost.

"You don't mind if we go, do you?" Anna asked. "We haven't had a chance to eat yet, so we're going to get a pizza or something."

I smiled. "No, of course I don't mind."

I waited by the door while Anna made her excuses to the artist and Marty fetched their coats. Those few minutes alone were enough to turn my depression into a dull ache of outrage. We went outside together. There was nothing now to stop us from going our separate ways. Me to my solitary house, the two of them to whatever they had planned. And eventually to bed.

"Would you like a lift?" I asked.

Anna shook her head. "No, it's okay, thanks."

"It's no trouble. It's too cold to be walking tonight."

"No, honestly, it's okay." She appealed to Marty. "We've not really decided where we're going yet, have we?"

"No. There's still a dispute about whether it's going to be Italian or Chinese. But thanks anyway." He held out his gloved hand, smiling. "It's been nice meeting you."

I shook it. They said good night and walked away. As I watched them go, I noticed that his feeble figure was no taller than hers. He put his arm around her, and I felt a sour, leaden feeling in my gut. To think that she had given herself to such a pathetic creature was unbearable. The full impact of my disappointment finally hit me. I drove home, imagining the two of them together. Now they will be in a restaurant, I thought. Then, later; now they will be home. And then; now they will be naked. The images were as vivid as though I were watching, but this time unwelcomely so. I had a sudden vision of his body on hers and quickly forced it from my mind. It was useless tormenting myself. Unworthy as Marty was, he was still Anna's choice. I could do nothing to change that.

I consoled myself with the thought that at least I was closer to her than I had been. Now the ice had been broken and I had seen her socially, I had something to build on. It was not much, but it was all I had. I would have to content myself with that.

It was only when even these crumbs seemed about to be taken from me that I felt compelled to act.

୧୦

I found out by accident. It was shortly after the exhibition. I was upstairs in the office, Anna was downstairs in the gallery itself. I had no idea she was using the telephone until I picked up the office extension and heard her voice.

I did not intend to eavesdrop. But there was something seductive about being able to listen without her being aware of it. And once I had hesitated, I had no choice. They had not noticed the click when I lifted the receiver, but if they heard me set it back down they would know I had been on the other end. So I had to listen.

The gist of the conversation escaped me at first. Then Anna said, "I know it's a big step, but I want to go," and I became more alert. The word "go" seemed fraught with dreadful connotations.

"So long as you're sure, that's all right," the other speaker, a girl, said. "But have you thought what'll happen if it doesn't work out? I know you won't like me saying it, but you haven't known each other that long, have you?"

"Oh, don't you start, Debbie. I've had all that from my parents. You know what my mum's like."

"Well, for once I can see her point. I mean, I really like Marty, but it's still a massive risk, isn't it?"

"I *know* it is, but I've got to take it. It isn't as though I'm doing it lightly. Sometimes I'm petrified when I think about it, but I can't just stay here and let him go by himself, can I?"

"Couldn't you go over later?"

"What's the point? If I'm going I might as well go with him. Why spend God knows how long apart, just until I'm sure I'm doing the right thing? There's only one way to find out, isn't there?"

The other girl sighed. "I know. And I suppose I'd do exactly the same if I were you. I'm just jealous that it isn't me who's being whisked off to America."

The room lurched. I tried to tell myself they might only be talking about Anna going on holiday, but then even that straw was snatched away.

"Have you told your boss yet?" the girl asked.

Anna's voice dropped lower. "No, not yet. It isn't for another couple of months, so I'll tell him nearer the time. We're going to need all the money we can get until I find a job over there, so I don't want him sacking me. I don't think he'll mind, but I daren't chance it."

I closed my eyes. I wished I had never picked up the telephone. Anna was leaving. Going to America with that sad excuse for a man. Not only was he wasting her, now he was taking her away. And she did not even dare tell me. I hardly heard the rest of the conversation. I had just enough presence of mind left to put the receiver down when it finished.

I sat there and tried to gather my wits, already feeling a sense of loss. And growing anger. This was Marty's fault. Anna would go to America with him, and I would never see her again. There was nothing I could do to prevent her: as poor a specimen as Marty was, I was a poorer rival.

It was the first time I had actually thought of myself as such. But I realized now that that was what we were. Rivals. As the concept established itself in my mind I began to consider what advantages I had over him. It was painfully obvious that there was only one. His ignorance. Neither he nor Anna perceived me as a threat to their relationship. Until that moment I had never considered myself as one either. Now I knew I had to be. I would do anything to keep him from having her. Anything.

The question was, what *could* I actually do? Common sense told me that, by myself, the answer was very little. It was then I hit upon the idea of bringing in outside help.

Two days later I called Zeppo.

Chapter

3

The same night I met Zeppo I had a peculiar dream. Normally I am a heavy and deep sleeper: if I have any dreams, as psychologists insist I must, I do not remember them. But this was extremely vivid. I was in the house I grew up in. I was lying on a sofa, and I presume I was a child, since everything in the room was much larger than it should be. A fire was burning nearby, and I felt warm and comfortable. My mother was sitting with her back to me, brushing her hair in front of a mirror, and I lay there, peaceful and secure, watching it catch the glow from the fire with each stroke.

That was all. Or at least as much as I could remember. Why I should remember any of it at all I had no idea. There was nothing about it that seemed exceptional. But the memory of it stayed with me after I had shaved and breakfasted, and it was still on my mind as I drove to the gallery.

I put my distraction down to that and my meeting with Zeppo the previous night. The traffic was moving slowly as I came into the center of London, the usual crammed lanes of early morning vehicles. I approached a junction and passed through the traffic lights, and suddenly there was a crunching jolt.

I was rocked violently as the car came to a sudden stop. A Range Rover had run into my left wing. I barely had time to recover from the shock when the cars waiting behind me began blaring their horns. I glared up at the other driver, a woman, about to gesture for her to pull away and wait for me, when she did the same, gesticulating imperiously before backing her car off mine. The discrepancy in heights had prevented the bumpers from locking, and they separated with only a slight jar. She edged around in front of me and, once clear of the junction, pulled over to the side.

My car had stalled on impact, and as I tried to restart the engine I found my hands were shaking. The clamor of car horns only made matters worse, and it took three attempts before the ignition caught.

A rasping, scraping noise came from my left wing as I pulled to the curb behind the Range Rover. I put on the hand brake and angrily climbed out. I was just formulating the first heated phrase when the woman slammed out of her car and pre-empted me.

"Are you blind? The bloody lights were on red!"

I was taken aback by her accusation. I had not expected her to have the gall to accuse me of being in the wrong. "Yours may have been. Mine were on green."

"Don't be ridiculous. I'd been waiting for them to turn. You went straight through!" She looked at the side of her car. "Oh, just look at this! I've only just got it back from the garage, and now you've broken the bloody side light!"

"*I've* broken it?" I was almost speechless. "*You* were the one who ran into me!" I bent to examine the damage to my own car. The front of the left wing was dented down to the wheel arch, which was buckled against the tire at one point. By comparison the Range Rover was hardly scratched.

"I want your number," the woman was saying. "Idiots like you shouldn't be allowed on the road. What if I'd had a child with me?"

"Hopefully it would have told you not to go through a red light!"

"Right!" She turned suddenly to the people who were walking past on the pavement. "Excuse me, did any of you see this

man run into me?" Faces turned and stared. One or two people slowed, although none stopped. My cheeks burned. She
appealed to an elderly man who was lingering more than the
rest. "Did you see what happened? This man just ran through
the lights and hit me as I was pulling out. I need a witness."

"I only saw you pull in. Didn't see him hit you."

This was ridiculous. "I didn't hit her! She hit me!" I looked
around for a witness of my own. The traffic was flowing past
steadily. The cars that had been behind me had disappeared.

"But didn't you see what actually happened?" the woman
persisted. The man had slowed to a stop. He shook his head
doubtfully. Other people passed by with curious stares.

"He's already said he hasn't," I said.

"I'm not speaking to you, I'm speaking to him. Did you see
him go through the red light? You must have done if you were
walking past."

The man shook his head and began to edge away "No. No.
Sorry."

"Just a minute," the woman called after him, but he had
turned his back and increased his pace, giving one last shake
of his head to exempt himself from further involvement. "Oh,
bloody typical!" She faced me again. "All right, give me the
name of your insurance company. I'm not going to stand here
arguing with you. I'll have your name and address, too. We'll let
them sort it."

She flounced back to her car and rummaged in the dash-
board. "Here." She scribbled her details on a piece of paper
and handed it to me. I did likewise. "I just hope you have the
decency to admit it was your fault after all this."

"I could say the same to—" I began, but she was not listening. The paper was snatched out of my hand.

"And on top of it all, now I'm bloody late," she snapped,
climbing back into her car and slamming the door. I stepped
back as she quickly cut into the traffic, forcing another car to
stop to let her in. She ignored his irate rebuke on the horn and
in seconds had disappeared among the stream of vehicles.

I went back to reassess the damage to my car. It was obvious even to me that it was not going anywhere. Fuming, I left a note in the windscreen for the benefit of traffic wardens and went to a telephone to arrange for my garage to pick it up. Then I went to the pavement edge to hail a taxi.

Typically, the only ones I saw were occupied. I waited ten minutes, my mood deteriorating with each second, until I finally turned away in disgust. A sign told me the underground was nearby. I headed toward it.

I had not taken the tube in years. I could remember it being busy, but I was not prepared for the mayhem that greeted me at the bottom of the escalators. I was pushed from behind and jostled from the front as I tried to guess which way to go. Everyone seemed sure of themselves except me. I looked around for someone to ask but could see only the countless moving heads of other commuters. The crowds parted and flowed around me as I stood indecisively. I saw a map on the wall and made my way over, finally deciphering that I needed to be on another line. I joined the flood of people heading in that direction and let myself be carried along a tiled, echoing tunnel to the sudden space of a concrete platform.

Compared with the tunnels, it was relatively empty. But it soon began to fill up. I had started near the front of the platform. Now I found myself squeezed steadily back until a press of people stood between me and the edge. I found myself wedged between a West Indian woman with a suitcase and a tall shaven-headed youth in a leather jacket.

A sudden rush of air preceded the appearance of the train. It pulled to a halt, and immediately its doors had opened, the crowd on the platform began pushing against the people getting off. The mechanical instruction to "Mind the Gap" was chanted over the top of the chaos. I felt panic-stricken as I struggled toward the nearest door without seeming to make any progress. Then, just as I thought I would not make it in time, a sudden surge practically lifted me into the train. A moment later the doors hissed shut, stopped, opened, shut again, and then the train lurched forward and picked up speed.

I had been deposited in the walkway between the doors. I

had thought the platform was crowded, but now strangers pressed against me from all sides, impassively intimate. The train gave a sudden jolt, and I was thrown against a young woman at my side. I stammered a low apology and quickly looked away from her cold stare. Bright light outside the windows announced that we had come to the next station on the line. The train halted, and I was nearly pushed off as people rushed for the platform. The corresponding influx of new passengers forced me further inside until I was jammed into the middle of the compartment, with no room to turn or breathe. The air was crammed with thick, unpleasant odors. Diesel, hair and sweat. I grabbed for a handhold as we lurched into motion once again. The blackness of the tunnel had only just engulfed us when the train slowed, chugged forward grudgingly and stopped.

No one seemed to notice. The darkness outside the window was complete. Inside, people sat or stood indifferently. I tried to mimic them, but the situation was alien to me. I felt smothered and isolated. When the train jerked forward once more, my heart jerked with it. We eased slowly through the tunnel, slowing several times but mercifully not actually stopping again. Then there were lights and faces outside the windows. The doors opened, and without knowing which station it was I blundered my way out onto the platform.

I gulped in the cold, diesel-smelling air, hardly noticing the knocks from the people passing. Above me was a sign saying EXIT, and I headed for it blindly, now moving with as much purpose as anyone else. I stumbled over a busker's open guitar case, ignoring his shouted insult as I sighted the final escalator. I emerged into gray daylight and, with vast relief, saw the line of taxicabs waiting outside the station. I climbed into one, gave my destination and sank back into the seat. The interior was warm, quiet and blessedly empty. I gazed out of the window at a world that was once more comfortably distanced. It seemed like the best drive of my life.

When I arrived, Anna had already opened the gallery. "I was just starting to get worried," she said as I walked in. I instantly felt that it had all been worth it. "I wondered where you were. Are you all right? You look shaky."

Her concern was balm for the morning's wounds. I lowered myself into a chair and closed my eyes. "I had a little accident on the way in," I said and told her what had happened. It sounded much better in the telling than it had seemed at the time, and my description of the idiot woman in the Range Rover actually had Anna laughing. I warmed to the story so much that I almost forgot what else I had to tell her.

"Oh, by the way," I said, before she could walk away. "I'm having a cocktail party next Saturday. I hope you and Marty will be able to come."

℁

The party had been Zeppo's idea. I had thought it was a good one until I learned he meant I should hold it myself.

"But I've never had a party," I had objected, appalled at the thought.

He had smiled. "Well, now's your chance."

The invasion began on Saturday afternoon with the arrival of the caterers. Cartons of cutlery, crockery and glasses littered the floor. My home was soon bustling with strangers. I fretted about breakages, stains and theft as I tried to keep an eye on everything that was going on. By the time the first guests came my nerves were in shreds. I hated the thought of countless people trampling through my home, making it as public as any bar. But as more people began to appear, and the onus of conversation was taken from me, I began to calm down a little. When Anna and Marty arrived the entire downstairs was already quite full. Even more surprisingly, everyone seemed to be having a good time. As far as I could see, every person I had invited had come.

Except one.

My impatience turned to anxiety. If Zeppo failed to show up, then the entire exercise was a complete waste of time. My smile became increasingly strained. I could not even bear to

talk with Anna and Marty for long. It was an effort not to constantly glance at my watch, and I had almost decided to telephone him when the doorbell rang.

I went to answer it, willing it to be him. It was.

"Zeppo! Glad you could make it!" I hoped he would notice
the barb in my voice. He only grinned.

"Wouldn't have missed it for the world. This is Angie."

The girl was obviously some sort of model, blond and flam-
boyantly beautiful. I said hello and stood back to let them in.
She took off her coat and held it out for me. Underneath she
wore a very short, very tight red dress that clung to her unde-
niably spectacular body. She was another of Zeppo's sugges-
tions. I had not been enthusiastic. Now, seeing her, I felt even
less so.

"Let me get you both a drink," I said. Zeppo caught my
look.

"I'll come with you. Won't be long, Angie."

We left her in the lounge and went to the drinks table.
"Where have you been?" I demanded, keeping my voice low.
"I thought you weren't coming."

He seemed unconcerned. "Blame Angie. I didn't think we
were going to make it at all. She wouldn't leave the house until I'd fucked her." I almost dropped the bottle I was holding.
Zeppo laughed. "Don't worry. We both showered afterward."

I tried not to let my distaste show. "I hope neither of you is
too tired to make a further effort."

"Oh no. We're both raring to go."

I looked over to where the girl was standing. Her pose was
self-conscious and displaying. "Are you sure she's suitable?" I
asked, doubtfully.

"Angie? Christ, I should say so. Stacked and goes like a bitch
in heat. What more do you want?"

"You don't think she might be . . . well . . . a little too obvious, do you?"

He popped a canapé into his mouth. "I'm sorry, Donald, but
I couldn't find a Girl Guide at such short notice. Come on, relax. I bet there's not a man in the place who's not panting at the

sight of her. Present company excepted, of course."

I wondered if he was drunk. But he seemed sober enough. I ignored the jibe. "What exactly did you tell her?"

"Just that we'd got to go to a boring party. I bet her she couldn't get off with whoever I picked out. To give us more chance I said she could have a week to do it in, so long as she makes a start tonight."

"And she *agreed*?"

"Oh yeah. Provided I didn't pick anyone who was either gay or too old to get it up."

"Good God." I looked at the girl again. Two men were already talking to her. "What on earth did you bet her?"

"Whoever loses has to be the other one's slave for a day. They have to do whatever the other wants." A rather unpleasant smile touched his lips. "I've already got one or two ideas if she loses." He shrugged. "But she'd still have done it if it had only been for a packet of crisps. Angie's game for anything. Now why don't you pour me a drink like you said and point the happy couple out for me."

I glanced around to check where Anna and Marty were. "They're over by the far wall to your left. What would you like to drink?"

"A Manhattan. Same for Angie, since you forgot to ask her." He glanced over. "The one with dark hair and the black dress?"

"Yes."

He raised his eyebrows. "Not bad. I see what you mean about the boyfriend. No wonder you're pissed off."

"Quite."

"He must have a big cock." I slopped the vermouth onto the table. Zeppo grinned. "Sorry."

I handed him the drinks and impassively mopped up the spilled liquid. "I don't really think that sort of talk is appropriate, do you?" I said. "I trust you'll be able to restrain yourself when you talk to Anna."

A smirk played around his mouth. "I'll be a perfect gentleman, don't worry."

In view of his strange behavior that was easier said than done. "When do you intend to start?"

He shrugged. "No time like the present. I'll get Angie away from those two before she drags them into the bedroom, and we can all go over."

Trying to ignore my misgivings, I led the way to where Anna and Marty were talking with a middle-aged woman, an acquaintance of mine who ran an interior design business.

"I don't think any of you have met Angie and Zeppo," I said. I performed the introductions, then turned to Marty. "There's someone over here you might like to meet. A fellow countryman of yours."

"Oh . . . yes, okay." He gave Anna a quick look as I guided him away, pretending not to notice his lack of enthusiasm.

"I'm sure you'll enjoy talking to him," I said, steering Marty toward the other American, a man I hardly knew and whom I had invited expressly for this purpose. I left them together and wandered off, catching Zeppo's eye and giving a brief nod. Shortly afterward I saw the girl he had brought detach herself and go to the drinks table. But instead of returning to Zeppo, she strolled over to where Marty was listening with a bored expression to the older American. He seemed pleased at the interruption.

I poured myself another drink and tried to relax. Then I noticed that the designer was still talking to Anna and Zeppo. I went over.

"My dear Miriam, I almost forgot! You must come and have a look at my new acquisition. I bought it for purely commercial reasons, and I would love your opinion. Personally, I think it's awful, so there's a good chance you'll like it."

She laughed. "In that case you're probably right."

I explained to Anna and Zeppo. "We have a long-standing argument over what qualifies as art and what's simply design, and I've been dying to fuel the fire with this particular monstrosity for ages."

"Donald, you're just a nineteenth-century throwback," Miriam said. "Sometimes I despair of you."

"Then there's hope for me yet. But I doubt even you can defend this abomination. I can't wait to sell it, to be honest. I only kept it here to show you." I took her arm and eased her away. The painting was in another room. As we went out I looked back. Anna was laughing at something Zeppo had said. At the other side of the room, Marty and the girl seemed deep in conversation. I took both as hopeful signs and tried not to speculate any further.

Zeppo and the girl left shortly after midnight. I did not have a chance to speak to him privately again, but as far as I could tell there was no repetition of the strange behavior he had exhibited earlier. At least, both he and the girl spent considerable time alone with their prospective—if ignorant—partners, which was encouraging.

"I'll phone you tomorrow," he said when I walked them to the door. I concealed my impatience and said good night.

Back inside, Anna and Marty were also getting ready to go. I had to leave them in the hallway while I attended to a glass of red wine one oaf had knocked over. Neither of them noticed when I returned. Marty was standing behind Anna, helping her with her coat, and as she shrugged it on, he leaned forward and gently kissed the nape of her neck. She smiled without turning around, bending her head slightly. The moment was spontaneous and private, and I could not bear to watch it. Clearing my throat, I quickly walked toward them.

"Ready for off?" I said, brightly. "Well, thank you both for coming."

They had moved apart when they heard me. Anna smiled. "Thanks for inviting us. We've really enjoyed it." Marty fiddled with his glasses and murmured in agreement.

I could not resist probing. "I'm sorry I've hardly had chance to speak to either of you all evening. I hope you managed to find someone interesting to talk to. I shouldn't say it, but I know some of the guests were a little dull, even if they are friends of mine."

"No, it's been lovely. Really."

They were clearly waiting to leave. I said good night and let them go. As I closed the door I felt a sense of anticlimax. The introductions had been made, and now all I could do was wait to hear from Zeppo. Frustration mingled with the now familiar hollowness the thought of Anna going home with Marty gave me. I stood in the hallway until both feelings had faded to a manageable level, then went back to the dozen or so guests who still remained. I gave them another half hour and then began to usher them out.

I no longer had any interest in being a host.

⊚

I tried unsuccessfully to contact Zeppo all morning, but there was no reply. Even so, when he finally telephoned me in the afternoon, I was too eager to hear what he had to say to complain.

He sounded pleased with himself. "There's good news and bad news. The bad is that Angie drew a blank with Mr. Universe."

"You mean Marty?"

"That was the idea, wasn't it?"

Disappointment welled up in me. "But I thought you said she was going to try for a week. Isn't she giving up rather easily?"

"You don't know Angie. If she thinks there's any chance at all, she doesn't give up until she's torn their trousers off. So if she reckons it's no go, then it must be."

"Perhaps she made the wrong approach."

"Not Angie. Believe me, Donald, she knows what she's doing. He just didn't want to know. Very polite and all that, but he still blanked her out. She was pretty pissed off about it. She's not used to being turned down, let alone by a geek like him. She thinks he must be either gay or some kind of freak."

There was an even more depressing prospect. I remembered the way Marty had kissed Anna's neck. "Perhaps he's just loyal to Anna."

"That's what I meant by freak. He must be even more of a sap than he looks to turn down something like that. I know Anna's not bad, but she's hardly in Angie's league."

I agreed wholeheartedly, but not in the way Zeppo meant. I had found the blond girl's beauty brash and glittering; entirely external. Anna's was something far finer.

"You said there was good news as well."

A low chuckle came over the line. "The good news is that Angie makes a great slave."

"She's not there, is she?"

"Calm down, Donald. She's in another room. She can't hear."

I tried to hold down my irritation. "Is that all you meant by 'good news'?"

"Now don't get agitated."

"Just tell me what happened between you and Anna."

"Nothing actually *happened*. I was only testing the ground. But she was putting out the right sort of signals."

"You're sure?"

"Of course I'm sure. The only snag is the boyfriend. If not for him I would've made a move last night. As it is, I'll just have to ease my way in a bit more first."

"But you don't think you'll have too much difficulty?"

He laughed. "Donald, look at him and look at me. There's your answer."

His confidence was reassuring, if a little irksome. "How long do you think it will take?"

"I've already told you it's not the sort of thing you can set to a timetable. I'll just have to see how it goes. There's no rush, is there?"

I hesitated. He had to know sooner or later. "Actually, there is." I told him about America.

I heard him swear. "Why didn't you tell me before, for Christ's sake?"

I was taken aback by his tone. "I only just found out myself," I said, annoyed by my own defensiveness. "But if it's not for two months, I can't see that it matters. It should still give you plenty of time, surely."

"That's not the fucking point!" He stopped. When he spoke again his voice was more controlled. "I just don't like having things sprung on me. Is there anything else I should know?"

There was. But he did not need to know it just then. Particularly not if he was going to take that attitude. "No. Do you think you'll have enough time?"

I heard him breathe a long sigh. "Yeah. I expect so. But I like to know exactly where I stand. So in future, no secrets, all right?"

"Of course." I could hear what sounded like a dog barking in the background.

"Hang on." Something was put over the receiver. The line became muffled. "Sorry about that," he said, a moment later. There was a laugh in his voice. "Where were we?"

"I was about to ask what you propose to do next?"

The laugh became more pronounced. "Look, I've got to go now. I'll call you next week. Don't worry. Once I've got her softened up she'll not want to look at the wimp she's going out with."

He hung up before I could say anything. I put the receiver down with mixed feelings. I was beginning to have my doubts about Zeppo. But I could not help but share his optimism.

Chapter

4

Since becoming involved with Anna I had found it increasingly difficult to apply myself with any real enthusiasm to the affairs of the gallery. Even auctions, which I had once always enjoyed, seemed to have lost their appeal. When I went to one the week after the party, I was apathetic to start with. Had I known who would also be there, however, I would never have gone in the first place.

The auction was of part of the estate of an elderly politician. It included his collection of eighteenth-century French oils, one of which in particular I had my eye on. So, unfortunately, did several other people. When the bidding approached the limit I had set myself, I had to choose whether or not it was worth going any higher. At one time, only weeks before, I would probably have decided it was. Now it seemed like too much trouble. I sat back and let the bidding go on without me and felt only mild regret when it stopped shortly afterward.

There were one or two other pieces I had been considering trying for, but all at once I could not be bothered. I eased my way along the line of chairs and toward the exit. The back of the room was crowded with people who had not found seats, and as I went through them I felt a tap on my arm.

"It's Mr. Ramsey, isn't it?"

The woman was a little younger than I. Her hair was just

starting to gray, and her eyes were magnified by a pair of large-framed glasses. She was smiling, hesitantly.

"Yes?"

Her smile grew, "Oh, good. I thought it was."

I continued to stare at her. I had no idea who she was. "I'm sorry, I don't . . ."

"Oh, it's these things." She took the glasses off. It made no difference. "Margaret Thornby. You ran into my car last week."

Then, of course, I recognized her. "Oh," was all I could think of to say.

"I spotted you coming out, but I wasn't entirely certain it was you until just now." She lowered her voice as the auctioneer began introducing the next item. "Shall we pop outside? We can't really talk in here."

I had no desire to talk to her anywhere. But she was already edging into the corridor. I had no option but to follow.

"There. That's better." She gave me a smile. I did not return it. I had belatedly realized that she had again blamed me for the accident, albeit in a much friendlier tone this time. "I'm glad I've seen you, actually. I've been wondering how you went on after our little bump last week."

She was unaccountably pleasant. "My car had to be towed away," I told her, rather more stiffly than I intended. "The wing needs to be replaced. I'm still using a courtesy car."

"Oh, I am sorry. Mine only needed the side light replacing, so it could have been worse."

I said nothing

"Actually, I've been meaning to get in touch with you," she went on. "When I'd calmed down I realized that I might have been a bit . . . well, a bit pushy. Not that I'm saying it was my fault or anything. But I think I might have gone a bit over the top."

An apology was not what I had expected. I was unsure how to react. However, she did not give me any chance.

"The thing was, I was in an awful rush. I was supposed to be meeting someone, you see, and I was late already. I don't

come into the City very often, and whenever I do as a rule I always avoid the rush hour. But I was meeting my son at the train
station—he's just got back from India, or rather he had just got
back—so there was no avoiding it. I was hoping to get there in
plenty of time, because I didn't want to leave him standing
around in the cold after he's been used to the hot weather. But
I misjudged it, and instead of getting there for half past eight,
as I'd planned, I was still stuck in the traffic at a quarter past.
So when we had our little accident, it was the last straw, and I
suppose I did rather take it out on you."

She pulled an apologetic face. "I never even thought to ask
if you were all right. You did look a bit shaken, but then so was
I, I suppose. And when I got to the station, I found that
Damien's train had been delayed by over half an hour, so it
turned out that I was in time after all."

She gave a little shrug. "Anyway, I'm glad I've seen you to
set the record straight. I daresay you must have got a horren-
dous impression of this fearful woman shouting at you like a
mad thing, and I'm not normally like that. Not often, anyway,"
she laughed. "Sorry, I'm running on a bit. But I was going to
get in touch with you anyway to clear things up. There's no reason for us to be unreasonable just because of what was an accident, after all. We might as well let the insurance companies
sort it all. That's what we pay them for, isn't it? And they certainly charge enough, don't they?"

She looked at me expectantly, waiting for my reply. Dazed
by her monologue, nothing immediately suggested itself to me.
"Yes, I . . . ah, that sounds . . ." I nodded, not quite sure what
I was agreeing to. She beamed at me.

"Oh good! I'm so glad we've been able to straighten things
out. Anyway, I'll let you go now. I don't want to keep you." My
relief was premature. She went on almost without pausing. "Are
you here on business or pleasure?"

"Oh . . . Business."

"Really? I'd no idea you were in the trade. I've got an antique
shop in Hampstead, that's why I'm here tonight. I don't nor-

mally bother coming to auctions in the City. I think you can pick up much better bargains out in the sticks, but I felt I really had to come to this, just to see some of the stuff that's going. And there's a rather lovely little doll's house coming up later that I'm going to bid for. I don't expect I'll have much chance of getting it, not with the prices the things have fetched so far, but you never know. Were you here for anything in particular?"

She had a disconcerting habit of staring at me very directly while she spoke. And she stood much too close. It was an effort not to move away. "An oil painting."

"Did you get it?"

"No."

"Oh dear. Still, never mind. Are paintings your speciality, by any chance?"

"Actually, I am an art dealer."

She blinked. "Really? Oh, and here's me babbling on about antiques. You must forgive me, I just assumed that you were in the same line as me." She laughed. "There I go again, jumping to conclusions. Do you have a gallery? I suppose you must have, mustn't you?"

"It's not far from the West End."

"The West End . . . let me think. It's not near that biggish, expensive one just called 'The Gallery,' is it? That's the only one I know around there."

"That is it, actually."

She stared at me. "Oh, *really?* I didn't realize you were anything to do with that." I remembered that I had written my name and address on a piece of paper instead of giving her a card. "A friend of mine bought a watercolor from you about two years ago. Dutch, I think. Nineteenth century. The name escapes me."

"I'm afraid . . ."

"No, of course you won't be able to remember it. Still it just goes to show what a small world it is, doesn't it?"

Too small, obviously. I looked at my watch. "I'm sorry, but I must be . . ."

"Oh, I'm sorry, I didn't mean to keep you. Yes, I'd better get back inside anyway. I don't want to miss the doll's house, do I?"

"No," I agreed, beginning to edge away.

She held out her hand. "Well, I'm glad I've had the chance to see you, Mr. Ramsey. Let's hope the insurance companies don't take too long sorting everything out. And the next time I'm nearby, I'll pop into your gallery."

"Yes, do." With a final goodbye I hurried away before she could say anything else.

I was so pleased to escape it never occurred to me that she might mean what she said.

⁊❡

It was a week of surprises. Zeppo had telephoned, in a rather more composed mood this time, and said he would call into the gallery on Thursday. But Anna preempted our plans. She had been rather quiet all week. Ever since my party, in fact. I did not feel secure enough with her to ask why. Then on Wednesday morning, she told me.

She seemed embarrassed when she asked if she could have a word. "Of course," I said. "Is it something important?"

"Well, yes, I suppose it is, really." A blush had spread from her face to her neck. I tried not to stare at where it disappeared into the top of her blouse. "I'm leaving."

The words came as a shock. I had not expected her to tell me for weeks, and my first thought was that she was planning to leave even sooner than I expected.

"Oh. When?"

Anna looked uncomfortable. "That depends on you, really. I'm going to America with Marty. New York. To live there. It's not for nearly two months yet, but I thought I ought to tell you straight away, to give you time to find a replacement. I'd like to stay on as long as I can," she added, hurriedly, "but if you want me to leave now, I understand."

Relief made my reaction unforced. "My dear Anna, that's

wonderful! I thought for one horrible moment that you meant you'd found another job and wanted to go immediately! Of course you mustn't leave yet!"

"You don't mind, then?"

"Of course I don't mind! I can't pretend I won't be sorry to see you go, but how could I possibly object? I'm happy for both of you."

Her face cleared. She smiled brilliantly. "Really? I was dreading telling you in case you'd ask for my notice now or something."

"I'm not that much of an ogre, am I?"

"No, of course not. I just . . ." She was becoming embarrassed again.

"Well, anyway, I'm glad you've told me. I think it's wonderful news." I had an inspiration. "In fact, I think this calls for a celebration. Have you anything planned for lunch?"

"No, nothing."

"In that case you have now. And if you try to refuse, I really will fire you, so let's not have any arguments. All right?"

Anna laughed. "It doesn't look as though I have any choice."

"None at all." I looked at my watch. "It's half past eleven now. There are one or two things I have to do first, so if we go at twelve o'clock we should still beat most of the rush. How does that sound?"

"Wonderful." She was smiling broadly.

"In that case I'll hurry up and finish what I was doing."

I went to the office and closed the door. Despite the fact that Anna's departure was now official, as it were, I felt elated. She had been under no obligation to tell me so soon. It implied a warming toward me. I picked up the telephone and called Zeppo. It rang a long time before it was answered.

"Yeah?"

"Zeppo? It's Donald Ramsey."

There was a groan. "Donald? What do you want? Christ, I'm still in bed."

"In that case I've done you a favor getting you out of it. I'm taking Anna to lunch. I want you to be there as well."

"Lunch? No way."

"It's important."

"Look, I've already got plans for this afternoon. And I've got someone with me."

"Get rid of her and cancel whatever you were doing. This is too good an opportunity to miss." I explained what had happened and told him where we would be. "We'll be there just after twelve o'clock. You can get there for half past. That gives you about an hour. If you rush you should be able to manage that, I think."

He sighed irritably. "Oh, okay. I'll get there as soon as I can. But this is really pissing me about."

"That's what I'm paying you for."

"Look, I've said I'll be there, all right?" His voice was petulant.

I was tiring of his moods. "Would it be too much to ask for you to be in a better frame of mind, do you think?"

"I'll be all sweetness and light," he said and hung up.

He was late. But I had expected as much and did not allow it to spoil my enjoyment of Anna's company. She was animated, on a high now that she had told me, and when Zeppo finally arrived I felt a momentary pang that I no longer had her to myself.

"That's your friend Zeppo, isn't it?" she asked, looking over my shoulder. I turned. He was at the bar. I waved him over.

"What are you doing here?" His smile included us both in the question. He seemed genuinely surprised.

"It's a celebration. Anna's going to New York."

He turned to her. "Fantastic! How long for?"

"Hopefully for good."

"She's going with her boyfriend. You met him at the party, I think."

"I remember. Marty. Well, that's great! Congratulations."

There was no sign of his earlier sullenness. Either he was an excellent actor, or he had managed to cheer himself up. I did not particularly care which. I was only thankful for the fact.

"Why don't you join us?" I asked. "Unless you're meeting someone, of course."

He looked at his watch. "I was supposed to, but he's not here. I'm late, though, so I might have missed him."

"In that case have a glass of wine. I'm sure we can squeeze one out of the bottle."

He sat down. I poured his wine and watched Anna as they chatted. She was resting her arms on the table, leaning forward slightly. Her dress was stretched taut where her breasts hung against it. I made myself look at her face.

Zeppo, of course, had been to New York. "It's great. London's got nothing on it. It's got a real buzz twenty-four hours a day. Is that where Marty's from?"

"Well, he lived there before he came to London, but originally he's from Boston. That's where his parents live, but Marty says it's too country club and snobbish for him. And he doesn't exactly hit it off with his family, either. So we'll stay in New York, at least until Marty's finished his doctorate, and then it all depends where the work is."

"I've never been to Boston. Apart from New York I've only been to California a couple of times. Now there's somewhere you've got to go."

Anna smiled. "I'd like to, but Marty's not too keen on the West Coast."

"Really? God, why not?"

"He's not really one for the beach lifestyle. He says he had sand kicked in his face so many times when he was a kid that the tide comes in on him."

We laughed dutifully. "It can be a bit like that," Zeppo said. "But you shouldn't let that put you off. Some of the beaches are incredible. It'd be a shame to miss them."

The implied censure was only mild, but it was there. The first overt move against Marty. Anna accepted it with a shrug.

"Oh well, we'll see. There are hundreds of places I want to go to. I expect I'll never get around to seeing half of them."

"Have you a job already lined up?"

Anna glanced at me. "Oh no, not yet. I'll just have to look around when I get there."

"If you'd like, I have one or two contacts in New York I could get in touch with," I said. "They may be able to help."

"Oh, would you? That'd be fantastic!"

I basked in her gratitude. "Well, I can't promise that they will, of course, but I can certainly try." I would at least go through the motions.

"Oh, that'll be great, Donald! Thanks ever so much. We'll be able to live on savings for a while, but the sooner I can find work, the better."

"Don't build your hopes up too much. But I'll see what I can do."

That put Anna in a better mood than ever. Watching her, I could almost forget the reason we were there. Then Anna excused herself, and Zeppo leaned toward me.

"I think now's as good a time as any for you to go."

The request took me by surprise. "Now? Why?"

"Because there's only so much I can do while you're playing gooseberry, isn't there? Don't look so upset. That's what you're paying me for, isn't it? You've got to leave us alone sometime or other."

I covered my disappointment. "Yes, of course. I just wasn't expecting it. What do you plan to do?"

"Not much. It'll give me a chance to get to know her a bit better, that's all. Then, if it goes well, I can rip her clothes off and take her over the table." He sighed at my expression. "Joke, Donald."

"I didn't find it funny."

Zeppo smirked. "I noticed. Anyway, think of an excuse before she comes back. Say you've remembered a meeting or something."

"Won't that seem rather suspicious?"

"Why should it? You're her boss, for Christ's sake, you don't have to account to her. Just make it something simple and leave it at that."

I stood up as Anna returned. "Anna, I've suddenly remembered I've got an appointment in half an hour. I'm going to have to go. I'm afraid you'll have to open the gallery yourself. You don't mind, do you?"

If it was flimsy, Anna did not appear to notice. "No, of course not. I'd better be getting back anyway. I've had far too long as it is." She began to pick up her coat.

"No need to go this minute. There's no hurry. Finish the wine first. I'm sure Zeppo won't mind running you back, will you Zeppo?"

"Of course not. My pleasure."

I left them at the table. Not without regret and, I admit, a touch of jealousy. And anger. Zeppo's attitude was becoming unacceptably insolent. But then he still believed he was doing this just for money. From choice. Soon I would have to let him see otherwise.

For the moment, though, I had time to kill. There was a cafe opposite the gallery that was as good a place to wait as any. I parked some distance from it, so Anna would not see the car, and started to walk back. No sooner had I set off than it began to rain. By the time I reached the cafe I was soaked. I bought a cup of coffee and sat in a window seat, uncomfortably damp. From there I could look over the road at the gallery. I doubted I would be noticed by anyone on the far side of the street. Plants cluttered the windowsill, and the glass itself was so misted I could barely see through it myself. I sipped the appalling coffee and settled down to wait.

I was just beginning to suspect that Zeppo might have lured Anna off somewhere when I saw his car pull in farther down the road. A moment later they were both running toward the gallery, sheltering under Zeppo's coat. I was pleased by this unexpected intimacy and felt more kindly disposed toward the rain. I watched as they went inside, and then the lights came on against the dark afternoon. Now I could see them clearly through the gallery's large windows, a silent pantomime. I wished I could hear what they were saying. Both of them seemed to be smiling a great deal. The telephone must have rung, because Anna suddenly picked it up and began writing something in the messages book. Zeppo watched her for a moment, then moved to the window and looked out. I drew back but he did not see me. After a while Anna hung up, wrote some more, then said something to him. He answered, nodding. They laughed.

I took another sip of coffee and was surprised to find it was cold. I was about to order another when I saw someone else going into the gallery. I could see it was a woman, but she had her back to me and it was only when she turned to acknowledge Zeppo that I recognized her. It was Miriam, the rather ridiculous designer who had been at my party. I hoped she would leave once she found I was not there. But she showed no inclination of doing anything of the sort, and when Anna disappeared and came back with three cups on a tray, I knew Miriam was planning to stay.

I cursed her and looked at my watch. Enough time had passed to justify my going back, and now that Anna and Zeppo were no longer alone there was no reason not to. I left the cafe and walked to my car, getting wet again in the process. I parked in back of the gallery and let myself in.

"Well, this is a full house," I said. "For one happy moment I thought you were customers."

"Sorry to disappoint you," Miriam said. "I was passing, so I thought I'd stop by and see if you were in. Anna was a lifesaver and made me a cup of coffee. Good God, Donald, you're soaked!"

"Yes, I got caught in it," I took my coat off and gave it a shake. "It'll teach me to find a nearer parking space in future."

"Would you like a coffee?" Anna asked.

"I'd love one, please. I take it your lunch partner didn't arrive?" I said to Zeppo. It was only after I spoke that I realized I wanted to catch him out. But he fielded the question smoothly.

"No, but it was probably my fault for being late. I must have missed him. How was your meeting?"

Now he had caught me unawares. "Oh . . . unproductive."

"That's a shame. It didn't take very long, did it?" He sipped his coffee. The observation could have been innocent.

"Not as long as I would have liked. But never mind." I turned quickly to Miriam. "This is a pleasant surprise. I didn't expect to see you so soon after the party. Is it a purely social visit, or do you have an ulterior motive?"

"You are a cynic, Donald. Actually, it's both. It's a purely social visit, but I do have an ulterior motive."

"That sounds intriguing."

"Don't get excited. Some friends of mine phoned yesterday and invited themselves up next weekend. So I thought I'd have a few people around for dinner. Take the burden of entertaining them off me for a while. I wondered if you'd like to come?"

I was about to make an excuse when Anna returned with my coffee. Before I could answer, Miriam added. "I was going to ask if Anna and her boyfriend—Zeppo, isn't it?—wanted to come as well?"

There was a moment's silence. Miriam had obviously seen them together at the party and drawn the wrong conclusion. Zeppo smiled.

"You've got the name right, but I'm not Anna's boyfriend, I'm afraid."

"Oh, I'm, sorry, I thought . . ." Miriam went red. Anna and Zeppo smiled at each other.

"It's okay. You did meet my boyfriend, but only for a minute. He's called Marty." A flush of color had touched Anna's cheeks as well, descending onto her throat.

"Oh, yes, of course, how stupid of me," Miriam blustered. "Well, if you and Marty would like to come, you're very welcome. And you too, of course, Zeppo."

Zeppo looked amused. "Thanks, I'd love to."

I followed his lead. "So would I. Miriam's an excellent cook." In fact she was nothing of the sort, but it would be worth risking indigestion to bring Anna and Zeppo together again.

Miriam laughed. "I think Donald's being kind, but I'll do my best not to poison you. Will you and Marty be able to come, or have you something planned?"

I willed Anna to accept. "No, I don't think so," she said. "Thanks very much."

I looked across at Zeppo. He held my eyes for a moment before looking away.

It seemed that fate was on our side.

Chapter

5

The dinner party was a disaster. Miriam's guests seemed to have been selected with the same sense of foolhardy experimentalism that she had used to decorate her house. It was a beautiful old Victorian villa that had been ruined by the combination of period features with a more severe, modernistic style. Bauhaus chairs rubbed shoulders with paneled doors, and splashes of vivid, designer art hung below the original wall and ceiling moldings.

The guests themselves were similarly ill assorted, and as soon as I saw the preponderance of cropped hair, dowdy clothes and wire-rimmed spectacles I knew we were in for a vegetarian evening. Even worse was the fact that Anna, Marty, Zeppo and I were not even allowed to sit near each other. Miriam, with a designer's love of arranging things, seated everyone apart from friends and partners, obviously with the intention of forcing conversation. The result was to stifle it altogether.

The evening droned on with forced small talk about the deplorable state of the country, the roads and the weather. Only when the topic focused on a television documentary about the horrors of factory farming did it become slightly animated. One woman, perhaps tipped off by his leather jacket and trousers, tried to draw a so-far silent Zeppo into the conversation by asking how he could see something like that and still eat meat. "You *did* see it, didn't you?" she asked.

He sipped his wine and smiled. "Yeah. Made me so hungry I had to go to McDonald's." The nervous laughter seemed unsure whether to take the comment as wit or insensitivity. Talk moved onto a safer topic.

Finally, after enduring coffee and the cheese board, it was a respectable enough hour to leave, which was a relief for everyone. Zeppo approached me as coats were collected and dispensed.

"What a fucking waste of time that was," he muttered. Only I was within earshot.

I had to agree. But I was loath to let an opportunity drift away. "It's still quite early. We can go on somewhere else."

Zeppo shook his head. "Forget it. I've wasted enough of a perfectly good Saturday night as it is. I've got better things to do."

The evening and disappointment had grated on my nerves. I was in no mood for his prima donna tendencies. "No you haven't," I said, keeping my voice low. "And if you have they can wait." For a instant he looked surprised, then he grinned.

"Ooo. Got teeth, have we?" I said nothing. We stared at each other, and as the moment stretched out I remembered where we were and felt my will buckle. But just as I was about to look away he shrugged. "Okay, fuck it. Might as well chuck the entire night down the pan." He said it easily, but I still felt a nugget of satisfaction at facing him down.

It was decided, on my suggestion, that the four of us share a taxi. Zeppo and I sat in the pull-down seats, facing Anna and Marty in the back. I waited for Zeppo to say something, but apparently his capitulation stopped short of taking the initiative. I looked at my watch. "Well, I don't know about anyone else, but I think we deserve a drink after enduring that. It's not too late. Would anyone like a nightcap?"

Zeppo, after pausing just long enough to make me worried, took the hint. "If anyone's interested, I'm a member of a private club not too far away. We could go there, if you'd like."

I did not like. I could well imagine the sort of club Zeppo would belong to. But it was too much to expect him to both co-operate and suggest somewhere civilized. I feigned enthusiasm. "That sounds like a good idea to me." I looked across at Anna and Marty. "Shall we?"

She glanced at him. He had been quiet all evening. I thought he seemed a little intimidated by Zeppo. I took a petty gratification from the idea. "Well . . ." he began.

"Come on, let's go," Zeppo coaxed, looking from him to Anna. "We deserve a drink after that. Just one, then you can get a taxi from there. It's practically on the way. Okay?"

Without waiting for a reply he turned and gave the driver fresh instructions. Marty looked at him, then at Anna. They exchanged a smile. It excluded everyone else. I saw Marty put his hand on Anna's knee and give it a little squeeze. When Zeppo turned around again, they were sitting as before.

"All set. We'll be there in five minutes," Zeppo said. Marty readjusted his glasses.

The club was not quite as bad as I'd feared. I had been expecting a nightclub and was relieved when there were neither flashing lights nor loud music. But it was still very much in keeping with the sort of place I imagined Zeppo to frequent. Garish, brash and superficial. It was full of glittering young people, liberally decorated with enough mirrors to satisfy even the most demanding narcissistic appetite. I felt utterly out of place, and Marty looked it, whether he felt it or not. Zeppo, however, was obviously very much at home.

"Hey, there's some friends of mine," he said, and set off toward a crowded table. We were left to follow.

"Have you been here before?" I asked Anna as we made our way over.

"No. I didn't even know it existed." She lowered her voice. "God, is everyone here a model?"

"I'm not," Marty murmured. "I don't think Donald is either. Do you think they'll serve us?"

Anna stared as a striking black girl in a bikini top and miniskirt went past. "I feel positively drab."

"You've no need to," I said. "You put most of these girls to shame." I meant it. Their sharp, characterless looks left me untouched.

Zeppo had already arranged seats for us at the table. "Everyone, this is Anna, Donald and Marty." He ran through a list of names I immediately forgot. Marty and I received dismissive smiles and nods: Anna merited more attention.

"I'll get some drinks," Zeppo said and disappeared without asking what we wanted. The people at the table continued their animated, slightly hysterical conversation as though we weren't there. Only when Zeppo returned did we exist for them again.

"The drinks are on their way." He suddenly seemed bristling with energy. "God, we've just been to the worst dinner party in the world," he announced. The group listened deferentially as he gave an exaggerated account of our ordeal. It was greeted with wild shrieks of laughter. "Honest, I thought I was going to fall asleep in the mange-tout!"

The drinks arrived. I found myself presented with a Mexican beer. "How come you know Zeppo?" a bronzed young man asked Anna.

"Through Donald." She indicated me. "I haven't really known him very long, though."

The young man showed no interest in how long I had known him. He was about to ask Anna something else when Zeppo cut in. "Donald's an amazingly rich art dealer." They looked at me rather more appreciatively. "Anna's lucky enough to work for him. And Marty here's an anthropologist."

Marty looked embarrassed as attention switched to him, pinning him in his seat. He studied his untouched drink.

"Anthropology? Oh, you mean like body language and stuff?" asked a vacuously pretty girl with bleached white hair and thick dark eyebrows.

"That's part of it. But there's a little more to it than that," Marty said.

"Like what?" a young man with dreadlocks wanted to know.

Marty adjusted his glasses. "Well, it's basically the study of Man. With a capital *M*, not a small one."

There were giggles from around the table. Zeppo turned to Marty, a faintly condescending smile on his face. "Are you studying us now?"

Marty smiled and shook his head. "You needn't worry. I don't do it all the time."

"It must be great to be able to know if someone's lying by the way he scratches his nose, though." Zeppo's mockery was dangerously obvious.

"Well, it's not quite as simple as that."

"No?"

"No." Marty's hand went to his glasses, touched them, came away again. "Nose scratching can be an indication that someone's lying, or nervous. Then again, they might just have an itchy nose. It's not an exact science."

"So you don't know what I'm thinking by the way I'm sitting," said the blond girl. She was leaning with her elbow on the table, chin on hand, gazing at him intently. She was also showing a considerable amount of cleavage. Marty glanced across and hastily looked away.

"Ah . . . no."

Zeppo's smile was perilously close to being a smirk. "Oh, I bet you're just being modest," he said. "I can't believe you can't tell more than that. What about me, for instance? What would you say my 'behavior' tells you?"

Marty looked uncomfortable. "I really don't . . ."

"Oh, come on. You must be able to hazard a guess after all the years of work you've done."

There were sounds of encouragement from around the table. Anna was looking at Marty a little anxiously. I hoped Zeppo was not being too heavy handed. Marty gave a reluctant shrug.

"Okay, if you really want me to." Zeppo smiled superciliously. Marty studied him and took a deep breath.

"Well, the way you're leaning forward, legs apart, facing me directly, suggests that you're feeling confident. Possibly even confrontational. You've been displaying signs of aggression for a while now, so I'd say you either feel threatened or want to assert your dominance over the other males in the group. If you were a gorilla you'd probably be beating your chest and roaring."

Zeppo shifted slightly in his seat. "Ah, now you're starting to feel a bit more uncomfortable," Marty went on. "You're drawing back slightly, moving your legs together, which suggests that you no longer feel quite so sure of yourself—and now you're leaning forward again, displaying more aggression characteristics, so perhaps you didn't like what I said. Now you're frozen and tense, which could mean either that you're nervous or that you're ready for sudden movement. And by the way your jaw muscles are bunching I'd say it's probably the latter, so I'd better stop before I really piss you off and get my teeth knocked out."

No one spoke when he had finished. The blond girl stirred first. "Wow, that's amazing!"

The spell was broken. There was a ripple of relieved laughter. Everyone began to move again.

"He's got you sussed, Zepp," the boy with dreadlocks said. Zeppo's mouth was set in a frozen smile. His jaw muscles were still working, I noticed.

"That's really brilliant! You can tell all that just by *looking* at someone?" The blond girl was plainly impressed.

Marty's hand went to his glasses again. He glanced at Anna, a half smile on his face. "No, not really. I was just making it up."

There was a moment's stunned silence. Then everyone burst out laughing.

"So all that was just bullshit? Honestly?" asked the blond boy. Marty nodded.

"Sure. Complete bullshit." He smiled across at Zeppo. "Wasn't it?"

Zeppo smiled tightly back at him. "Yes." He relaxed and grinned. "Serves me right for being pushy." I wondered if anyone else could see how angry he was. I was so pleased I took a drink of the beer before I remembered what it was. Marty had done himself no favors. Zeppo was not the sort to take humiliation lightly. Now he had a grudge to help motivate him. As the conversation ran on, centering on Marty, Zeppo stood up and went toward the toilet. I followed.

"If I were you, I would be inclined to keep the contest purely physical in future," I murmured as we went in.

"Oh, piss off," he said and locked himself in a cubicle.

Chapter

———

6

By halfway through the next week, I had heard two pieces of gossip stemming from that evening. One was good, one bad. The bad came from Miriam. She came into the gallery on Monday afternoon, brimming with apologies and scandal.

"You're becoming quite a regular visitor," I said.

"I know. I'll be buying one of your bloody paintings next. Is there any chance of a coffee? I'd kill for some caffeine."

"I'll get it," Anna said.

Miriam flopped down into a chair. "I've come to apologize."

"Whatever for?"

"Saturday bloody night. It was awful."

"Of course it wasn't!" I lied.

"Donald, we both know perfectly well it was. I'm afraid I'm just not cut out in the hostess mold. And to be honest, I'd forgotten how boring some of my old friends are. That's university friendships for you. Ah, thank you." She took the coffee from Anna. "Mm. That's better. Anyway, just wanted to make sure you were all still talking to me."

"Really, it wasn't that bad."

She sipped her coffee. "Donald, you're a lovely man, but a liar. I'm sure it must have been thoroughly boring for Anna and Marty." She waved aside Anna's polite reassurance. "And I'm sure poor Zeppo wished he'd never got roped into it."

"Oh, I wouldn't worry too much about Zeppo if I were you," I said. "He tends to take things very much in his stride."

She hesitated. "Yes, so I've heard," she said, pointedly. "How do you come to know him, anyway?"

I was instantly wary. "Through mutual friends, really."

"He's not a close friend of yours or anything, then?"

"Well, I don't suppose I've known him very long, but he seems likeable enough," I said, torn between endorsing him and not wanting to be too closely affiliated in case she knew something incriminating.

"Ah." Miriam sipped her coffee. It was clear she had information to divulge. I was by no means sure I wanted to hear it. Certainly not then, in front of Anna. But it would have seemed unnatural not to ask.

"Why?" I hoped I sounded casual. Miriam put down her cup. I could see that nothing could have prevented her telling us anyway.

"Oh, I just wondered. I was talking to someone yesterday who knew him. Or knew of him, at any rate."

"Who was that?"

"An old friend of mine. Zeppo went out with her niece for a while."

I was relieved. Whatever she knew, it was not the same information I had. That would have been disastrous. "I gather she told you something about him?"

"She did indeed. According to her, he's a real monster. Gave her niece a terrible time. Walked all over her, let her know he was seeing other girls. All sorts of things. Finally, the silly girl threatened to cut her wrists. I suppose she was hoping to frighten him. The next day she had a parcel delivered. A packet of razor blades in a red velvet box."

I instinctively glanced at Anna. She looked shocked. "She didn't use them, did she?"

"No, thank God. When he did that she came to her senses. Realized what a shit he was and pulled herself together."

"Perhaps he's just a shrewd judge of human nature," I said, furious with her. "That could have been what he intended."

Miriam was unconvinced. "It might have been, but my friend seemed to doubt it. And even if it was, he was still taking a hell of a risk."

She chatted some more, but she had finished what she came to do. An apology on the one hand, a character assassination on the other. When she had gone, I turned to Anna.

"That was rather surprising about Zeppo. I didn't think he was the type to do something like that."

"No, neither did I. Just goes to show you never can tell."

I busied myself with a catalogue. "If that is what happened. Miriam's stories do tend to be a bit apocryphal at the best of times, and a thirdhand version from someone's aunt hardly seems to be the most reliable source. I'm sure Zeppo wouldn't do a thing like that." I stopped before I became too defensive. It was best to dismiss it. I closed the catalogue. "Anyway, if her taste in art was anything like Miriam's, I couldn't blame him if he had."

We laughed.

The second piece of slander came from Zeppo and was much more encouraging. I had not heard anything from him since Saturday and suspected that his silence was a display of petulance after his loss of face. But by midweek he had presumably licked his wounds enough to feel like talking to me again.

"It's Donald," I said when he answered the phone. "I've been trying to get in touch with you." I kept my voice neutral.

"I've been away. I can go away, can't I?"

"Of course. I simply wondered where you were. I've been trying to get hold of you for days."

"Well, now you have, so what's your problem?"

"The problem is that in future I would appreciate it if you would at least let me know when you're planning to take a holiday." I had not intended to be drawn into an argument, but I was not going to be spoken to like that.

"Oh, I'm so sorry. What would you like, a written apology on your desk by tomorrow morning? With detention for spelling mistakes?"

"There's no need to be facetious."

"Stop acting as though you fucking own me, then! If I want to go away for a day or two days or a fucking month, I will, and I don't expect you to get on my back about it! Okay?"

I was astonished by his outburst. "May I remind you that I'm paying you for this?"

"You're paying me to do a job, and I'm doing it. I don't have to take shit from you as well. If you're going to start acting the big boss, you can find someone else to get into your girlfriend's pants. If you can. Understand?"

I took a deep breath. I realized this was only Zeppo's way of reasserting himself after Saturday. It was better to let it pass. I still had a trump card he was unaware of, but I was not going to throw it away in the heat of the moment. It would be all the sweeter when Zeppo finally realized that, whether he wanted to or not, he would do as I told him.

"I think you've made yourself perfectly clear," I said.

"Good."

Neither of us spoke for a moment. I cleared my throat. "If you've got that out of your system, I called because I thought you ought to know Miriam came into the gallery yesterday."

"So?"

"Apparently you used to be . . . acquainted . . . with a niece of one of her friends." I repeated what she had told us about the razor blades. It immediately put him in a better mood.

"Christ, I'd forgotten all about that." He laughed. "Shit, what was her name? Carol? Jenny? I can't remember. Did she use them?"

"Don't you know?"

"Why should I? I was hardly going to phone her to see if she'd committed suicide, was I?"

"Well, she didn't. Apparently the razor blades shocked her out of it."

"Pity. I liked the idea of someone killing themself over me."

"Yes, well, as sorry as I am to disappoint you, that's not the main issue, is it? The point is that Anna knows about it."

"So what?"

"So it hardly shows you in the best of lights, does it? We've spent all this time trying to create a good impression, and now this happens!"

"Donald, you worry too much. And you might have been trying to convince her that I'm nice and wholesome, but I haven't. That doesn't get you into bed with someone. The idea is to fire her with passion, not get her to vote me neighbor of the year."

"Yes, but even so—"

"Trust me. It'll only make me seem more exciting. Girls love bastards. All it's going to do is make her more intrigued." He paused dramatically. "And from what I've been told about Marty, she's probably desperate for somebody to give her a good time."

I was clearly supposed to ask what that meant. I did.

"Do you remember the guy with dreadlocks on Saturday night?" he went on, appeased. "Well, he's gay, and guess who he said he's seen hanging around gay clubs?"

I was incredulous. "Marty?"

"Bingo."

"Are you sure?"

"Stevie was. After you'd all gone he said he recognized him from a club called the Pink Flamingo."

"Is he certain it was Marty?"

"He said so. He remembered him because he was always alone and never spoke to anyone. Just sat there by himself."

"That doesn't necessarily mean he's homosexual, does it?"

Zeppo laughed. "If you can think of any other reason for going to a place where the waiters are topless and wear leather chaps, I'd like to hear it."

I was prepared to believe almost anything of Marty. But this seemed too incredible. "Perhaps he didn't realize it was a gay club."

"Be serious."

I still could not accept it. "But what about Anna?"

"What about her? He might be bi, or trying to go straight."
He chuckled. "Face it, Donald. Our Marty's a closet queen."

"My God." I did not know what to make of this at all. "Why
didn't you tell me straight away?"

"What for? I've told you now, haven't I? You couldn't have
done anything if I had."

Zeppo's revenge on me for laughing at him. "Do you think
Anna knows?"

"I've no idea. I think she ought to, though, don't you?"

"You're going to tell her?"

"It's worth thinking about. But not just yet. It could easily piss
her off at me if I'm not careful. Particularly if she already knows.
So I think we should just bear it in mind for now and see what
happens. It's always nice to keep something in reserve."

I could not agree more. "So what do you intend to do next?"

"Well, all things considered, I think it's time to make a
move."

"So soon? I thought you were going to take things slowly?"

"What do you think I've been doing? Jesus, you don't think
I normally wait this long, do you?"

"I still think it's too early. We can't afford any setbacks."

"There won't be any."

"I don't know . . ."

"Look, I don't tell you how to run a gallery, do I? So don't try
and tell me how to fuck a girl."

His crudeness grated, but I thought it wiser to overlook it.
"I'm not. I simply don't want anything to go wrong."

"Donald, believe me, I know what I'm doing. She's primed
and ready. It's Tuesday today. By next weekend, I'll have had
her."

Despite his indelicacy, I felt my chest tighten with excitement. "You're sure?"

"Positive."

I hesitated, wondering how much to tell him. "There's one
thing. I don't want you to do anything without letting me know
first."

"What?"

"I want you to tell me when you think something's actually going to happen. I want to know beforehand."

"You're joking!"

"No."

There was an incredulous pause. "So if Anna decides to tear her pants off and throw herself at me, I've got to say, 'Hang on, I've just got to tell Donald?' "

"I'm sure someone with your experience can arrange things better than that."

"For Christ's sake, though, why? What difference does it make?"

"Probably none. But I still want to know."

I heard him snort, exasperated. "Are you frightened I'll make it up or something? What do you want to do, examine the sheets afterward?"

"I simply don't want to find out after the event, that's all." It was not all, but it was all he needed to know just then. "If anything happens without my knowledge then the entire arrangement is off. I won't give you a penny. Is that clear?"

"Jesus! Yes, all right, Donald, I get the message. Thy will be done. I promise not to shaft her without asking your permission first. Okay?"

"Thank you."

"Am I permitted to come into the gallery tomorrow and speak to her? Or is that asking too much?"

"There's no need to be childish. What do you have in mind?"

"I thought I'd take her out to lunch. If that's all right with you, of course. You'll have to be too busy to come with us. Don't worry though, we'll go to a no-screwing restaurant."

I ignored the comment.

⊙∿⊙

I was nervous all next morning. Apart from anything else, I was still worried how Anna would feel about Zeppo after what Miriam had said. But when he arrived she seemed to act normally toward him. When he offered to buy lunch, however, I noticed that she glanced at me to see what my answer would be. I declined. "The two of you will just have to make do without me," I added, hoping to force her hand. Anna hesitated briefly, then accepted.

I watched them as they left the gallery. They looked right together. Anna was laughing as they walked past the window. If she had been disturbed by Miriam's story, she was not showing it now. I continued looking out through the window after they had gone and then turned and faced the empty gallery. I had an hour to pass before they returned.

I telephoned for a sandwich to be delivered. While I waited I wondered what Zeppo would say to her and tried to imagine how she would respond. I pictured various scenarios, but the only ones I could visualize clearly all ended in failure. When I imagined Anna throwing wine in Zeppo's face and walking out, I stopped myself. I looked at my watch. Only ten minutes had passed. They would only just have reached the restaurant.

My sandwich arrived, but I had no appetite. I listlessly picked the prawns from it and dithered about the gallery, straightening frames, adjusting magazines. Anything to pass the time. I looked at my watch again, restraightened the same picture frames. There were people I could telephone, but my lack of interest outweighed the time it would occupy. I could concentrate on nothing except the increasingly slow progress of the hands of my watch.

Then, suddenly, there were only fifteen minutes left. The minutes that had crawled by now seemed to run away, and I grew more nervous as each one disappeared. My stomach began to complain. I went to the office where I kept a packet of indigestion tablets, and as I chewed one I heard the door open downstairs.

I looked at my watch. She was early. I tried not to think what that could mean and forced myself to take the stairs at a reasonable pace. I was so convinced that it would be Anna that when I emerged into the gallery and saw someone else standing there I was dumbfounded.

The newcomer turned toward me. "Hello," she said. It was the woman who had wrecked my car with her Range Rover.

"I'm sorry, have I disturbed you?" she asked, looking anxious. I made an effort and smiled.

"No, not at all. I'm sorry, I was just . . ." Nothing offered itself, and I let the sentence trail off. Luckily, she was not one to allow time for an awkward silence.

"I was in the area, so I thought I'd drop in and see how you were. I hope you don't mind?"

"Not at all," I said, finally recovering. "I was just a little surprised, that's all. Pleasantly," I added, smiling more naturally this time.

"Sorry to disappoint you if you were expecting a customer. Although I suppose I might even be one, if I see anything. Anything I can afford, that is," she laughed.

"Yes, well—" I began, but she was already going on, walking to the nearest painting.

"Oh, I say, that's rather nice, isn't it? Who's it by?"

"Flint."

She studied it, head on one side. "I can't say I've heard of him, but then, paintings aren't really my forte. I know what I like, but that's about all. How much is it?"

I told her.

"Gosh." She laughed. "Well, at least it shows I've got good taste, if nothing else. Still, it is rather lovely." She stared at it for a second or two longer, then abruptly turned to me. "So. How are you?"

"I'm fine, thank you." Still wondering what the reason for her visit was, I almost forgot to add, "And you?"

"Oh, can't complain. Well, I could, but it doesn't do any good, does it?" I smiled politely. She looked around the gallery. "I must say, you've got some wonderful pieces. I do like a more traditional style. I'm not one for any of this modern stuff myself."

"No, neither am I," I said, mollified somewhat.

"My daughter's at art college. Talented girl, but some of the things she's done leave me stone cold. I say to her, 'Why don't you paint something that actually looks like it's supposed to, Susan? There's enough of these intense art students running around, all daubing away at the most hideous things,' but will she listen?" She spread her hands, helplessly. "Still, what can you do? They're all intent on making a 'statement' now. I'm probably old-fashioned, but I like a painting to look like something. If an artist's got talent, what's the point of hiding it?"

I could not have agreed more. But before I could say so, she had already left the subject behind. "How's the car, by the way?"

I struggled to keep up with this change of tack. "Oh, it's . . . I've got it back from the garage, at last."

She beamed. "Have you? Oh, good." She was walking toward me. "And what about the insurance? Have you heard anything from them, yet?"

I made a conscious effort not to step back as she advanced. "No, not yet. But—"

"No, neither have I. I was on to them the day before yesterday, to give them a rocket. They're quick enough to take the money from you, but when it comes to paying it out again they don't want to know, do they?"

"No, I suppose not." I held my ground as she stood in front of me. Her perfume was cloying and thick, not at all like the cleaner fragrance of Anna. At the thought, I remembered that she should be back any second. Almost desperate, I wondered how I could get rid of the stupid woman before then.

"I managed to get the doll's house, by the way," she said, while I was still wondering.

"The doll's house . . .?"

"From the auction. The one I saw you at."

"Oh, I see . . . Oh, good."

"Yes, I was quite pleased myself. I didn't really expect to get it, but for once no one else seemed very interested. Well, not as interested as I was worried they would be, at least. It's Victorian. Quite a beautiful little thing. In fact I'm by no means sure I want to sell it. It's quite heartbreaking, sometimes, buying a piece you like only to have to sell it again. Still that's what business is all about, isn't it? I suppose you feel exactly the same way about some of your paintings."

"Well, yes . . ." There were very few that appealed to me enough for me to want to keep them, but it was simpler to agree. I looked at my watch, hoping she would take the hint. It was already past the time when Anna should have returned.

"I'm sorry, I'm chattering away. Am I keeping you from your work?"

"Actually, I am expecting someone any second. A client."

"Oh, I am sorry. You should have said." She reached out and touched my arm as she apologized. I only just stopped myself from flinching away. "That's my trouble. I'm a bit of a chatterbox. In case you haven't noticed." She laughed. "Anyway, I'll not stay. I actually called in to see if I could treat you for lunch or a coffee somewhere, but you're obviously busy."

Surprised, I was about to regretfully agree when the door opened again. I looked up. It was Anna.

She glanced at the woman and smiled a greeting.

"Sorry I'm late."

"That's all right." I was suddenly very conscious of the woman's presence. She had turned and was smiling across at Anna. I was about to introduce them, reluctantly, when I realized I could not remember the woman's name.

"Anna, there's a catalogue on my desk. Could you fetch it for me, please?" It was the only thing I could think of to save me from the imminent social embarrassment.

She was hanging up her coat. "Yes, of course." With another smile at the woman, she went upstairs.

"That's my assistant," I said needlessly.

"Pretty girl." Again, she touched my arm. "Anyway, I'd better be getting off. I don't want to be here when your client arrives. Next time I'm going to be in the area, I'll give you a ring, shall I? Perhaps we can manage a coffee or something when you've more time."

"Yes, of course." I was prepared to say anything to be rid of her. I began to walk her to the door. She stopped in the doorway and offered me her hand.

"Nice seeing you again. And I do like the gallery, by the way. Very impressive."

I smiled and said something or other in the way of thank you. Then, finally, she left. I closed the door, resisting the impulse to lock and bolt it behind her. As I went back into the gallery, Anna was coming downstairs.

"I can't find any catalogue on your desk, Donald. Are you sure it's there?"

"It doesn't matter," I said. "I'll look for it later."

"Was that a client?"

"Hardly. She's the woman who ran into my car."

"I thought you looked a bit flustered. Is everything okay?"

"Now she's gone, yes. She offered to take me out for lunch."

Anna raised her eyebrows. "Really?" She smiled. "Could be she wants more than just the insurance."

I felt a jolt of alarm. "What do you mean?"

"Well, you're an eligible bachelor."

I could feel blood rush into my cheeks. "Oh no, I don't think it's anything like that. No, I'm sure . . . oh, no."

Anna was grinning. "Well, you never know. Is she married?"

"She must be, she has children."

"Ah, but has she mentioned a husband?"

I thought back. I could not remember her saying anything about him. Anna laughed.

"Don't look so horrified, Donald, I'm only kidding."

"I'm sure it's nothing like that."

"No, I know. I was only kidding. Really." She made a visible effort to stop smiling. I decided to change the subject and with a start remembered where she had been.

"Nice lunch?" I asked.

"Yes, thanks."

I waited for more, but she said nothing else. I tried to think of a way to sound her out further but could think of nothing that did not sound suspicious. "I'll be in the office," I said.

I went back upstairs. I had told Zeppo to telephone me as soon as he could. I sat down behind my desk and waited for his call. The telephone rang almost immediately. I snatched it up.

"Hello?"

It was a customer. Struggling to hide my impatience, I dealt with the inquiry as quickly as I decently could and hung up. I waited again. Zeppo's interpretation of "as soon as possible" was apparently different from mine. It was almost an hour later before he called.

"How did it go?" I asked, breathlessly.

"I'll tell you tonight."

"But—"

"I'll be at your place at seven."

"Zeppo—!" I almost shouted and heard a click as the connection was cut.

I banged down the receiver in frustration. I did not know what to think. It did not seem promising, but Zeppo was quite capable of tormenting me just for the fun of it. I picked up the telephone again and tried his number. There was no answer. He had either not called from home, or else he was ignoring me. Whichever, there was nothing I could do about it. I would have to wait until that evening.

I took two more indigestion tablets.

Chapter

7

The rest of the day was awful. It was an afternoon when everything seemed to take spiteful pleasure in going wrong. My accountants called to tell me they had lost half of my records when their computer crashed. Shortly after that I discovered that a prospective customer had died and would therefore not be collecting the watercolor he had bought only two days before. Furthermore, a full refund would be appreciated, his daughter, a mercenary-minded young harpy, informed me. And to cap the day off, my pen leaked in my jacket pocket, creating an indelible blue stain the size of a fifty-pence piece.

My stomach burned irritably. Even the fact that Anna wore only a thin shirt, tantalizingly hinting at the shape of her breasts, failed to improve matters. Normally I could have watched her indefinitely, but right then, not knowing what had happened between her and Zeppo, the sight only tormented me.

I decided enough was enough and closed the gallery early, stopping off at the chemists for a stronger stomach treatment on the way home. I cooked myself a bland meal of scrambled eggs, washed the dishes and was just wondering what to do next to pass the time when the doorbell rang. I looked at my watch. It was only half past six. Much too soon for Zeppo. I went to the front door and opened it.

Zeppo was standing on the top step. "Oh. I wasn't expecting you yet," I said stupidly.

"Are you going to let me in, or do I have to stand out here all night?"

I moved to one side to let him pass. "You're early," I repeated, moving into the lounge. Nerves and his premature arrival conspired to make me clumsy and self-conscious.

"Do you want me to go and come back later?"

"No, of course not. I just . . ." I cut my losses. "Drink?"

He accepted, tersely, and sat down. I poured one for myself, despite my indigestion. Zeppo's manner implied I might need it. If he was baiting me, he was taking it to extremes.

I handed him his drink and tried to appear relaxed. "So," I said. "What happened this afternoon?"

He took a heavy mouthful of whisky. His jaw muscles bunched and worked.

"The bitch blew me out."

The room seemed to tilt. I stared at him. "What do you mean?"

"I mean she said no."

"No?"

"Yes, no! Christ, do you want me to spell it out?"

I still could not accept it. "She actually turned you down?"

"Yes! She actually turned me down! Is that clear enough now?"

It was beginning to be. I sat opposite him. "Why?"

"Because the stupid bitch won't two-time that scrawny little prick, that's why!"

"You surely didn't ask her as bluntly as that?"

He sneered at me. "Oh, credit me with a bit of sense! Of course I didn't! I didn't have to, she stubbed me out before I had a chance to ask anything!"

I closed my eyes, kneading them. "I think you'd better tell me exactly what happened."

"I want another drink first."

I took his glass and refilled it, topping up my own as well. Zeppo received his drink without thanks.

"She must have been expecting something," he said, after swallowing half of it. "It was going fine at first. We were having a laugh, getting along great. Then I asked her if she wanted to go out for a drink with me one night, and she said she didn't think that would be a good idea. I asked why not, and she said because Marty wouldn't like it. So I said that he needn't know, and she just said, 'I think I know what you're leading up to, and I'd rather you didn't.' I thought she was just playing hard to get, you know, wanting me to coax her, so I gave her the full works, about how I couldn't help how I felt and all that sort of shit, but she didn't budge. She just cut me dead! Came out with crap about how she'd had a feeling this was coming and that she was flattered, but that she loved Marty and she'd rather we'd leave it at that. Then the bitch even had the fucking nerve to say she valued me as a friend! Me! I couldn't believe it! I felt like knocking that fucking understanding look off her face!"

I was too numb to react to his language. "What did you say to her?"

"What the fuck could I say? She made it pretty plain she didn't want to play ball. She's not interested in anyone except that wimp!"

I took another drink. The spirit seared my stomach. I barely noticed. "So much for your assurances. I thought you said she was 'primed and ready,' I think it was?"

"Don't get fucking smart with me! How was I to know she was a freak? Jesus, I could have a dozen girls better looking than her just by snapping my fingers!"

"Then it's a pity she's as immune to your digits as she is to the rest of you! I knew this was too soon!"

"Oh, and you're such an expert, aren't you? If you're so experienced why don't you see if you can do any better yourself?"

With an effort, I bit back further recriminations. "I suppose what's done is done. Arguing isn't going to change it. We'd better decide what we're going to do next."

Zeppo stared moodily into his glass. "What can we do? She's made it clear she doesn't want to know."

"You're surely not going to give up that easily?"

"You tell me what else we can do, then! If we'd got more time, all right, but we haven't! She's emigrating in a few weeks, for fuck's sake!"

"So that's it, then? One refusal and you let yourself be beaten by someone like Marty?"

"It's not my fault there's a deadline!"

"Perhaps it's just as well there is. At least it gives you an excuse."

"Don't push it, Donald."

"I'm not. I'm merely stating the obvious. I expected better from you than this."

"Tough shit."

This bickering was getting us nowhere. "There must be something we can do!"

He shrugged. "Short of drugging her, I can't think of anything." He looked at me. "That's not a bad idea, come to think of it."

"No!" The thought appalled me.

"Suit yourself." He tossed back the rest of his drink. "I just wish I'd told the bitch that her precious boyfriend is as bent as a butcher's hook. See how romantic she felt about him then."

I had forgotten all about that. "You didn't say anything about it?"

He shook his head. "No, I wish I had. I was so surprised I didn't think about it until afterward." He looked at me, smiling nastily. "Mind you, it's not too late, is it?"

I took his glass and went to refill it. "Coming from you now, it would only sound like sour grapes."

"So what? It would still drop Marty in the shit, wouldn't it? I can't see her wanting to rush off to America with him then."

"But what if she already knows? That would finish your chances once and for all."

He took the glass from me. "They're not exactly brilliant anyway, are they?"

"No, but if you antagonize her they'll be even worse."

He shrugged. "Okay. I'll get Stevie to do it, then. He's the one who saw him, after all. We can arrange for him to meet them accidentally, and he can drop it into the conversation."

I was only half listening. An idea was starting to form. "I don't like the idea of involving anyone else. It only complicates things."

"So what do you suggest? We've only got a few weeks left. What else can we do?"

"That depends." I spoke slowly. "Perhaps we've been approaching this from the wrong angle."

"What do you mean?"

"We've been concentrating on seducing Anna away from Marty. We might have better luck trying the other way around."

He frowned. "You mean work on him again?"

"It's worth a try. And this time, now we know which way his preferences lie, we can try someone more suitable than your femme fatale."

Zeppo looked thoughtful. "Yeah, that's not a bad idea. I could have a word with Stevie. It might cost, but I'm sure we could work something out."

I swirled the liquid in my glass, choosing my words carefully. "I wasn't thinking about using him. As I said, I don't want to involve anyone else."

Zeppo stared at me. "You better not mean what I think you do."

"Why not? It seems to make the most sense."

An incredulous smile spread across his face. "Hang on a minute. Let's get this straight. Now you want me to try and seduce *Marty*? Is that right?"

"In a nutshell, yes."

He began to laugh. "I've got to hand it to you, Donald. You don't do things by halves, do you? First you hire me to get Anna into bed, and now you want me to try with her boyfriend! Jesus Christ!"

"I realize you'll probably want a higher fee, of course."

"Oh, that's very decent of you. But there's no need. I'm not doing it."

"I really think you should reconsider."

"Forget it." His laughter had gone. "What the hell do you think I am?"

I made the mistake of trying to be humorous. "To paraphrase an old joke, I think we both know what you are. It's just the price that's in doubt."

Zeppo slammed the glass down. "Get fucked, Donald!" He began to walk to the door.

I followed him. "I'm sorry if I've offended you, but I really can't see where the problem is."

He turned on me. "Oh, come on! I'm sure even you must have a pretty good idea! She's a girl. He's a boy. So am I."

"Does that make any difference?"

"Of course it fucking does!"

"Is that your only objection?"

"Christ, isn't that enough?"

I stood up. "Wait here." I went past him to the door. "Help yourself to another drink."

I left him standing there, enjoying the bemused expression on his face. I went into my study, to the small wall safe there. I opened it and took out a large brown envelope. I was about to play my trump card.

Zeppo was sitting down when I returned. He had refilled his glass, I noticed. I thought, not without satisfaction, that he would need it. I handed him the envelope and sat down opposite him.

He looked at it. "What's this?"

"Open it and see."

I watched as he put down his glass and slid out the photographs. He looked at the first one and stiffened. Then, with studied casualness, he flicked through the rest.

"Where did you get these?" He set them down beside him. His voice was calm but not reassuringly so.

"From a business associate. He specializes in rather more—shall we say 'rarified'?—types of art than most dealers. I was surprised to see these there. Normally he doesn't deal with photographic material, but I suppose the strong classical themes of these helped sway him. And they are quite well done. I daresay you could justifiably call them art instead of pornography, although I'm not sure everyone would agree."

"How long have you had them?"

I picked them up and replaced them in the envelope. "Quite a while. I actually came across them months ago, long before I had any inkling that I would be needing your services. I recognized you straight away, of course. That's one disadvantage of having such a memorable face. Not that I thought anything of it at the time. You were just someone I'd bumped into at a couple of dinner parties, and since I'm not particularly interested in photography, whatever the subject matter, I was only mildly amused. In fact I forgot all about it until I decided I needed help with Anna and Marty. Then you seemed like the ideal candidate. So I went back to my associate, and as luck would have it, he still had the photos."

Zeppo was looking at me coolly. "What are you planning to do with them?"

"Do with them?" I shrugged. "Nothing at all. But I thought this was as good a time as any to let you know I had them. Particularly since several of them show you engaged in the sort of activity we're discussing now."

He made an attempt at sounding blasé. "So what? I'm a model, not a politician. In my line no one gives a toss about gay pictures."

I smiled. "Possibly not. But some of your partners do look a little . . . young, shall we say? Not quite school-leaving age?"

His face was white. "Listen, you old bastard, don't try and blackmail me. You wouldn't like it."

"I'm sure neither of us would. Although if copies of these were circulated to certain people, I'm certain you'd like it even less. I don't imagine this sort of thing does anyone's career much good. But you needn't worry about anything like that from me. We have a perfectly good business relationship, and I wouldn't dream of spoiling it. No, I simply wanted to remind you that I'm not suggesting anything you haven't done before, that's all."

"That was different. It was a long time ago, and I needed the money."

"Zeppo, you don't have to justify yourself to me. I'm merely pointing out that what you've done once for money, you can do again. And this time for considerably more."

"What's to stop me from taking these with me?"

"Nothing at all. In fact you could give some to your friends. I have several copies. In different places, of course."

He glared at me. For the first time, I realized he was capable of violence. "You fat, smug, pompous old cunt."

"That sort of talk helps no one. Now, do we have a deal?"

He did not answer at first. Then he gave a short, grudging nod. "All right. But you're making a mistake."

I thought he was threatening me. "And why's that?"

"Because it's a bad idea."

"You seem to have suddenly changed your mind. You said a moment ago it was worth a try."

"Yes, with somebody else. Not with me. What if Anna finds out? I thought the whole point was for me to end up in bed with her. If she finds out I'm trying to screw her boyfriend, she's not going to be too thrilled about that idea then, is she?"

"If we handle this properly she'll never know. I can't imagine Marty telling her about it. Can you?"

He gave a sullen shrug. "Perhaps not. But in that case, what's to stop her still going to America with him?"

"You are. Once he's, ah, compromised himself, he'll be vulnerable and open to persuasion. You'll be able to manipulate him any way you like. The last thing he'll want is for Anna to find out he's had an affair with another man. It'll be much easier for him to simply cry off and go back alone than admit that. Assuming, of course, that he still even wants to take her."

Zeppo ignored my gallant attempt at a joke. "It'd be a lot easier just to blackmail him now. This is getting too complicated."

"Not at all. For one thing, the only item we have to blackmail him with at present is an uncorroborated sighting in a gay nightclub. This way we'll have him in a stranglehold."

He was unconvinced. "I still think it's too risky."

In retrospect, I realize he was right, and I wonder now if I was not already pushing for the eventual denouement even then. But if I was, I was unconscious of the fact.

"Of course it isn't," I said. "You're just looking for excuses."

Zeppo sighed and threw his hands up. "Okay. We'll do it your way. Just don't blame me if it goes wrong."

"If I didn't know better, I'd say that you've lost confidence in yourself. Has Anna made you lose faith in your own abilities?"

"Look, I've said I'll do it. Don't push your luck." Without asking, he got up and poured himself another drink. "We'll have to think of something to get Anna out of the way for a while."

"Don't worry," I said. "I'll take care of that."

Chapter

8

"*Amsterdam?*"

Anna stared at me. I nodded. "I know it's asking an awful lot, and if I could think of another way around it, I would. But I can't." I looked apologetic. "I do realize I'm springing it on you, and you have got a lot on, but if you could possibly manage it, it would be helping me out enormously. If you can't, though, you must say. I don't want to force it on you."

She seemed completely taken aback. "No, no, of course. It's just, well, it is rather short notice. And I've never bid at an auction before."

I nodded. "I realize that, and if you can't go, then that's quite all right. Quite all right. I'll think of something else."

"I'm not saying I can't," she said, hurriedly. "You've just caught me by surprise, that's all." She bit her lip. "Look, you don't need to know right now, do you? Can I tell you this afternoon? I'm meeting Marty for lunch, and that'll give me chance to work out what I've got to do and talk it over with him. Is that all right?"

"Of course it is! I don't want to rush you. I'm sorry to have to ask you at all, but there's no way I can go myself, so . . ." I brushed it away. "You have a chat with Marty and let me know this afternoon. Whatever you decide will be fine by me."

It was two days after my meeting with Zeppo. It had taken

me that long to think of a way to remove Anna from the scene. I had found it in the list of forthcoming auctions. Two were being held in Amsterdam the following week, with a day's gap in between. Neither had anything I was really interested in, but Anna wasn't to know that. I had invented a visit from an important buyer as the reason why I couldn't go myself, and if I could persuade her to go on my behalf, that would leave Marty alone for three full days.

She came back from lunch with a smile on her face. "I've spoken to Marty. He says there's no reason why I shouldn't go. It's only for a few days, and it'll be good experience, won't it?"

"Excellent experience," I enthused. "And I'm certain you'll enjoy it. I can't tell you what a load that's taken off my mind. I really don't know what else I would have done."

Anna was obviously excited by the prospect now she had accepted it. "Don't be too relieved. I've never done anything like this before. I might make a total mess of it."

"My dear, you'll be fine. I have every confidence in you. Just keep putting your hand up until either you've beaten everyone else, or the bidding goes beyond your limit. There's nothing to it."

"Well, if you're sure you trust me." She laughed. "It's quite exciting, really. I've always wanted to bid at a big auction."

"In that case I'm glad I've given you the chance before you leave. I can't tell you how grateful I am. So long as you're positive it won't be too much of an inconvenience. You mustn't feel obliged to go."

"I don't. Really. I'm looking forward to it."

"And you're sure Marty doesn't mind?" I found it easy to consider Marty's wishes when I knew they did not interfere with my own.

"Of course not. I dare say he'll be able to survive without me for a few days." Her face suddenly lit up. "In fact, there's nothing to stop him coming along, is there? We could pay the extra airfare and the difference for a double room. If you don't mind, obviously."

I managed to smile. "Of course I don't mind. But wouldn't it be rather boring for him? Sitting in an auction room isn't everyone's idea of fun."

It was no good. "Oh, Marty won't mind that," she said. "And he doesn't have to come to them if he doesn't want to. We can spend the rest of the time together."

"Yes, I suppose so."

She looked at her watch. "I'll give him another fifteen minutes, and then I'll phone him. He should be back at the university by then."

I could see she was completely taken with the idea. I went to the office, where I did not have to sustain a facade of enthusiasm. I had not anticipated this. If Marty went with her, I would have gone to all that trouble—and considerable expense—for nothing. Worse, I would have to try and think of another way to isolate Marty, and there would be precious little time left for that.

I felt a fresh surge of antipathy for him. Even in this he was obstructing me. It was yet another grievance to add to my list. Brooding on it, I sat and waited.

After a while the office extension pinged as Anna picked up the telephone downstairs. I resisted the temptation to try and eavesdrop. I had managed it once, by accident. I did not trust my luck to hold a second time.

It seemed a long time before a second chime told me their conversation was over. Steeling myself, I went back downstairs. Anna was still by the telephone. She looked reassuringly crestfallen, and my spirits immediately lifted.

"I've just spoken to Marty," she said. "He can't come."

"Oh, what a shame."

"I know. But he says there are too many loose ends for him to tie up at the university." She smiled, trying to hide her disappointment.

"Well, it's only for three days, isn't it? And you know what they say about absence."

"I suppose so."

"I know it's no consolation, but I will be giving you a bonus to show how much I appreciate this."

"Oh, you don't have to do that! I'm getting what amounts to a free holiday anyway."

Relief had made me expansive. "You're still pulling my coals out of the fire, and I'm very grateful. When you get back I want you and Marty to go to whatever show or restaurant you like. On me."

Anna leaned forward and kissed my cheek. Her lips were cool, but my flesh felt branded by the contact.

"If you're any nicer to me, I don't think I'll be able to leave at all."

"I may just hold you to that," I said, blushing.

⟲⟳

There were no further hitches. On the morning of Anna's departure, I drove her to the airport. Marty came too. They sat together in the back of the car, and when I parked in the airport terminal I saw that they had been holding hands. Both of them seemed a little subdued as Anna waited to check in, and when they said goodbye to each other outside the departure lounge, no one watching would have dreamed the separation was only for three days.

I stood discreetly in the background. Anna's last, impulsive hug pulled Marty off balance. His glasses were knocked askew, and he adjusted them, absently, as he watched her disappear through the glass doors. He stared after her for a moment before turning toward me.

We walked back to the car in silence.

"Is Anna going to call you later?" I asked, to break it.

"She said she'll phone me tonight."

"You're not going out, then?"

"No, I've too much to do."

"Yes, Anna said you were busy. It's a shame you couldn't have gone with her. I hope you didn't mind my asking her to go?"

"No, not at all. It'll be a good experience for her. And it'll all help when she's looking for work in New York. Have you had any feedback from that, by the way?"

"Feedback?"

"You were going to contact some people you knew, to see if they could help her. Have you heard anything?"

Not only had I not heard anything, I had also forgotten I had offered to try. But I resented him feeling he had the right to ask. "No, not yet. They should have got my letters by now, though. I'll give them another week, and if I've not heard from them by then I'll try telephoning." I changed the subject. "I expect it'll seem strange being in the flat alone."

He nodded. "I guess."

I made an attempt at jocularity. "Do you think you'll be able to manage?"

A faint smile touched his mouth. "Sure. Anna's going to call every day, so if I run into any trouble I can always yell for help."

That was interesting to know. "Have you arranged a set time? In case I need to contact her," I added.

"She's going to call between six and seven. I'm usually back by then."

I dropped Marty at the university and drove to the gallery. It seemed empty and lifeless without Anna. I shook off the feeling and telephoned Zeppo.

"She's gone."

"Good. Any problems?"

"No. And I found out that Marty's staying in tonight."

"Tonight's no good."

I wondered if Zeppo was trying to make excuses. "Why?" Some of my suspicion must have carried into my voice, because he laughed.

"Now, now, Donald, don't snap. Tonight's no good because it's the first night she's been away and he'll probably be wandering around the flat crying and sniffing her perfume and trying to tell himself he's missing her. Tomorrow will be better."

"Isn't that just wasting a night?"

"Is this the man who lectured me about doing things too soon?"

I conceded. "All right. I suppose you know what you're doing. But whatever it is, leave it until after seven o'clock." I told him what Marty had said about Anna telephoning then. "I don't want her to know he's seeing you."

"You're all heart. Are there any other instructions, while you're at it? Perhaps you'd like to tell me exactly what you want me to do with Marty?"

"I'll leave that side of things up to you."

I heard him laugh, drily. "You're a true leader, Donald."

ᘒᘒ

That night I had the dream again. It was the same setting as before. I was lying on the sofa, drowsily watching my mother brush her hair in the firelight. She was sitting with her back to me. This time I noticed she was wearing the same white silk robe she often used to wear when I was a child. The room was quiet except for the sound of the fire crackling in the grate and the whisper of the brush. I felt warm and snugly content, hypnotized by the golden highlights in my mother's hair. Then, distant but jarring, there was another, more intrusive noise as, in the dream, the doorbell rang.

I awoke with a start. The alarm clock was clamoring next to my head. I reached across and turned it off, then lay back to gather myself. I felt disoriented and confused. The dream was still vividly with me. I could remember every detail, but now the glow of contentment it had given previously had gone. In its place I felt only a vague sense of unease.

It had lifted a little by the time I sat down to breakfast but still not disappeared completely. I put it down to having a lot on my mind and tried to ignore it. I had enough to think about in the real world without worrying about any dream. Dismissing it, I set off for the gallery and more immediate concerns. Namely, that Anna was due to telephone sometime that morning. Her first auction was at ten o'clock.

She rang shortly after eleven.

"Donald, I've got it!"

Her excitement cut through the bad connection. "You've got it?" For a moment I had no idea what she meant.

"The Hopper! I've just come straight out to tell you! God, it was great! And I got it for five hundred less than you said you'd go to!"

I put all the enthusiasm I could muster into my voice. "That's fantastic! How on earth did you manage it?"

"I just kept bidding. I thought one man was going to keep on going. He kept up with me right to the end, but then he dropped out! Oh, I can't believe it!"

Neither could I. I had selected a painting from each auction and authorized Anna to stop bidding at a figure well below what I imagined each would go for. Clearly, I had miscalculated. Now I was several thousand pounds poorer and the proud owner of a painting I did not want. "You've done marvelously well!" I said.

She laughed. "Well, all I did was keep sticking my hand in the air like you said."

"You outbluffed another bidder and got it for well under your limit. That's no mean feat. I'm proud of you."

"Thanks. God, I'm still out of breath! I think the adrenaline must still be pumping."

"In that case I recommend you buy a bottle of champagne to calm your nerves. Put it on expenses."

"I can't drink a full bottle by myself!"

"Nonsense. And if not, you can always save some for after the next auction." At which I sincerely hoped she would be less successful.

"I'm tempted, I must admit. Oh, I can't wait to tell Marty!"

I felt a hard knot of bitterness. Marty again. Always Marty. "Are you going to call him now?" I asked.

"No, I can't. He'll be at the university, and I don't want to disturb him. I'll have to wait until tonight."

"No doubt he'll be waiting by the telephone."

Anna laughed again. "He better be. I'm bursting to tell him. Oh, I'm going to be cut off," she said suddenly.

"I'll talk to you the day after tomorrow. Well done, again."

"Okay, I'll phone after the—" The line went dead. I held the receiver to my ear for a moment longer, reluctant to relinquish the link between myself and Anna, before setting it back in its cradle. In spite of the news of my unwanted acquisition, it had been good to hear from her. If this was what it was like when she was away for a matter of days, I dared not imagine how I would feel if she went to America.

A mood of restlessness settled on me. In the past I had never lacked for anything to do. But now, with two days to go before Anna returned and a day and night before I learned how successful Zeppo had been with Marty, the hours stretched endlessly ahead of me.

Boredom made me eat an ill-advised lunch, after which my stomach steadily deteriorated. Acid seared my chest, and by early evening my fears of an ulcer had given way to something more sinister. I contemplated calling for a doctor, half convinced I was having a heart attack. For a while I allowed the thought to occupy me, losing myself in fantasies of hospitals and deathbeds, and as my thoughts became more morbid, so they were taken from the subject that had prompted them. Either that or the indigestion tablets finally did the trick: it was almost with surprise that I realized the pain had finally eased.

I felt better still when I realized my maudlin self-indulgence had occupied a considerable portion of the evening. Suddenly, the morning no longer seemed a lifetime away. Almost cheerful now, I made a light, bland snack and considered how to pass the rest of the time. The anodyne of television has never appealed to me. I refuse to have one in the house, preferring instead to read or listen to music. Or retreat into an even more private world. It was this last I chose now.

My private gallery is in a windowless room on the first floor. Inside are the pieces that comprise my secret collection, started when I bought that first snuffbox. I let myself in and turned on the lights. The atmosphere was cathedral quiet; restful. The anxieties of the day sloughed off as soon as I closed the door. I paused for a moment to savor the feeling.

In my preoccupation with Anna, I had not been in the room for weeks. Now it was like a homecoming. I knew every painting, every line drawing intimately, but their attraction had never palled. Each was erotic in its own way, some strikingly so, others more subtle in their appeal. There was an eighteenth-century pastoral scene, typical in every way but for the shepherdess's bare breasts and the shepherd's hand beneath her petticoats. Next to it, an engraving of Leda embracing the swan, burying her face in its feathers as its neck twined around her back. Further along was a scene of two naked girls supine on a bed, sensual and languorous after their passion.

I lost myself amongst them, sometimes lingering over a particular piece, sometimes only pausing briefly before moving on to the next. One, however, drew me back time and time again, and after a while I moved a chair closer and sat down to study it more comfortably. It showed a couple making love in front of a fire, while from behind a screen a man watched unseen. Gradually, I forgot about the other pictures.

The watcher's face was rapt as he crouched behind the screen, only feet from where the couple lay. They appeared oblivious to him. The man's head was thrown back in the extremity of his passion, the girl's eyes closed in ecstasy. One arm curled around her lover's neck, the other lay flung out, apparently in abandon. Or was it? Palm upward, stretched out toward the screen, it could just as easily have been extended in invitation. It was that ambiguity that fascinated me. That outstretched arm transformed the entire picture, implicating the watcher in the lovers' union, elevating him from mere voyeur to an actual participant.

I gazed at the scene, hypnotized. The girl became Anna, the man, Zeppo. The fantasy took form, began to move. I crouched behind the screen, invisible. I moved closer, lingered on the edge of Anna's outstretched hand. On a level with them, I looked directly into Anna's face as her head turned. Her eyes opened, and she smiled at me . . .

I woke with a start. I was still in the chair, facing the now lifeless, two-dimensional picture. My neck ached. I rubbed it gingerly, my thoughts still sleep muddied. I had a vague impression that something had awakened me, and then I heard the noise again. Muffled and distant, a faint chiming noise, followed by a dull but violent banging. The last wisps of sleep disappeared, and I stood up.

Someone was at the door.

Chapter

9

I looked at my watch as I hurried downstairs. It was two o'clock. Uncaring of the time, the banging grew louder as I neared the front door. I unlocked it without thinking. I suppose I already knew who it had to be.

As soon as I opened the door, Zeppo pushed inside. He was soaking wet.

"Have you any idea what the time is?" I said, closing the door on the rain. His hair was flat to his head, trickling water over his face. It was already pooling around him. "Look at the mess you're making on the carpet!" I was aware of how inane I sounded even as I spoke.

Zeppo was breathing heavily, his lips curled. "Fuck the carpet!"

Strangely, I did not feel surprised to see him. Nor was I in any hurry to hear why he was there. "Take your shoes off and get yourself a drink in the lounge," I said. "I'll get you a towel."

When I came back from the kitchen, the trail of muddy footprints on the pale carpet told me that Zeppo had ignored at least one of my instructions. He stood in the center of the lounge, drink in hand, clearly daring me to object. Restraining myself, I handed him the towel.

"Well? I presume this isn't a social call?"

Zeppo glared at me. "He's fucking straight!"

I poured myself a drink. "What are you talking about?"

"Oh, take a fucking guess! Where have I been tonight?"

"You mean Marty?"

"You're like fucking lightning, aren't you? That's right, Marty. I saw him tonight, just like you wanted, and guess what? He's not queer. He's straight. Hetero. So can you guess what happened when I made a pass at him?"

I felt amazingly calm. Even his language failed to bother me. "I presume all this is a preamble to telling me it didn't work."

His face twisted. "Of course it didn't fucking work! I knew it wouldn't! I never should have listened to you!"

"As I recall, it was you who claimed he was gay in the first place, so you can hardly blame me because he's not. I refuse to be a scapegoat for your failure."

Zeppo's glass shattered against the wall. *"Don't start, or I'll break your fucking neck!"*

He faced me with clenched fists, his face contorted. Surprisingly unconcerned, I went to the cabinet and poured him another drink. I took it over to him.

"Try not to throw this one. It's a rather good single malt, so if you feel the urge to break something, tell me and I'll get you a blended whisky in a cheap glass."

For a moment he did not move. Then, reluctantly, he accepted it. A little of the violence ebbed away from him. I sat down.

"Now, if you feel capable of it, why don't you tell me exactly what happened?"

He hesitated, then flopped into a chair. "Jesus, what a fucking night." He rubbed his hand across his face. "I met him in this gay club in Soho—"

"Did you have any difficulty persuading him to go?"

"Not really. He was a bit wary at first, so I told him there was something I wanted to talk about that I couldn't discuss over the phone."

"What time was this? After Anna had called him?"

"Yes! I'm not fucking stupid, now do you want to hear this or not?" I said nothing. Nostrils flared, he continued. "I got to

the club early so I could watch his face when he came in.
There's no way you can miss what sort of a place it is, but he
didn't bat an eye. Didn't even flinch. Just ordered a mineral water and sat down. So I thought Stevie must have been right."

He took a drink, grimly shaking his head. "Anyway, he asked
what I wanted to see him about, so I said I wanted to apologize for being a bit of a bastard the last time I saw him and that
I didn't want him to get the wrong idea about me." He snorted.
"Christ, him get the wrong idea about *me*.

"Then a stripper came on, so I said, 'He's good, isn't he?' and
he said, 'Yeah, I've seen him before.' " Zeppo spread his arms,
carried away by his narrative. "What the fuck was I supposed
to think? I thought he was letting me know he bent both ways.
I asked where he'd seen him, and he told me it was at the Pink
Flamingo. That was where Stevie had spotted him. I said I'd
never been, but I'd heard it was pretty good and we should
both go sometime."

He closed his eyes. "Jesus, I can't believe I let myself in for
this." He emptied his glass and held it out to me. I refilled it,
this time pouring the blended scotch instead of the single malt.

"Then what?"

Zeppo took a swig of whisky. "He said, 'I didn't know you
went to that sort of place,' so I said, 'Well, sometimes it doesn't
pay to advertise.' He looked a bit uncomfortable and asked why
I was telling him all this, but I thought he was just embarrassed
at being found out. So I said—oh, shit—I said, 'Because I was
jealous when I saw you with Anna.' " His face screwed up at
the memory. "Oh, fucking hell, why did I listen to you?"

"What did Marty say?"

Zeppo blew out a long breath. "He started stammering that
he thought I should know he wasn't gay or anything. I thought
he was still trying to pretend or something, so I asked who he
was trying to kid and said—oh, Jesus—I said Anna need never
know about it."

He took another gulp of whisky. "I thought he was just another queer trying to fool himself he was straight."

"Are you sure he's not?"

"Of course I'm fucking sure! The little shit started patronizing me! Him! Patronizing *me*! I couldn't believe it! He said I'd got the wrong idea and he was sorry if he'd given me that impression, but he really wasn't gay. So I asked how come he went to places like the Pink Flamingo, then, and guess what he said?" Zeppo looked at me, thin lipped. "He's doing it for research. Fucking research! He's been going to different types of nightclubs to study 'behavior patterns.' Not just gay clubs. All types. It's part of his fucking *thesis*!" He spat the word out and finished the rest of his whisky in one go.

"Could he have been using that as an excuse?" I asked, not really believing it. Zeppo gave a terse shake of his head.

"No. I could tell he wasn't lying. He got all involved when he started telling me about it. I wasn't even listening by then, though. I just couldn't believe what a cunt I'd made of myself."

"I wonder what his thesis is actually about?" I mused. Zeppo looked startled.

"Does it fucking matter? He made a fool of me! He even had the fucking nerve to say he was *flattered*! Christ, I should think he was!"

"Calm down."

"Why? I've just been humiliated by that little runt for something I didn't want to do in the first place!" He ran his hand through his hair. "I told you it'd be a mistake, but you wouldn't listen, would you?"

"We've already been through that."

"Fuck that! You weren't the one who had to sit there while some little shit made you look stupid, were you? No, you just got me to go out and do it instead!"

"Did you try to deny it?" I asked, hoping to distract him.

"How the fuck could I *deny* it after I'd just made a pass at him? I just sat there like an idiot and wished you were dead. Then he said he thought he'd better go and that he wouldn't tell anyone about our 'misunderstanding.' "

"Well, that's something, at least."

He stared at me. "Oh, yeah, it's a great consolation. And I bet he means it."

"Don't you think he does?"

"Oh, come on, Donald! You seriously think he's not going to tell Anna? *I* would. It's too good a chance to miss. I can just imagine it. 'Oh, you know Zeppo, the macho male model? Well, he made a pass at me, and I turned him down.' Then Anna can say, 'That's funny, so did I.' Face it, Donald, we're fucked." Abruptly, he stood up. "Where's the toilet? I need a piss."

I answered without thinking. "Upstairs, at the end of the landing."

He went out. I mulled over what he had told me. For some reason, I did not feel surprised. It was almost as though I had expected it. But before I could follow this line of thought further, a far more urgent one seized me. The toilet was on the same floor as my private gallery. And I had left the door open.

I almost ran upstairs. The bathroom was at the far end of the hall. The door was closed. Relieved, I hurried to the room that housed my collection and froze. Zeppo was inside, standing in front of the cabinet that held my snuffboxes.

I tried to keep my voice level. "The toilet is at the end of the hallway."

He turned and grinned at me. "I know."

I held the door open. "If you don't mind, I'd like to lock up in here now."

"Not yet. I haven't finished looking."

I could feel myself shaking. "This is my private collection. It's not for public viewing."

"I'm not surprised." He laughed. "You randy old bugger, Donald! You've kept these quiet, haven't you?"

I moved toward him. "Will you please get out of here?"

"Hey, hey, hey, no need to be hostile. The door was open, I saw the pretty pictures and came in to look. That's what art's for, isn't it?" He peered at the print next to him. "Is that swan shafting her or what?"

"Get out."

"Donald, don't be so pushy. I'm not hurting anything. I'm interested, really I am. I've never seen antique porn before."

"This is not pornography!"

"Well, it's not Enid Blyton, is it? Is there a Readers' Wives section as well?" He strolled around the room. "God, look at the size of that fat bitch! You should have told me you were into this sort of stuff. I could have got you the real McCoy. None of this soft-porn shit. I mean, there's not one penetration shot in the lot of them. And those dykes look like they've fallen asleep."

"I told you to get out!"

He looked at me. His smile was unpleasant. "I heard you. But I like it here. I feel more at home." To prove his point he pulled over the chair I had fallen asleep on earlier and sat down. "Don't let me keep you, though, Donald. You go if you want to."

There was nothing I could do. The more I let him see how much his presence there bothered me, the longer he would stay. "If you insist on being childish, I suppose I can't stop you."

"That's right, you can't." He looked around. "So this stuff turns you on, does it?"

"Not in the way you seem to imagine. I find it aesthetically stimulating, if that's what you mean."

"Bullshit, Donald. If you're only interested in their 'aesthetic value,' how come they're all about people having it off? Or is that just a coincidence."

"I don't deny that they're erotic. But first and foremost, they're erotic art, although I don't suppose that distinction means anything to you."

"So you're trying to tell me it's only the art you're interested in and not the erotic?" He laughed.

"I would hardly expect someone like you to understand what I mean."

"Now, now, don't get snotty. If you get your rocks off over blue paintings, that's up to you. Far be it from me to call you a dirty old man." He stretched out his legs. "Anyway, down to business. You and me have got some settling up to do, haven't we?"

"Settling up?"

"That's right. For services rendered." He leaned forward. "I want paying. Then I'll leave you to enjoy your 'art' in private."

I laughed. It did not sound too unconvincing. "I'm sorry, Zeppo, I'm not with you. I was under the impression that our arrangement was for payment on completion."

"It's as complete as it's going to be."

"Do I take it that you intend to give up?"

"Give up? Donald, what the fuck are you talking about? There's nothing *to* give up. It's over and you owe me."

"Owe you? What do I owe you for? As I recall, the agreement was for you to seduce Anna. You haven't. Then we agreed that you would do the same to Marty. Again, you haven't. So I'm afraid I don't really see how I owe you anything."

My refusal was motivated as much as anything by a desire to hit back at him. I felt a spiteful pleasure as his complacency began to crack. "Don't stick the blame for Marty onto me! That was all your idea!"

"Based on your information that he was homosexual. Which was apparently wrong."

He took a deep breath. "Look, I've been fucked around enough. If you think I'm going to let you welsh on the deal, forget it."

"How am I welshing? I hired you to do a specific job, which you haven't done. And now you want paying for it?" I knew I was provoking him, but I did not care. I shook my head. "I'm sorry, Zeppo, but as I see it you're the one who's welshing. I'll gladly pay you—when you've done what you said you would."

He threw up his hands. "Oh, for Christ's sake! Tell me what else I could have done! Come on, tell me!"

"I've no idea. That's why I hired you."

"Jesus Christ, Donald, don't you listen? Look—read my lips—forget it! I've tried everything I could. There's not enough time left for anything else. They're only interested in each other! That's it! Finito!"

"And you're prepared to accept that?"

"Yes!"

"In that case I fail to see why I should pay you a penny."

The chair toppled over as Zeppo jumped to his feet. "Fuck this!" His voice was low, his face hard. "So I've not slept with that frigid bitch. I don't care. I want what you owe me. Now."

With a shock, I realized he was close to attacking me. And with that threat of violence, the thought that had been at the back of my mind began to push its way forward. I shied away from it, reluctant to confront it too soon, even while I accepted its general direction.

"I must say, I expected more of you, Zeppo," I goaded him, conscious now that I was walking a very fine line. "After all your boasting, I certainly didn't think you'd let yourself be put off so easily."

He was glaring at me. "You're really starting to piss me off, Donald."

"The feeling's mutual. Although I'm more disappointed than anything else. I didn't think you were the type to let someone like Marty beat you. Obviously, I came to the wrong man."

"Don't push it."

I sighed. "Well, if you're prepared to admit that an American academic, who is half your size and indisputedly unattractive, is a better man, perhaps we should part company after all. If you can't even cope with competition like that you're no use to me anyway. I'll pay you a settlement fee. Let's say ten percent for trying, shall we?"

"Let's say all of it, or I smash every picture in here and then start on your fucking face!"

"It's a pity you can't show such aggression where it's needed. Perhaps Marty wouldn't be waiting to laugh at you with Anna if you had."

"I'm warning you, Donald—!"

"Go ahead and warn me! It still doesn't alter the fact that you let a worm like Marty get the better of you. Wrecking my paintings and beating me up won't change that!"

Zeppo took a step toward me, then stopped. His fists were balled. "I want my money. Now."

"Earn it."

"Now, or I'll break your fucking neck!"

I sneered. "Are you sure you're man enough?"

I miscalculated. Before I could say anything else he had grabbed me by the shirt and flung me against the wall. I felt a frame break beneath my back, and something sharp dug into my flesh. Part of me fretted over the damage, trying to guess which picture it was, then Zeppo punched me in the stomach. I doubled up, struggling for breath, and as he seized hold of me and yanked me off the wall, in a rush the thought I had been suppressing surged forward and formed itself into speech.

"It's not my neck you should break, is it?" I gasped.

I was slammed back against the wall. But his rage had been pierced. Zeppo blinked. "What?"

I could feel his breath on my face, sweet with whisky. "You heard." My voice was hoarse and choking. "If you're going to kill someone, at least make it someone worthwhile."

A flicker of uncertainty crossed his face. "What the fuck are you talking about?"

He had me pinned up against the wall, his fists bunching my shirt under my throat. I wriggled slightly to ease the pressure on my windpipe. "It's not me you should be angry at. It's Marty. He's the one who's responsible for all this. He's the one who's humiliated you. If you want to kill someone, kill him."

I could feel his hold on my shirt slacken. He stared at me. "You're not serious."

"Aren't I?"

"Kill Marty?"

"Why not?"

His hands dropped away. He stepped back. "Jesus, you mean it, don't you?"

I massaged my throat. My shirt was torn. "A few moments ago you were ready to kill me. So why not him?"

"Oh, this is . . ." He turned and walked a few paces away, shaking his head. "This is getting stupid."

"Just think about it."

"Think about what? Committing fucking murder? Forget it, Donald! I'm not interested!"

"Why?"

"Why? What do you mean, 'why'? Why do you think? Okay, so I lost my temper just now, but that doesn't mean I'm going to top someone just for the sake of it!"

"I'm not asking you to do anything for the sake of it. Just tell me why you won't at least consider killing Marty? You're obviously capable." My stomach ached where he had punched me. I tried to ignore it.

Zeppo shook his head again. "Oh, for Christ's sake! I've no intention of spending the rest of my life in prison just because you want to get rid of somebody's boyfriend! Jesus!"

"And if you could do it without anyone knowing? Would you consider it then?"

"Oh, I suppose you've already got the perfect murder worked out, have you?"

"No. But assuming we could think of something?"

"No!"

"Why not? If you could be assured of not being caught? Why not?"

"I can't believe you're even talking about this."

A small part of me shared his surprise. Even as I was speaking I wondered how long this intention had been brooding in my subconscious. "Give me a reason. Why wouldn't you?"

He turned to face me again. "All right, then. Why should I?"

My argument came as smoothly as if it had been scripted in advance. "For the same reason you do everything else. Money."

He gave a short laugh. "Oh no. Even I draw the line somewhere, and this is it."

"Are you trying to tell me you object on moral grounds?"

"If you like."

"I'm afraid I don't believe you."

His finger stabbed out at me. "Well, fuck you and fuck your stupid ideas. I want my money by tomorrow afternoon, or I'm going to tell your precious Anna exactly what her sweet old boss has been trying to do!"

"She's in Amsterdam."

"Then I'll tell her when she gets back!"

"In which case the vice squad will receive some very interesting photographs. With your name and address." I smiled. "As they may do anyway." He took a step toward me. "And as they certainly will if anything unfortunate were to happen to me," I added.

Zeppo halted, then closed his eyes and pressed his palms into the sides of his head. "Jesus, how did I get into this?"

"Blame it on being imprudent enough to pose for unsavory photographs with minors." I advanced toward him. "Look at it as a choice between being well paid to remove an obstacle. Or a prison sentence and the end of your career."

He gave a bitter laugh. "Oh, right! And I suppose there's no penalty for murder? What do you get for that, a pat on the head and a bag of sweets?"

"Zeppo, I assure you prison holds no appeal for me either. If we can't find a safe way, then so be it. All I'm saying is let's examine the possibilities."

He stood uncertainly. Abruptly, he shook his head. "No." He went toward the door.

"I really think you should." He hesitated, hand on the door handle. "There's something else you might like to consider as well."

He looked back at me warily. "What?"

"It's downstairs. In the study." I went past him into the hall-way, leaving him to follow.

"What is?"

"A picture you might be interested in."

"Shove it," he said. But the words were mechanical and without energy. He trailed me downstairs.

"I think you might like to see this one." I opened the door to the study. He paused.

"What are you up to?"

"Don't be such a cynic, Zeppo. I merely want to show you something I think you'll be interested in." I waited. Curiosity won. He went in. I closed the door behind us.

"It's this one." I indicated a small canvas on the wall. "What do you think of it?"

He gave a cautious shrug. "So-so. Why?"

"It's a sketch by Jean Cocteau. Have you heard of him?"

"Yeah." I could not tell from his expression if he had or not. I went on anyway.

"In that case you'll know how rare this is. Cocteau's famous for his films, but he also made a few quite celebrated sketches in the twenties. This is one of them. It was given to me as a present many years ago, which was the only reason I held on to it. I've never really liked it. At the time it had some value as a curio. Do you know how much it's worth now?"

"No."

I told him. He appeared unimpressed. "Congratulations. I hope you've got it insured. What's that got to do with me?"

"I thought, with you being in a field related to the film industry, that you might like it?" He looked at me in surprise. "Kill Marty and it's yours."

For once I had the pleasure of seeing Zeppo thrown completely off balance. "Are you serious?"

"Perfectly."

"You'd give me that to kill him?"

"That's what I said."

He looked at the painting, then back to me. "Is it real?"

"Of course it's real! You don't think I'd hang a copy in my own home, do you? Or anywhere else, for that matter."

He regarded the sketch again. I let the idea sink in.

"It's really worth as much as that?" he asked at last.

"Oh yes. Obviously, it could be a little more or a little less. But that's approximately what it would fetch at auction if you decided to sell it. You can always make your own inquiries if you don't believe me. So long as you're subtle about it."

He studied it again. I doubted it was out of any aesthetic appreciation. I wondered which was the greater lure, the value of the sketch or the name of the artist. As well as being avaricious, Zeppo was also a poseur. I knew the thought of possessing such a piece would appeal to him.

Slowly, he began to shake his head. "No. Nice try, Donald, but no. No way." Something about the way he said it made me keep silent.

"No, it's . . . it's . . ." He shook his head more emphatically. "It's too risky." I said nothing. "Sleeping with someone's one thing, but this . . ." He looked at me, waiting for my response.

"It's your choice."

He began shaking his head again. But his eyes continually strayed to the picture. "No . . . I mean, how can we be sure that we wouldn't be caught?"

I had him. Trying not to smile too smugly, I took him by the arm and led him back into the lounge.

"Why don't we have another drink while we discuss it?" I said.

Chapter

10

I telephoned Marty shortly before six o'clock the following evening. As I expected, there was no answer. But instead of hanging up I let the phone ring on emptily. I wanted it to be ringing when he arrived home. And if I was on the line, no one else could be.

Anna had called me that morning. I had not gone into the gallery until late. It had been five o'clock before Zeppo and I had finalized everything, and I had slept through the alarm. I had only just opened when she rang, and for once I did not feel inclined to talk to her.

"Is everything all right?" I asked.

"Everything's fine. I'm sorry to bother you, but I was thinking about tonight's auction. I wondered, since we got the Hopper for less than you expected, if I should go a bit higher for the Burns? I wouldn't do it without asking you, but I thought you might want to use the money you'd saved."

It was an effort to apply myself to the question. "No, I don't think so. I don't really want to pay any more for it. Just stick with the existing limit."

She sounded disappointed. "Oh. Okay. You don't mind me asking, do you? Only I started thinking about it last night, so I thought I'd better ask you about it."

"Yes, I'm glad you did." Suddenly, it seemed too much of an

effort to make excuses. "In fact, I've changed my mind. Yes, go up to . . ."—for a moment I could not remember the amount— "that much extra," I said lamely.

"Shall I? You think it's a good idea, then?" Her eagerness was touching, but my mind was elsewhere.

"Yes, very good. Well done."

"Thanks. I can't wait for tonight. Shall I call you afterward? It shouldn't be too late."

"No, don't bother. I may be out. I'll hear all about it when you get back tomorrow." The last thing I needed that evening was any distraction. Particularly from Anna. She must have noticed my lack of enthusiasm.

"Is everything all right?"

"Yes, fine! I'm . . . with a client."

"Oh, I'm sorry! I didn't realize."

"I don't want to seem abrupt, but I'd better not keep him waiting."

"No, of course not. I'm sorry if I've disturbed you."

"That's all right. I'm glad you did. It was a good idea. But I'm going to have to go now. Good luck for tonight. I'll see you at the airport tomorrow morning."

She had said goodbye, and I had hung up. Belatedly, I had realized I should have checked what time she was going to telephone Marty. But it was perhaps as well I had not. I was not sure how casual I could have sounded, and I did not want her to remember the inquiry later. I had poured myself a coffee and waited for Zeppo.

It had been late afternoon when he arrived. He came to the back door, as I had instructed. "Have you got everything?" I asked.

"Yeah. But you didn't give me enough money. I had to put in some of my own, too. So you owe me fifty quid."

"Fifty?" I had given him a hundred. I had no idea how much that sort of thing cost, but a hundred had seemed more than enough. He had also insisted on being given a postdated check, which he would hold against the Cocteau sketch. Ours was not a relationship based on trust. "Have you got receipts?"

He gave an exaggerated sigh and handed me several slips of paper. "Oh ye of little faith. The dust sheets alone cost nearly fifty. And if you're thinking of putting those through the books, I wouldn't. You don't really want anyone asking what an art gallery needs with DIY and gardening equipment, do you?"

"Of course not." I had asked for the receipts automatically, but Zeppo was right. I tore them up and dropped them into a bin. "Where is everything?"

"In the car out back. Shall I bring it in now?"

"No, not yet. Wait until I close the gallery."

He hesitated. "Are you still sure about this?"

"Of course I am. I hope this isn't cold feet I detect, is it?"

"No. I'm only asking."

"Good. I don't want you letting me down at an embarrassing moment."

"I won't. I've already told you I won't." His tone was aggressive. But I thought there was also some uncertainty there, and while I enjoyed seeing cracks in his self-assurance, I did not want it to collapse altogether.

"In that case we'll say no more about it," I said. And neither of us had.

Now he sat silently in the office as I held the receiver to my ear, waiting for Marty to answer. When he finally did, it seemed so sudden that it startled me.

"Hello?"

"Marty? This is Donald. Donald Ramsey." My voice sounded rushed. But that was not such a bad thing.

"Hi. What can I do for you?"

"Are you alone?"

"Yes, why?"

The first hurdle, at least, was over. I ignored his question. "Has Anna called?"

"Not today. I spoke to her yesterday. Why, what's the matter?"

I looked across at Zeppo. "I think you'd better come over here right away."

"Why, what's wrong?" I could hear the sudden urgency in his voice.

"Now don't panic, Marty. I'm sure everything's all right, but the Dutch police have contacted me—"

"The *police*! What's happened?"

"I'm not entirely sure, but it seems as though there's been some kind of shooting incident."

"Oh God. Is Anna okay?"

"I don't know, the police wouldn't tell me. They just said that a number of people had been injured and that some had been arrested as well, on drug charges—"

"*Drug* charges? For Christ's sake, what's going on?"

"I can't tell you any more than that, Marty. The police were very vague. They only said a number of people were involved and that Anna was one of them. It all seems very confused, I don't think they're even clear themselves."

"They must know if she's all right! Has she been hurt or arrested or . . . or *what*?"

"Marty, I don't know! That's all they told me. I think . . ." I hesitated. "I think they're having problems identifying some people. Some of them were killed, and—"

"Oh no. Oh Jesus."

"Marty, we don't *know* Anna was one of them! She could be fine. This could all be a misunderstanding!"

"Who did you speak to? Give me his number."

"The line's constantly busy, I've been trying. Listen, I think it's best if you come over here as soon as you can. Pack a few clothes and bring your passport. I'll find out when's the next flight to Amsterdam and book seats on it. We'll be able to find out much more if we're actually there." I was relying on shock to stop him thinking clearly, make him let me take the lead. "Take the tube, not a taxi. It'll be quicker. The front door will be locked, so come to the one at the back. And until we know more, I wouldn't mention this to anyone. Just get over here as soon as you can."

The telephone clicked as he hung up. I put the receiver down on the desk without breaking the connection. If anyone tried to call him now, the line would be engaged. I motioned for Zeppo to be quiet until we had left the office. If Marty happened to pick up the telephone again, I did not want him to hear us talking.

"He's on his way," I said.

"What if he takes a taxi anyway? Or tells someone?"

"I don't think he will. He's in no fit state to think for himself at the moment. He's far more likely to do as I told him."

"But what if he doesn't?"

"If he tells anyone, we'll have to postpone it, obviously. I'll just have to pretend that I've been the victim of a particularly sick hoax."

"And what if he gets a taxi instead of the tube? Are we still going to go through with it then?"

I sighed. Zeppo had swung between moods of supreme confidence and uncertainty all afternoon. I was beginning to tire of it. "Can you really see a London taxi driver remembering one insignificant fare out of hundreds? And the date and time as well? I can't. I'm only being cautious. I really don't think it matters."

I looked at my watch. "Now, he'll be here in less than an hour. I suggest we go downstairs and get everything ready."

Marty made the journey in slightly more than forty-five minutes. The buzz of the doorbell seemed incredibly loud when it came. Zeppo and I looked at each other. Neither of us spoke. Then he nodded, and I went to answer it.

I paused in front of the door, took a deep breath to steady myself and opened it. Marty was standing outside, suitcase in hand.

"Have you heard anything?" he asked. His face was white and stricken.

"No, I still can't get through." I moved to one side to let him in, then closed the door and went past him. He followed me inside. "Did you come by taxi or tube?"

"Tube. So you don't know anything else at all?"

"Nothing. Have you brought your passport?"

"Yes. What did they say, exactly?"

We were in the short corridor that led to the storeroom. He was close behind me. "You haven't told anyone, have you?"

"No, I came straight over."

I opened the storeroom door and went inside. The cotton dust sheet slid a little on the underlying polythene as I walked on it. "So no one knows you're here?"

"No! Dammit, will you tell me what they said?" he shouted, and then Zeppo stepped out from behind the door and swung the crowbar against the back of his head. I moved aside as he pitched forward and fell face down onto the floor. His glasses skidded off and came to rest at my feet, and I held up my hand as Zeppo raised the crowbar again.

"Wait." The suitcase had dropped loosely from Marty's fingers. I moved it out of the way and draped a fold of the dust sheet over his head and shoulders. He was breathing noisily, twitching a little but otherwise still. I stepped back. "All right."

Zeppo brought the crowbar down. The end was wrapped in a towel to prevent blood splashing on the initial blow, but not enough to significantly deaden the impact. By the third swing, patches of red were already beginning to soak through the white dust sheet. I let him swing once more, then motioned for him to stop.

I crouched and took hold of Marty's wrist. Incredibly, there was still a flutter there. I stood up and moved out of the way. "Not quite."

Zeppo hefted the crowbar and brought it down several more times before he stopped and waited for me to check Marty's pulse again. There was an unpleasant smell. I wrinkled my nose against it and counted up to sixty. Then I put his wrist back down. "That's it."

"Is he dead?" Zeppo was breathing heavily.

I straightened and looked at the bloodstained sheet. It clung wetly to the broken object underneath. "I think we can safely assume so, yes." My voice was amazingly steady.

Zeppo's shoulders sagged. "Thank God for that." His

cheeks were flushed, but the rest of his face was pale. He made to set the crowbar on Marty's body.

"I wouldn't put that down just yet," I said.

He jerked back. "Why? He's dead isn't he?"

"Yes. But now we've come this far, we might as well do the job properly."

"What are you talking about? How much more properly can you get than that?" He nodded at the figure on the floor.

"He can be identified from dental records if his teeth are intact."

Zeppo stared at me. "You want me to smash his teeth?"

"I think it's a sensible precaution, yes."

"No way! You didn't say anything about that before."

"It hadn't occurred to me before. But I think we should."

"No, you mean you think *I* should! Well, forget it! If you want his teeth smashed, you do it!"

"I don't see what you're being so squeamish about. They hardly matter to him now."

"I'm not breaking his teeth!"

I could see he meant it. "All right, if you feel that strongly about it. I don't suppose it really matters. It was only an idea." I still thought it was a good one. I had also brought paint stripper to remove his fingerprints. But there was no point now. "We'd better start to clean up."

Zeppo emptied Marty's pockets and removed his wristwatch. Then we wrapped him in both the cotton and polythene dust sheets and manhandled the entire bundle into a large refuse sack. By the time we had finished, I was exhausted, and Zeppo was sweating heavily.

"Jesus, I need a drink," he said.

"You can have one later. The last thing we need is for the police to stop you for a Breathalyzer test."

"Oh, come on, Donald! One isn't going to do any harm! I need something after that!"

"No."

We stared at each other. In spite of what I had just seen him do, I did not feel at all threatened by him. Far from it. He seemed unnerved, his aggression more petulant than arrogant. I held his eyes until he shrugged and looked away.

"Oh, all right, all right, I'll not have a bloody drink. Can I at least go for a piss? Or is that too risky as well?"

While Zeppo was at the toilet, I went through the articles he had taken from Marty's pockets. There was a wallet containing credit cards and a relatively small amount of money, a passport and an address book. I took the money from the wallet and then, as an afterthought, bent each credit card in half. I did not want Zeppo to succumb to temptation. Leaving all this in a small pile, I opened the suitcase.

There was nothing of any interest in it. A few clothes, hastily packed. A soap bag, a checkbook, and some more money. Marty had obviously been a prudent person. I put everything except the money in the suitcase and was just closing it when Zeppo returned.

"Doing a spot of grave robbing, are we?" he asked, grinning.

"If it offends your principles, I suppose you won't want the cash he was carrying."

He picked up the thin bundle of notes and counted through them. "Waste not, want not, eh?" His eyes were unnaturally bright. He seemed to have suddenly recovered his self-assurance. I wondered if it was reaction.

"If you're ready, I suggest we see about getting that"—I nodded at the bulky plastic sack—"into the car."

"You'll have to give me a hand to lift it." There was a hint of malicious pleasure in his voice. I had the suspicion that he was quite capable of managing on his own but said nothing as I went to help. Much of the weight seemed to fall onto me before Zeppo finally announced that he had it.

I switched off the light in the corridor before I opened the back door. It was dark outside. The alley at the rear of the building was unlit, and the lights from the street failed to penetrate into it. There was no one in sight, and when I opened the car boot it shielded us from anyone who might be passing. Inside was a brand-new spade and pickaxe, overalls, Wellington boots and a pair of gloves—the rest of Zeppo's purchases. I took them out and beckoned to him. He staggered out and quickly lowered the sack into the boot. While I put everything else back inside, Zeppo fetched the crowbar and Marty's suitcase from the storeroom. The crowbar, now wrapped in plastic, went on top of the sack, the suitcase onto the backseat. That done, I handed Zeppo the car keys. I had reluctantly decided that my gray BMW was less conspicuous than his red sports car.

"Have you got the map?" I asked. He patted his pocket. "And you're sure you know where you're going?" We had put much thought into where to dispose of Marty's remains, finally deciding on the North Yorkshire moors. The exact spot would be left to Zeppo's discretion.

"If I get lost I'll ask a policeman."

He got into the car and turned on the ignition. The lights came on, dazzlingly lighting the alley. I watched as he slowly edged out into the road and pulled away. The noise of the motor quickly died in the distance. I went back inside and closed the door on the darkness and smell of exhaust.

Without the sheeting, the storeroom looked the same as ever. I looked around for any sign that Marty had been there, but there was none. The last half hour might never have happened. Feeling utterly calm, I turned out the lights, locked up and made my way home.

Chapter

11

I was waiting at the airport when Anna arrived next morning.
I felt a proprietorial thrill when I saw her walk through the cus-
toms area. She smiled as she came toward me, but her smile
faded as soon as we had greeted each other.

"I didn't get it," she said. For a moment I did not know what
she was talking about. "It went for eight-seven in the end." She
gave an apologetic shrug.

"Oh well, win some, lose some," I said, realizing what she
meant. "It can't be helped."

"A Japanese woman bought it. Someone else stayed with her
up to eight-five but then dropped out. I'm afraid they left me
well behind."

"That's how these things are. If someone's determined to
buy a piece, there's very little you can do to stop them. Unless
you want to spend a ridiculous amount of money. Never mind.
At least you got the Hopper, and that was the one I was most
interested in."

I could see my condolences were unnecessary. Anna was not
really listening.

"Have you heard from Marty?" she asked.

"Not since we saw you off. Why? Is anything wrong?"

"Oh no. I just wondered, that's all. I thought he might be
here." Her casualness was unconvincing.

"Well, I did call him last night to see if he wanted to come with me, but he wasn't in."

"What time was that?"

"Oh . . . about eight, I think. Is there something the matter? You look worried."

She smiled. "No, not really. It's just that I couldn't get in touch with him yesterday."

"At home or the university?"

"At home. I called him last night, but there was no answer."

"Perhaps he was working late."

"Yes, probably." We walked a few more steps. "Do you mind if I try again now? Just to tell him I'm back?"

"Of course not. I'll wait here." I watched as she went over to the row of telephones and joined the smallest queue. I yawned. It had been another late and almost sleepless night. I had waited up until after half past four for Zeppo to call and tell me he was safely back. There had been no problem. Once on the moors he had followed minor roads and finally stopped at a particularly isolated spot. He had carried Marty well clear of the road and buried him in an area of bracken.

"It's just started to grow now," he had told me. "In another few weeks it'll have covered over completely."

The shovel, pick and crowbar had been thrown in a flooded quarry pit. The overalls, gloves and Wellingtons had been brought back. Along with Marty's clothes and suitcase, they would be cut up and torn into strips, mixed with household rubbish and discarded at several dumping sites around London. Marty's more personal belongings, such as his passport and credit cards, would first be burned and then similarly disposed of.

That was what Zeppo was doing while I was at the airport. He had left my car in the overnight car park where his own was waiting, locking the keys inside. Using my spare set, I had collected it earlier that morning and run it through a car wash before going to meet Anna. Later, I would have it cleaned more thoroughly and have the tires changed. I wanted no trace of mud or dirt from the moors left on it.

Anna had finally reached a telephone. I could see a small furrow appear between her eyebrows as she held the receiver to her ear. I felt a mild shock when she began to speak, before I realized that she must have telephoned the university. The furrow remained after she had cut the connection and dialed again. This time she waited without speaking. After a while she replaced the receiver.

"Any luck?" I asked, as she came over.

"No. I called the university, but he isn't there. And there's still no answer from the flat."

I patted her arm. "Don't look so worried! He's probably on his way to the university right now."

"But it's not like him to be late. And when I tried the flat from the hotel this morning, there was no answer then, either."

"Well, perhaps your telephone's out of order."

"I don't think so. It was ringing. And the first time I called last night it was engaged, so it must be working."

That would have been me. "Not necessarily. It might not be ringing out at the other end. That happened to mine once. Or you might have been connected to the wrong number the first time. There could be any number of reasons."

The furrow faded a little. "You're probably right. It's just not like him not to be in, that's all."

"And if your telephone's on the blink he's probably still at home now, thinking it's not like you not to call him."

She laughed, a little abashed. "I know, I'm being silly."

"Not at all. In fact, if you'd like, I'll take you back home first. I daresay I won't get a stroke of work out of you until we've set your mind at rest."

Anna looked instantly relieved. "Would you? Are you sure you don't mind?"

"Of course not."

I put her bag in the car boot—I had already checked to make sure it was empty—and we set off for her flat. At first we chatted about her trip, but as we drew nearer she fell silent. I felt tense myself. I could not be entirely sure that Marty had left nothing behind to indicate where he had gone. There was no reason why he should, but I would be happier once I knew for certain.

I had never been to Anna's flat before, and once we reached Camden she had to give me directions. "This is it," she said. I parked outside the terrace house.

"Shall I stay here?" I asked, hoping she would not say yes.

"No, it's okay. Come on in."

I followed her around the back of the house and up a flight of wooden steps to a first-story door. Anna unlocked it and we went inside.

"Marty?" she called. I stayed in the kitchen while she went through into the rest of the flat. It smelt pleasantly of herbs and spices, with a rather sour underodor of stale coffee from a dried filter cone. A dirty cereal bowl, beaker and spoon lay in the sink, testimony of Marty's last breakfast.

Anna came back into the kitchen. She looked more worried than ever. "There's no note or anything. I can't understand it. He knew I was coming back this morning."

"But he wasn't expecting you to come straight here, so he wouldn't have left you a note, would he? Why don't you try the university again?" I smiled reassuringly. "While you're doing that, I'll pop the kettle on, shall I?"

She went back into the lounge to make the telephone call. I filled the kettle and was searching for the tea when she returned, moments later.

"I've just spoken to the head of the department. He was about to ring here himself. Marty was supposed to be meeting him half an hour ago and hasn't turned up. No one knows where he is."

I looked a little concerned. "Well . . . perhaps he forgot about it."

"He wouldn't do that."

"Now calm down, Anna. Don't work yourself up over nothing. I'm sure there's a perfectly good explanation."

"But he knew I was going to phone last night. When I spoke to him the night before I *told* him I was, and he said, 'I'll talk to you the same time tomorrow'!"

"Well, sometimes things crop up unexpectedly. You said yourself that the line was engaged when you first tried. So he must have been here then, mustn't he?"

"I suppose so."

"And as far as he was concerned, I was going to pick you up from the airport and take you straight to the gallery. So if he's going to get in touch with you, he'll try there rather than here, won't he?"

She nodded, clearly not convinced. "We'd better be getting back anyway. I'm taking up all your time."

I waved the objection away. "Let's have that cup of tea first. It'll give you chance to calm down a little. And if he calls the gallery in the meantime, he'll leave a message on the answering machine." I was in no rush to leave. I liked the sense of intimacy of being with Anna in her home, surrounded by her belongings. It was my first excursion into her private life. The kettle boiled.

"Now, where's the tea?"

As I poured the water into the pot, Anna went into the lounge, and I heard the telephone being used again. I took the milk out of the fridge, smelling it to make sure it was not sour, and poured it into two mugs. I wondered when Anna would notice that some of Marty's things were missing. It was a temptation to suggest that she check, but I resisted it. She would find out soon enough. I put the tea and mugs onto a tray and carried it into the lounge.

Anna was still on the telephone. As I walked in, she said, "Okay, Al. Thanks anyway," and hung up. "I've called everyone I can think of who he might have gone to see, but no one knows where he is." Her anxiety was barely under control.

"Drink this." I gave her one of the mugs. "Getting yourself into a state isn't going to do any good."

"Yes, but where *is* he?"

"I don't know, but I'm sure you'll find out soon. Try to see things in perspective. It's only quarter to twelve. Don't you think it's a little soon to start panicking?"

She said nothing. Her tea remained untouched. I knew it

was only a matter of time before she would want to go to the gallery to see if Marty had called.

"May I use the toilet?" I asked, to forestall it.

"It's down the hall, the door on the right." Anna did not even look up as I left the room. I closed the door behind me. The hallway was small. One door led off to my left, one to my right. The one on the left would be the bedroom. I hesitated and then opened it.

A double bed faced me, almost filling the room. A stripped pine wardrobe and dresser took up most of what little space was left. The scent of Anna's perfume hung in the air. Afraid to linger, I was about to close the door when I saw the framed photograph on the dresser.

It was of Anna and Marty on a beach. Both wore bathing costumes. Marty was as pale and runtish as I had imagined, but I barely noticed him. It was the sight of Anna that hypnotized me. She was wearing a white bikini and had obviously just been swimming. Droplets of water glistened in her hair and clung to her body, faceting her deep navel. Her nipples were clearly visible as they pressed against the wet fabric of the bikini top, and the brief pants were cut high on her hips, plunging in a deep vee to her crotch, which bulged out in a small, raised mound. In the center of this, a faint, vertical indentation was just visible.

My chest tightened as I stared at the photograph. At that moment, I would have given anything to own it. It took all my willpower to come away and close the door. I went into the bathroom and washed my face with cold water. More in control of myself, I looked around the bathroom for further evidence of Anna's personal life. Bottles and jars cluttered the shelf above the washbasin, and the top of the bathroom cabinet was similarly full. I opened it. The first thing I saw was a large carton of sanitary towels, in plain view. I hurriedly closed the door again.

Flushing the toilet without using it, I went back into the lounge.

"Shall we go to the gallery?" Anna asked immediately. I agreed. I had no excuse not to.

There were several messages on the answering machine, none of them, of course, from Marty. I made more reassuring noises, but by now Anna's concern was growing fast.

"I know you think I'm being silly," she said, after calling the university yet again, "but this just isn't like him. I can't understand why he hasn't let me know where he is."

"I don't think you're being silly, I just think you're overreacting a little. I'm sure he'll turn up soon."

"But where is he?"

"I don't know. But I'll bet he comes home tonight at the usual time, with a perfectly good explanation." I smiled at her. "Now. What about lunch?"

Anna insisted on staying in the gallery in case Marty telephoned. I had sandwiches delivered, but she left hers untouched. As the afternoon passed she grew more and more pensive. She called the university again and even contacted the operator to check if her own line was faulty. Whenever the telephone rang, she froze, and if I answered it she watched me anxiously to see who it was. Finally, at four o'clock, I told her she could go home.

"Are you sure?" she asked.

"Quite sure. In fact, I'll drive you, if you like."

"No, really, there's no need." It was obvious that she wanted to be alone. Reluctantly, I decided not to insist. "If Marty calls, tell him to ring me, won't you?"

"Of course," I said. "And don't worry. I'm sure he's fine."

When my telephone rang that evening, I felt sure it would be Anna. I could think of no one else it could be. I had already spoken to Zeppo, and few other people called me at home. But the voice that answered was patently not hers.

"Mr. Ramsey?"

"Yes?" The brief elation I had felt disappeared.

"It's Margaret Thornby here."

The name meant nothing to me. Then I put it together with the voice, which seemed vaguely familiar, and my spirits sank even lower.

"Sorry to bother you," she went on, "but I wondered if you're going to be busy next Wednesday?"

Still disappointed that she was not Anna, I was slow to see what was coming. "Next Wednesday? Ah . . . I'm not . . ."

"The thing is, I've arranged to see someone next Wednesday morning," she said. "And I did say I'd let you know the next time I was nearby, so I thought I'd give you a ring and see if I couldn't offer to buy you lunch."

She gave a jolly little laugh that left me entirely cold. "I'm giving you a bit more notice this time. I could see I caught you unawares when I called into the gallery the other week, so I thought it was only fair to give you plenty of warning before I descended on you again."

I frantically racked my brains for an excuse. "Ah . . . next Wednesday . . ." I had a brainwave. "Just let me check in my diary."

I moved the telephone away from my mouth. After a while I put it back. "Now, Wednesday . . . That's the . . . ?"

"The sixteenth, I think."

"Yes, the sixteenth. Oh, what a shame. I'm out of town all day."

"Are you? Oh, what a pity." If we had been in the same room, I felt sure she would have put her hand on my arm again.

"Yes, I'm sorry about that, but you know how these things are . . ."

"Well, that's business, I suppose." She laughed. "It would be worse if you weren't busy, wouldn't it?"

Reprieved, I laughingly agreed. "Perhaps the next time we might have more luck."

"Well, I'm not sure when it'll be. As I said, my trips into the center tend to be few and far between." For which I was grateful. "But I'm sure we'll be able to meet up sometime or other."

We chatted for a while longer about the progress, or lack of it, of our respective insurance claims, and by the time I put the receiver down, relief at my narrow escape made me feel quite well disposed toward her. Then I remembered what Anna had said.

I had given little thought lately to her joking suggestion that the woman might have designs on me. But now the idea lodged in my mind. First she had called into the gallery. Now she had telephoned me. That was not normal behavior toward someone whose car you had run into. Or, as she claimed, had run into you. Disturbed, I poured myself a drink. The more I thought about it, the more it seemed that Anna might have been right.

I felt a sudden need to talk to her. She answered the telephone on the second ring.

"Hello?" She sounded rushed and expectant.

"It's Donald. I thought I'd call to see if Marty was back."

Her disappointment was dishearteningly obvious. "Oh, hello, Donald. No, he's not."

"Have you heard anything from him?"

"No. Nothing at all."

Now I had called, I was unsure what to say. "Are you all right?"

She attempted a laugh. "I'd be better if I knew where Marty is. No one's seen him since yesterday. I don't know whether to phone the police, or . . . or what." She drew a long, shaky breath. She seemed to be controlling herself with effort.

"Would you like me to come over?"

Her voice had a slight tremor. "No, it's okay, thanks. A friend of mine's going to stay."

It was my turn to feel disappointed. "Well, let me know as soon as you hear anything."

"I will. Look, I'm going to have to go, Donald. I want to keep the phone free in case he rings."

"Yes, of course. And don't worry about coming into the gallery tomorrow. Just . . . well, just see how you feel."

"Okay. Thanks." She sounded distant and uninterested. It was clear she did not want to talk to me. I said goodbye and put the receiver down, feeling worse than before I made the call. It had only let me see that, in spite of everything, Anna still only regarded me as her employer. Not a friend or confidant. I tried not to be disheartened and told myself that I could expect nothing else. Obviously, she had other people she would turn to before me. I would just have to be patient.

It was still early days.

The next day it was almost lunchtime before Anna arrived. She looked pale and tired. Her eyes were red and puffy.

"Have you heard anything?" I asked, brushing aside her apologies.

She shook her head. "Not from Marty. I've just had the police around to the flat. That's why I'm late."

"The police?" I was glad I was behind her; she could not see my face.

"I reported Marty missing, so they sent a couple of policemen to take the details." Her voice was dull.

"What did they say?"

"Not much, really. I did find one thing out, though." She tried to smile. "Wherever he is, he's taken a suitcase with him."

"A suitcase?"

"One's gone. Along with some of his clothes and his passport."

I looked shocked. "When did you notice this?"

"This morning, when the police were at the flat. One of them asked if anything of his was missing, and I said no, because I didn't think it was. I'd seen his clothes in the wardrobe, so it never occurred to me to check if anything had actually gone. And I didn't think it would have. I thought if he'd gone anywhere he would have told me. But then they asked if they could search the flat, and when I went around with them I realized one of the suitcases wasn't there. So then I had another look through his clothes and saw some of them had gone as well. Then one of the policemen asked if I knew where his passport was, and I looked but couldn't find that, either." She did not look at me as she spoke.

"Is anything else missing?"

"Not really. Most of his clothes were still there. His checkbook's gone too, but that's all. Nothing of mine's missing, if that's what you mean. The police made me check."

"Anna . . . I don't know what to say."

"Not much to say, really, is there?"

"Have you any idea where he might have gone?"

"No. None at all." She stared at the tabletop. "I just can't understand it. He wouldn't just go off somewhere without letting me know. He'd have left a note or something. And he certainly wouldn't go all this time without phoning me."

"Is there anyone he might have left a message with?"

"No one I've not already phoned. Except his parents, and I can't see Marty telling them anything. And I don't know how to get in touch with them anyway. Their number's in his address book, and he carries that with him."

I knew. I had given it to Zeppo to burn. "I don't want to pry, but can you think of any reason why he might have left?"

She shook her head. "That's just it, I can't! It's not as if we've had an argument or anything. The last thing he said when I phoned him was that he was missing me." Abruptly, she covered her face. "Oh, Christ, I feel so confused!"

Just as suddenly, she recovered. She wiped her eyes. "Sorry."

I offered her a handkerchief, awkwardly. "Here. It's clean."

"No, it's okay. I'm all right now. Really." She gave me a shaky smile to prove it. "It's just that I don't know what to think, that's all. One minute I want to kill him, the next I'm certain something's happened to him. I keep going round and round in circles."

I nodded sympathetically. "Are the police going to do anything?"

"They've already checked with all the hospitals, but nobody answering Marty's description's been admitted recently. That's something, I suppose. So now they just list him as a missing person, which means they'll keep an eye out for him at airports and train stations, places like that. But I can't see them trying very hard. Not when it looks as though he's packed up and walked out."

"Is that what they said?"

"Not in so many words. They were polite enough, but I could see what they thought. I'm just some neurotic girlfriend whose boyfriend's left her. I suppose you can't really blame them, can you?"

I sidestepped the question. "What about his work at the university? Has he been under pressure from that lately?"

"No more than usual. Not enough to make him do anything like this. And he loves it, anyway. He wouldn't just drop out without saying anything. That's what I can't understand. I know

what it looks like, but I can't believe he'd just walk out like this."
She looked at me. "What do you think, Donald? Honestly?"

It was my turn to shake my head. "I really don't know, Anna.
I can't claim to know him well enough to say."

"Yes, but what do you think?"

I sighed. "Well, let's say I'd perhaps be more concerned for
his welfare if his luggage and passport were still here. As it
is . . ." I spread my hands.

"I know. It looks like he's left me."

I said nothing. Anna was quiet for a moment. "But in that
case, why didn't he take everything with him?" she burst out.
"Most of his clothes are still here. And all his personal things
as well. If he was leaving he'd take everything, wouldn't he?"

"I don't know, Anna."

"And why hasn't he got in touch with me? Or the university?"

"Perhaps—" I stopped. "No, it doesn't matter."

"No, go on. Please."

"Don't take this the wrong way, Anna. I'm not saying he has.
But . . . well, perhaps he felt he needed some time to think."

"What do you mean?"

I spoke cautiously. "Well, perhaps he hasn't been in contact
because he was afraid to. I don't want to upset you, but it does
seem a coincidence that this has happened only weeks before
the two of you were to leave for America."

She frowned. "You mean he might have had second
thoughts?"

"All I'm saying is that it's a possibility."

Anna considered this only briefly. "No. No, he wouldn't do
something like that without telling me. Besides, he's as keen
on the idea as I am." She was emphatic.

I inclined my head. "Obviously you know him best. But try
and look at it objectively. I know it's hard, but if you look at the
bare facts, forgetting for the moment who's involved, then they
do seem to suggest something like that. Marty spends two days
on his own, and the day before you arrive back he disappears
with a packed suitcase and his passport."

"You mean he might have gone to America without me?"

I had not actually meant that, but it seemed a useful idea. I gave a helpless shrug. Anna was silent as she considered this new possibility.

"No, he wouldn't do that," she said after a while. But she seemed less certain than before. "Not without saying something. And most of his things are still here. He must be planning to come back. He could have just taken his passport because . . . because . . ."

I said nothing. She smiled sadly. "I can't get away from that, can I? Why has he taken his passport unless he was planning to use it?"

"I'm sure there could be any number of reasons," I said. But I did not attempt to give any.

Anna stared into space. "I just hope he gets in touch soon."

I patted her arm. "I'm sure he will."

A sort of tense calm settled over the next few days. Anna was quiet and withdrawn. She contacted the police regularly, as much to make sure they were actually trying to find Marty as anything else. They claimed to be doing everything they could, but Anna was not convinced. And her own helplessness weighed on her almost as much as Marty's disappearance. She declined my offer of time off. "I'd rather work than just sit at home and wait," she said.

I began to feel cautiously optimistic. I had given Zeppo an indefinite holiday, telling him I would be in touch when he was needed again. There was a tacit agreement that the original bargain, to seduce Anna, still stood. Whether this was because Zeppo himself saw this as unfinished business, or simply because it never occurred to him to question it, I have no idea. I was only glad he seemed to take it for granted. In any event, I had not expected to call on him again for weeks. I could not see Anna welcoming another man's attentions so soon after

Marty's disappearance. But what with the apparent lack of police concern, and her growing acceptance that Marty had left of his own accord, I began to think Zeppo might be able to resume his campaign sooner than planned.

Unfortunately, my optimism was premature. Interference was about to come from an unexpected quarter.

Chapter

13

Since Anna was unable to contact Marty's parents, I had assumed it was safe to disregard them. From what I had heard, they had not been particularly close to their son, and so it seemed reasonable to suppose they would remain ignorant of his disappearance, at least for the foreseeable future.

However, some things are simply unpredictable. When Anna walked into the gallery, a week after Marty had disappeared, I could see at once that she was upset.

"What's wrong?" I asked

She made an attempt to sound normal. "Marty's father phoned last night."

"His father?" I searched for a suitable response. "Has he heard from him?"

"No. That's why he called. It was Marty's mother's birthday two days ago, and he didn't send a card or phone. His father was going to tell him off for forgetting." Anna looked young and frightened. "It's the first time he's not been in touch on a birthday."

I tried not to let my irritation at the news show. Things had been going so well. "Anna, people forget birthdays all the time. It doesn't necessarily mean anything."

"But Marty's always thoughtful about anything like that. And his father said he's never forgotten before."

I could think of no way to convincingly defend Marty's lapse of memory. "What did you tell him?"

She shrugged. "What could I tell him, except that Marty had disappeared about a week ago, and I hadn't a clue where he was? He wanted to know why I hadn't let him know straight away. I said I couldn't because I hadn't got his number, but I could tell he didn't believe me."

"He didn't actually say that, surely?"

"No, but he let me know that's what he thought. He asked why Marty had left, and when I said I'd no idea, he said, 'Well, have you at least done anything to find him?' As if I'd just not bother!" She angrily brushed tears from her eyes with the heel of her palm.

"Come on. Sit down." I took hold of her arm and led her to a chair. My fingers retained a tactile memory of the contact. I poured us both a coffee and sat down opposite her. "Did you tell him you'd been to the police?"

She nodded. "Yes, but when I told him what they were doing, he said, 'So in actual fact, they're doing nothing.' Then he wanted to know what else I'd done, and when it actually came to saying it, it sounded like nothing at all. He made me feel like a callous bitch."

"You're hardly that."

"No, but he just . . . oh, you know, made me feel like I wasn't even *trying* to find Marty. I could tell he thought I knew more than I was telling him. He obviously thought I must have done something to make Marty leave."

I felt outraged for her. "That's nonsense!"

"I don't know, I'm starting to wonder." Her voice was on the edge of breaking. She held her coffee cup in both hands, as though she were trying to warm herself from it. She looked very vulnerable.

"Well, you shouldn't! Don't let him upset you, he was probably just hitting out at you because you were there. Didn't you say that Marty didn't get on with him?" She nodded. "Well, then, there you are! Now you know why. If he jumps to conclusions like that, he's obviously completely unreasonable!" I was prepared to dislike the man already.

"I know, you're probably right," Anna said, a little calmer. "But he still made me realize that I'm not *doing* anything. Marty's missing, and I'm just sitting and waiting for him to come back. That's not enough."

"You've done everything you can. Did Marty's father suggest what else you could have done or offer to do anything himself? Or was he just content to criticize you?"

She sighed, tiredly. "He's going to go to the State Department to see what they can do, so I said I'll go to the embassy here as well." She shook her head. "I should have thought of that myself."

So, perhaps, should I. "Will they be able to help?"

"I don't know. They might be able to put some pressure on the police to try a bit harder." She did not sound too hopeful. "Something needs to. I called them last night to tell them what Marty's father had said. I thought it might make them take it more seriously, but I might as well not have bothered." Her mouth tightened at the memory. "I spoke to this . . ."—she struggled for a suitable description—"this *pig* of a sergeant who just said he'd make a note of it. So I asked what else they were going to do, and he said that Marty was already listed as a missing person and they'd carry on keeping an eye out for him." Her agitation was growing as she relived the conversation. She put her coffee down, angrily. A little slopped into the saucer. Anna did not notice.

"I told him that 'keeping an eye out' wasn't enough! I mean, Marty's *disappeared*, for God's sake! You'd think they'd at least make an attempt to find him! Especially now, when even his parents are getting worried! But he just got all shirty and said he was sorry my 'young man' had left me, but they weren't a detective agency and can't be expected to find everyone who decides to leave home."

She paused, making an obvious attempt to calm down. "God, I was just so angry. I didn't bother saying anything else. If I had I'd only have regretted it. What with him and Marty's father, I just felt like . . . like screaming." She drew in a long breath. "I just hope to God the embassy does something. I can't stand sitting around like this much longer, not knowing anything. If I don't do *something* soon I'm going to go mad!"

Reluctantly, I realized that Anna was no longer going to passively resign herself to Marty's absence. There and then, I decided to change my tactics.

"All right," I said briskly. "Let's try and think what you can do. You've already done everything you can as far as the police are concerned. Now what about the embassy? Have you spoken to them yet?"

"I phoned them last night, but the person I need to speak to wasn't there. They told me to call back this morning." She looked at her watch. "He's probably there by now."

"Well, you give him a ring and make an appointment to see him. Insist that it's urgent and that it must be this morning. Don't take no for an answer." I doubted that she would have anyway. "I'll take you over whenever you have to go."

"There's no need to do that. I'll be all right."

"I'm sure you will, but I can still give you moral support. And while we're about it, what paper does Marty read?"

She looked puzzled. "The *Guardian*. Why?"

"We can put an advert in the personal columns. Appealing to him to get in touch."

Anna was brightening visibly now she had something to do. "I don't think he generally reads the personals, but it can't hurt, can it?"

I smiled reassuringly. "Not at all."

It was after lunch before Anna was able to see anyone at the American embassy. I overruled her protests about closing the gallery but allowed her to persuade me that she would rather be seen alone. "That way I'll look less like an hysterical girlfriend who needs looking after," she said.

I waited for her in the reception area. The room was white

walled and plain. A few paintings decorated it, but they were drab and uninspiring. I picked up one of the less dog-eared magazines from the low table and tried to find something interesting in it. The chairs ran around the walls of the room, facing the center. After a while another man, gray haired and quite distinguished looking, came in and sat down, shoes squeaking on the parquet floor. We ignored each other. The room was very quiet, except when one of us cleared our throat or turned a page.

I looked up as a door opened farther down the corridor. A middle-aged man held it open as Anna came out. "Please get in touch if there are any further developments," he said. Tight lipped, she walked down the corridor without answering him. I rose, giving her a questioning look.

"They're very sorry, but they can't interfere in 'domestic' affairs," she said. Her tone was bitingly caustic—a side of her I had not previously seen. "He said that if the police have already listed him as missing, there's nothing more they can do about it. Since his visa's not expired and everything indicates that he left of his own free will, apparently there's no reason for the embassy to become involved. The fact that no one's seen him, and that he's just abandoned years of research work, doesn't matter." She walked so fast I had to hurry to keep up with her. "What does it take, for Christ's sake?"

I hid my satisfaction. "I really don't know what to suggest, Anna. But at least you've tried everything you can. We'll just have to hope he responds to the advert in the *Guardian*."

She said nothing. We went outside. It was cold and drizzling, already growing dark although it was still only mid-afternoon. Anna was quiet on the way back to the car. I respected her silence. We were driving away before she spoke again.

"I've been thinking about what that policeman said. About them not being a detective agency." There was a determined look about her. "If they won't try to find Marty, I'll hire someone who will."

This was unexpected. "You mean a private detective?"

She nodded. "I should have thought of it before."

"Isn't that . . . well . . ." I stumbled for words. "Do you think that would do any good?"

"I don't know. But I don't have many options, do I? It's either hiring a detective or doing nothing. No one else is going to look for him."

I tried to hide my reluctance behind practical objections. A car pulled out in front of me, and I only just managed to avoid bumping into it. I forced myself to concentrate on the road. I had already caused myself enough trouble through one accident. "How would you get hold of a private detective?" I asked.

"I don't know. Yellow Pages, I suppose."

"But how would you know if he was reputable or not? I've always had the impression that some of these people operate on the fringe of the law. You could just be paying someone to do nothing."

"Well, I've got to try."

"Have you any idea how much someone like that would charge?"

"No, but the money hardly matters, does it?"

There was a note of censure in her voice. I retreated from it. "Of course not! I was only meaning that you might not be able to afford it."

"I can use the money I've saved for America."

My objections had antagonized her. I hurriedly tried to repair the damage. "There's no need for that," I said. "All I was trying to say was that I'd be only too pleased to pay for someone. If you'd let me."

She quickly looked at me. "Oh no, I couldn't do that!"

"Why ever not?"

"Because I just couldn't! You've done enough already!"

"My dear Anna, I've done nothing at all, except act as a chauffeur. I couldn't possibly let you spend your hard-earned savings. There's not much I can do to help, but at least let me do this."

"No, really, Donald. Thank you, but there's no need."

I was warming to my theme, enjoying the opportunity to be generous. "I know there's no need, but I would *like* to. Call it an indefinite loan, if you'd rather."

"Thanks, but I couldn't. Really."

"If you don't I'll be offended." Anna looked uncertain. "Please?"

She hesitated a moment longer, then gave in. "Okay. I . . . well. Thanks."

Before she looked away, embarrassed, she smiled at me gratefully. And, I was sure, with genuine affection.

It was payment enough.

☕

Anna was right about finding detective agencies in the Yellow Pages. It had never occurred to me before that such things would be so easy to locate. There were comparatively few but still more than I would have expected. She made her selection almost randomly, singling out the ones with bigger, more expensive advertisements in the hope that this reflected their professional expertise and success. Of these, any with melodramatic names were quickly discounted. Finally, we were left with a choice of five, after Anna dismissed one because he claimed "twenty years' experience as a detective sergeant."

"I already know what the police think," she said. "If he was a policeman for that long, he'll be no different."

The first number Anna called had an answering machine: she hung up without speaking. The second was more promising. I sat opposite Anna in the office while she gave brief details of what she wanted: I noticed the hand not holding the telephone was trembling slightly. She said goodbye and put the receiver back in its cradle.

"I've an appointment with Mr. Simpson at four o'clock."

"Is that who you spoke to?"

"No, just a secretary. She said he's out until this afternoon."

"Are you going to try the other numbers?"

She shook her head. "I think I'll see how this turns out

first." She gave an awkward smile. "To be honest, it feels a bit weird. Asking complete strangers to look for Marty."

I was instantly contrite. "You should have said something! I could have done it for you."

"Oh, no, I didn't mean that. I'd rather do it myself. But it just seems . . . well. You know."

I nodded understandingly. "Would you like me to come with you?"

"It's up to you. I don't want you to think you have to. You're doing enough as it is, and I've already taken you away from the gallery once today."

I could see that she did not relish the idea of going alone. I felt warmed by the fact that she wanted me with her. "I've already told you not to worry about that. This is far more important."

"You're sure you don't mind?"

"Of course I don't. I'd like very much to go with you."

Anna suddenly smiled. "If Marty knew where I was going, he'd love it. He's a big fan of the old detective stories."

"I've read one or two of Sir Arthur Conan Doyle's," I said. "I quite enjoyed them."

"Marty's into the American hard-boiled school. Chandler, Hammett. James M. Cain. All those."

All things considered, I thought that was quite apt.

The Simpson Investigation Agency bore little resemblance to any of its fictional counterparts. The first-floor office in Finchley had neither the opulence of Holmes's residence, nor the seedy masculinity of the American private eye's headquarters. Blandly anonymous, it could have housed anything from a double glazing company to an insurance broker's. A selection of framed certificates proclaimed the usual obscure qualifications. Sitting at the desk in front of them, Simpson himself looked as though he would be more at home with tax returns than problems of detection.

He shook both my and Anna's hands and told us to sit down. He was a balding, innocuous-looking man lost somewhere in his forties. A smell of after-shave and peppermint clung to him.

He offered us tea or coffee and seemed disappointed when we declined.

"Now, Miss . . . Palmer?" He looked at Anna inquiringly. She nodded. "I believe you want to locate your boyfriend."

"That's right."

"And what's his name, please?"

"Marty Westerman." Anna fretted with her hands as she told Simpson about Marty's disappearance. He made notes on a printed sheet of paper, waiting until she had finished before asking any questions. He wrote her answers down diligently.

"Have you a photograph?"

Anna fetched a small snapshot out of her bag. I looked at it jealously, but it was only of Marty. Simpson attached it to his notes with a paper clip.

"What do you think the chances of finding him are?" Anna asked. She looked and sounded nervous. Simpson pursed his lips.

"It's difficult to say. From what you've told me, it looks as though he left deliberately. Why he went and why he hasn't been in touch remain to be seen. It's no good my even trying to guess. All I can do for now is try and trace his movements, find out who was the last person to see him, if anyone's seen him since. I must warn you that I can't promise anything, though. If anyone is really determined not to be found, then to be honest finding them's pretty much a matter of luck."

Anna was sitting on the edge of her seat, listening intently. "Do people normally come back in cases like this?"

Simpson gave an apologetic smile. "You can't really make comparisons. If he just wanted some time to himself, then I'd say, yes, there's a good chance. But since we don't know why he went in the first place, it's best not to jump to any conclusions one way or another. I know it's difficult for you, but I don't want to raise your hopes too much at this stage. Let's just see what we can find out, shall we?"

He stood up, offering his hand again. "You've given us enough to be going on with. If you'd like to have a word with the secretary in reception, she'll give you details of the fees.

I'll get in touch with you in a few days to let you know what we've come up with." He gave Anna a reassuring smile. "Don't worry. We'll do our best."

On the way out, I found myself hoping that their best would not be good enough. I could not see any way he might pose a serious threat. But at the same time, the irony of hiring someone to uncover the very thing I wanted to remain a secret was not lost on me.

I hoped I was not being too clever for my own good.

14

"*You're fucking* joking*!*"

That was Zeppo's reaction when I told him about the detective. It was not a task I looked forward to. I had not imagined he would be pleased. I was right.

"You've *hired* a private detective? Are you fucking *mad* or *what?*"

"I didn't really have any choice."

"You didn't have any *choice*? Jesus *Christ*, why don't you just *tell* her what happened?"

"If you'll calm down a moment, I'll explain."

"Go on, then! Explain!"

I already had my argument prepared. I disliked having to account to Zeppo, but I had to admit that, on the surface, my actions did seem a little counterproductive. "Anna was going to hire someone anyway. Since I couldn't persuade her not to, I thought the best thing to do was offer to pay for it myself. At least this way I'll know as soon as Anna does if he finds anything. Besides which, I hardly think anyone is going to suspect me if I'm paying for the investigation."

I heard a thump as Zeppo hit something. I was glad I had chosen to tell him over the telephone. "This isn't fucking Agatha Christie, Donald! We fucking killed someone, and now you're trying tell me you're playing at psy-fucking-chology with a detective? Jesus Christ!"

"If we're talking about taking risks, I hardly think you should be talking like that over the telephone."

"Oh, for fuck's sake! You've hired someone to find Marty and you're worrying in case someone's tapping the fucking phone line? Oh, that's a real risk, isn't it?"

"I don't think hiring a detective constitutes any real danger—"

"Well, *I* fucking do! Why didn't you talk her out of it?"

"If you'd listen, I've already told you I tried! Would you rather I objected so much it began to look as if I had a reason?"

"You didn't have to go with her, though, did you?"

"I've already explained—"

"Don't give me that shit! All right, so you thought it'd be a good idea to pay for a detective. You could still have let her go by herself! You didn't have to hold her hand while she saw him, did you? Now instead of just being Anna's boss you've connected yourself to Marty! Whether you like it or not, you've made yourself part of that dickhead's investigation! How can you be so fucking *stupid*?"

To be honest, that had not actually occurred to me. But I was not going to admit it to Zeppo. "I still think you're overreacting. I can't see how he can possibly begin to suspect either of us."

"Why take the fucking chance, for Christ's sake?"

"Apart from anything else, it puts Anna under an obligation."

"An *obligation*? How much of a fucking *obligation* do you think she'll be under if she finds out you had her boyfriend clubbed to death?"

"It won't come to that."

"It better fucking not. Because if I go down, you go down! And if it's because of your fucking stupidity, you better hope the police get to you before I do—you know what I'm saying?"

I felt it was time to assert myself. "May I remind you who is paying whom?"

"I don't give a shit. And don't start with the big boss routine because of the photos, either. I've got just as much on you now as you have on me, so we wouldn't want the police sniffing round over a few fucking cock shots, would we? We're both in this, and in future if you get any more bright ideas I want to know about them first! Clear?"

I forced myself to swallow what he was saying. I did not want to risk an argument at this stage. "Perfectly," I said icily.

"Good. And I want to know whatever the detective finds out, as soon as he tells you. Jesus!" He hung up.

Infuriated, I banged down the receiver. But then, as I thought about what Zeppo had said, I felt a vague unease. I had thought at the time that going to see the detective with Anna was the best course of action. Now I was no longer so sure. And also at the back of my mind was the nagging fear that if I had overlooked one thing, there could be others.

It did not make for pleasant thinking.

࿔

Anna was almost cheerful the next morning. Not just because she now felt something was being done to find Marty but because she had also found out something for herself.

"Marty didn't take the plane tickets!"

For a moment, I was confused. "Plane tickets?"

"To America! They're still at the flat! What with Marty gone and everything, I'd forgotten all about them. But then yesterday, after I said I could use the money I'd saved for America to pay for the detective, I suddenly thought about them and checked to see if they were still there. And they were!"

I could not see why this should excite her. "Ah. Good."

My reaction must have been disappointing. She felt compelled to explain. "Don't you see what that means? He must be planning to come back! If he was going to leave for good, he would have taken at least one of them with him, wouldn't he?"

I answered without thinking. "Not necessarily. If he doesn't want anyone to know where he is, he'll hardly use a plane ticket you know about. And he might not want to go back to America now anyway."

Anna turned on me. "Thanks, Donald. That's really poured cold water on that idea, hasn't it?"

Astonished, I stared at her. But she was immediately contrite. "Oh, I'm sorry, I didn't mean that."

"It's . . . it's quite all right."

"No, I shouldn't have spoken to you like that." She seemed suddenly deflated. "I'm sorry. You're right, I was building my hopes up over nothing."

"No, no, I shouldn't have tried to dampen your spirits." Seeing how dispirited she had become, I genuinely regretted it.

"Yes, you should. I was getting all excited over nothing." She sat down, her animation gone. "I suppose I was still on a high after hiring the detective. You know, knowing that somebody was finally going to *do* something at last. Then when I found the tickets it was like Marty hadn't completely gone. I talked myself into thinking it was a good sign." She gave me a sad smile. "But you're right. They don't mean anything one way or another, do they? I was just being stupid."

"You shouldn't say that. You've got to have hope."

"Yes, but kidding myself isn't going to do any good. And neither is snapping at you. You were only saying what I already knew. I didn't even mention anything about the tickets to Marty's father last night, because I could guess what he'd say and didn't want to hear it." She sighed, shaking her head. "I'm really sorry, Donald. I was being a cow. You didn't deserve that."

I patted her hand. "Nothing to be sorry for. Don't even think about it." Then, casually, I asked, "I take it Marty's father called you again?"

She shook her head. "I phoned him. I'd thought he'd be pleased to know I was doing something."

"And was he?"

"If he was, he didn't show it. He certainly wasn't any nicer." She shrugged. "I don't know, perhaps I'm being a bit harsh on

him. It is his son who's gone missing, and as far as he's concerned I might be just some floozy who's led Marty on or
something."

The suggestion was distasteful. "Hardly."

"No, but he doesn't know that, does he? He's bound to be a
bit suspicious. And he'd had no more luck with the State Department than I've had with the embassy here. I don't think
that helped."

I thought she was being overly generous. "There's still no
cause to take it out on you."

"I suppose not, but I can understand him being worried."
She smiled. "I've just bitten your head off, and you've done
nothing, have you?"

I remembered what Zeppo had said and felt a sudden chill
at the thought of Anna finding out what had actually happened.

"Don't even think about that," I told her, not wanting to
myself.

I waited almost as anxiously as she did for the first news from
the detective. No matter how much I told myself there was
nothing to worry about, there was still a doubt that refused to
go. My stomach began to suffer.

The first results, however, were encouraging. "A neighbor
saw him leaving your home address with a suitcase around
teatime on either the eighth or ninth of this month," Simpson
told Anna. He had called at the gallery, and with his briefcase
and tweed jacket, he looked like an insurance collector. The
smell of after-shave and peppermint had come with him.

"A neighbor?" Anna frowned. "Who? I asked everyone one
I know."

He glanced at the thin cardboard folder open on his lap. "A
Mrs. Jenner. An old lady. She lives almost directly opposite, at
number thirty-two."

Anna looked surprised. "I know an old lady lives opposite

us, but I've never spoken to her. Was she sure it was Marty?"

"She seemed to be. She also said she'd seen you leaving a day or two earlier, also with a suitcase."

"She doesn't miss much, does she?"

Simpson smiled. "Every neighborhood's got someone like that. It can be useful."

My stomach had coiled at the mention of a witness. "You said she saw him on either the eighth or the ninth. Didn't she know which?"

"No, she couldn't be any more exact than that. She was quite upset about it. Her TV had broken down, otherwise she said she'd have remembered the day by what was on."

"I went away on the seventh," said Anna. "And I spoke to Marty that night and the next, so it must have been the ninth. The Wednesday."

Simpson looked at his file. "It could have been the night before, after you'd spoken to him. But since he went into the university the next day I think we can assume it wasn't. You say you telephoned him just after six and the line was engaged, so it looks as though he spoke to someone and then immediately afterward left with a packed suitcase." He looked at Anna. "Any more ideas on who he might have been speaking to?"

She shook her head helplessly. "No. None."

"You can't think of anyone who could have made him leave the house like that?"

"I've asked everyone I know. All our friends, the people he knows at university. No one spoke to him."

"All right. Keep on trying to think about it anyway." He briefly looked at the file again. "I think it's safe to say that, wherever he was going, he took either a bus or the tube. If he'd been planning to go by taxi, he would have ordered it from home." I offered up a silent prayer of thanks that I had told Marty not to take one. "I've been trying to contact the bus crews who went through your area at around that time. We've not spoken to all of them yet, but so far no one can remember picking up anyone who fits Marty's description. I've also spoken with the ticket office at the tube station nearest to you, but no one there can remember anything, either." He gave an apologetic little shrug. "The problem is that it's getting on for two weeks ago now. A lot of faces have passed through since then."

"So it's a dead end," Anna said flatly.

"Well, I can't pretend he's left a blazing trail, but it's still early days. And we've only just started looking. Airports and hospitals we leave to the police. They'll automatically be contacted if he turns up there. But there are plenty of other places he could be, so we'll concentrate on those. I've already been in touch with the Salvation Army, and they're going to see what they can do."

Both Anna and I looked blank. "The Salvation Army? How can they help?" Anna asked.

"They're very good, actually," Simpson said. "Most people don't realize it, but they've got a missing-persons bureau and an intelligence network that's pretty much as good as the police's. In fact, the police sometimes use it themselves. It can save a lot of time and footwork. And there's always the chance that we'll get lucky and find that he's staying in one of their hostels."

Anna looked dubious. "I can't really see that."

"Perhaps not, but it doesn't hurt to try. We've also been in contact with the YMCA to see if he's stayed with them. No luck so far, but we'll contact them every few days, just in case." He glanced down at the file again, then looked at Anna.

"There is one more thing that's worth mentioning. He's got to live on something. You said he'd taken his own checkbook with him. You don't have a joint account in either a bank or building society he can have access to, do you?"

Anna shook her head. "No. We keep our money separately."

Simpson looked disappointed. "Ah well. If you had, you could have got the bank to run a check on any withdrawals. Found out what checks he's written lately and where they've been cashed."

"Can't we do that anyway?"

"I wish we could. It would make things a lot easier, but no

bank will just release that sort of information unless it's a jointly held account."

"Not even if I explain what's happened?"

"No, I'm afraid not. Even the police haven't the authority for that. Not in this sort of situation."

"What do you mean, 'this sort of situation'?" I asked.

He spoke cautiously. "Well, I mean that at present there are no grounds for concern for Marty's actual well-being. I realize that you're very concerned about him yourselves, obviously," he added hurriedly, before Anna could say anything, "But there are no . . . let's say 'suspicious circumstances,' about him going. If there were it would be a different matter. If there was anything to indicate that, heaven forbid, something might have happened to him, then the bank would cooperate with the police. But not as things stand at present."

He smiled. "I know that doesn't exactly help us find him, but in a way it's a good sign that we can't have access to his account. If you see what I mean."

I did. And although I was not sure how Anna felt, I certainly found that reassuring.

෮௳

Anna invited me to her flat that weekend. Or, rather, she accepted when I offered to call around. I was still a little wary of forcing my company on her, but now I felt justified in seeing her out of working hours. And I was sure she seemed genuinely pleased.

I had expected to have her to myself, but I was disappointed. When I went into the lounge there was another girl on the sofa.

"You've not met Debbie, have you?" Anna asked.

"No, I don't think I've had the pleasure."

"This is Donald, my boss," Anna said to the other girl. I was stung by the way she qualified the introduction. But the injury was soothed a moment later.

"I've heard a lot about you," the girl said, and I felt almost childish pleasure at the implicit compliment. Her voice sounded familiar, but I did not immediately place it. Then I put her name to it and remembered. Debbie. The girl Anna had been talking to when I overheard them on the telephone. I felt a bristle of hostility toward her.

"I was just making a drink," Anna said. "Would you like tea or coffee?"

"Whatever you're making."

"Well, I'm having tea and Debbie's having coffee, so you can take your pick. I've got some orange pekoe, if you'd like it?"

"That would be lovely." Again, I felt a surge of pleasure. That was my favorite tea. I was sure Anna had bought it specially.

There was a moment's silence after Anna left me alone with the girl. She had a round, rather doughy face, unappealingly draped with straggly hair.

"I'd just like to say I think you've been great to Anna," she said out of the blue.

I was taken aback. "I've not really done very much."

"You're paying for the detective, for a start. I call that a big help. But not just that, you've given her support, and that's what she needs right now. I really appreciate it."

Her patronizing attitude irritated me. "I've only done what I can." I tried not to sound too stiff.

"Well, I think it's great. And I know Anna's grateful."

"There's no need for her to be."

She smiled. "I'm sorry. I'm embarrassing you. I just wanted to tell you while Anna was out of the way. She's taking it well, isn't she? I mean, it can't be easy."

"No, I'm sure it isn't."

"If it was me, I'd be going out of my mind. Not knowing what's happened to him. I couldn't stand it."

"No."

"I mean, I wouldn't say so to Anna, but to be honest, it doesn't look very good, does it? If it was my boyfriend, I'd be worried sick. For him to just walk out like that in the first place, and then for her not to hear anything. Well . . ." She looked at me, meaningfully. "I really wouldn't like to say what's happened. I mean, I really *wouldn't* like to say."

I had the feeling that, like it or not, she would anyway. She did. "Either he's got cold feet or found somebody else or something's happened to him," she went on. "I mean, if he was going to come back, or at least get in touch, he would have by now, wouldn't he? So he's either not going to or can't. Either way, it doesn't look very good for Anna, does it?"

"I suppose not."

"I mean, I know he could have suddenly had a breakdown, or got amnesia or something, but it's not very likely, is it?" I inclined my head, noncommittally. It did not satisfy her. "What do you think's happened to him?"

"I really couldn't say. I don't know him very well."

"Well, none of us do, really. I mean, I know Anna's been going out with him for nearly a year, but once she'd started seeing him they kept themselves pretty much to themselves. I must admit, I'd got my doubts about this whole America thing from the word go. It seemed a bit soon to me. I mean, don't get me wrong, I really liked Marty, from what I saw of him, but how well can you get to know anyone in a few months? Mind you, having said that, he never struck me as the type who would just walk out like this."

She shook her head. "You just don't know what to think, do you? One minute I'm convinced he's run off, the next I start thinking that something horrible must have happened to him."

"The police don't seem to think so."

She snorted. "The police? They wouldn't, would they? Unless it's something blindingly obvious, they don't want to know. They'd rather sit on their backsides than do anything constructive." She stopped and grinned, apologetically. "Sorry. Bit of a hobbyhorse of mine."

Thankfully, Anna came back with the drinks at that point. "Have you two got me all sorted out, then?" she asked. I was horrified at the thought of complicity with her awful friend, but Debbie only laughed.

"Of course. That's what friends are for, isn't it, Donald?"

I was saved from having to respond by the doorbell. "I'm popular today," said Anna, lightly. But I had seen her jump when it rang, and she was tense as she got up and went out. I wondered how long it would be before she was able to answer either the door or the telephone without flinching.

I heard the front door open, and then brief, murmured voices. Anna came back into the room. Her face was white. A man was behind her.

"This is Marty's father," she said.

Chapter

15

I would have known who he was even if Anna had not introduced him. He had the same runtish characteristics as his son, but without even the few redeeming features that youth had lent to Marty. As I stood up to offer my hand, I reflected that I had at least spared Anna the ordeal of growing old with someone like that.

He shook my hand reluctantly, dropping it almost straight away. He said not a word, making no attempt to be civil or explain his presence.

"This is a . . . a complete surprise," Anna said. "I had no idea you were planning to come over." She seemed shellshocked. Her friend Debbie stood wide eyed beside me, as though this was some kind of new and fascinating spectator sport.

"I wasn't. But I didn't seem to have much choice. Not if I want this cleared up quickly."

The criticism was so blatant it bordered on the insulting, and the tone of the man's thin, waspish voice made it clear that that was how it was intended. Anna colored up and seemed on the point of reacting. But all she said was, "You should have let me know. I could have met you at the airport."

He rebuffed the pleasantry. "That's okay. I'd rather settle in by myself. Although I hope all your taxi drivers aren't as incompetent as the one who drove me here. I almost had to find the way for him." He cast a brief glance toward where I was standing with Anna's friend before addressing Anna again. "Now, if you don't mind, I think we have a lot to talk about."

I was so astonished by his lack of manners that I was slow to realize this was a dismissal. There was a moment's stunned silence. Then Debbie began collecting her things together.

"I'd better be going anyway, Anna," she said, moving toward the door. "I'll call you later. Goodbye, Mr. . . . ." Her mouth worked as she groped for Marty's surname.

"Westerman," his father said, curtly.

Reluctantly, I followed her cue. "Yes, I'd better be off, too." I resented being ousted in such a way, but there was no excuse for me to stay. Westerman and I exchanged brief nods as the girl and I left. Anna came with us into the kitchen.

"I'm sorry about this," she whispered.

Debbie gave her a hug and kissed her cheek. "Don't be, it's not your fault."

"I'd no idea he was coming! Why didn't he *tell* me?"

"He's just being an awkward sod." Debbie said. "Don't let him get to you. Look, do you want me to stay?"

"No, I'll be all right. Thanks."

"I'll be at home all afternoon if you want me," I said, not to be outdone. Anna nodded, but I could see she was not really listening.

"I'd better go back. I'll talk to you both later."

"God, poor Anna!" Debbie said, as we went down the steps. "Can you believe how *rude* he was? What a pig!"

I found myself agreeing with her, something I would not have thought possible ten minutes earlier. I was even moved to offer her a lift and found I did not object to her garrulousness half as much when it was directed against someone I disliked.

After I had dropped her at the nearest tube station, I went home. I had told Anna I would be there, and now my visit had been interrupted I had no other plans.

For a while I was able to occupy myself with making lunch. Eating it took up a little more time. But after that I was once again faced with an empty day. The only subject I could concentrate on was Anna. I sat and waited for her to call, wondering what was being said in my absence. Nothing else seemed worth thinking about.

It was then I remembered my private gallery. With surprise I realized I had not been in it for weeks, not since the night of Zeppo's visit. I had not even thought of it since and felt mildly amazed that my former passion had gone neglected for so long.

The prospect of an afternoon of self-indulgence seemed heaven-sent to take my mind off Anna. I deliberately stretched out the moment, delaying going upstairs until I had washed the lunch dishes and had a cup of tea. Then, with a sense of reward, I went up to the gallery.

The anticipation was better than the fact. I turned on the lights and closed the door and waited for the usual sense of contentment to wash over me. When it did not, I began my study of the pictures anyway, consciously trying to manufacture the mood. It would not come. I found I had wandered past several pieces without really seeing them and tried to force myself into a more receptive state. But all that achieved was to make me notice the flaws in each work. The sensuality, the beauty of them was lost to me. Faults I had previously been able to overlook, even considered a part of their charm, now seemed clumsy and glaring.

In desperation, I went to the piece I had spent so much time over on my previous visit; the lovers and their hidden observer. The chair was still lying where Zeppo had knocked it over. Righting it, I sat down and stared at the trio, searching for my earlier absorption. All I found was an irritating awareness that the girl's feet were too small for her body and that the artist was weak when it came to depicting hands.

Finally, I gave up. I set the chair back in the center of the room, turned out the lights and closed the door. My collection no longer held any pleasure for me. Anna had spoiled my palate.

The telephone rang as I was going downstairs. I almost fell in my hurry to answer it and picked it up breathlessly.

"Hello?"

"Hello, Donald. It's Anna. I thought I'd better apologize for what happened earlier."

My restlessness dropped away. "There's no need for that. You're not responsible for the man's manners. He has gone now, I take it?"

"Yes. He didn't stay long."

"Did he improve after we'd left?"

"Not so much that you'd notice." She sounded very low.

"Did he give you a rough time?"

"A little. But he'd just had a long journey. He was probably tired as well as worried."

"That's no excuse. Was he very unpleasant?"

"Well, he let me see what he thinks of me. Which isn't very much."

I felt a flare of anger. "Then he's a fool as well as a boor. What did he say?"

"More or less what you heard. That it was time something was done, and he could do more here than in America. He made it clear that he begrudged having to come, but he obviously thinks that no one's trying to find Marty. And I don't think he trusts me at all."

"That's ridiculous!"

"I know, but . . ." I heard her sigh. "Well, that's the impression I got, anyway. He asked to look through Marty's things, and when I stayed in the bedroom with him, he seemed to actually resent me being there. As if I was trespassing on his son's property or something. I don't know, perhaps I'm being too touchy."

"Having met the man, I doubt it."

"I just can't understand what I've done. I know he's bound to be worried and upset, but so am I. I can't see why he's got to be so nasty. We should be helping each other, not arguing. He treats me as if I'm some sort of . . . of gold digger or something who's led his son astray. I'm starting to think I *must* have done something wrong. I just don't know what."

"That's silly, Anna. This isn't your fault and you know it."

"I don't know. I just . . . He makes me feel so *guilty*!"

"And I daresay that's exactly what he wants. You said yourself that Marty didn't get on with him. He's probably jealous of you, and so he's trying to make you suffer for it. Don't let him."

"But he's so sure of himself! I really tried to be friendly, to make him less hostile, but he didn't want to know."

"Anna, the man's clearly nothing but a bitter-minded, petty little tyrant. He's not worth upsetting yourself over."

There was a pause, and then she gave a low laugh. "You don't like him, do you, Donald?"

I smiled, realizing how worked up I had become but glad I had given Anna at least some light relief. "Not the slightest bit."

"Thank God for that. I was worried it was just me."

"No, I think it's a perfectly reasonable opinion."

She laughed again. It sounded wonderful. "Well, hopefully he'll be able to do some good now he's here. He's asked me to go to the embassy with him on Monday morning. He even managed to make that sound as if he was doing me a favor. I said I would, because I didn't want to give him the chance to say I'm not trying, but I still wanted to clear it with you. You don't mind, do you?"

"Of course not. I only hope they'll listen to him."

"So do I. I would think they'll have to. He's Marty's father, and he's come all the way from America. Surely they'll have to do something, won't they?"

"I'm sure they will." I wondered what. "Are you seeing him again before Monday?"

"No. I asked him if he wanted to come here for something to eat tonight, but he said no. He wasn't exactly gracious about it, but I can't pretend I'm disappointed."

"I can't say I blame you." On impulse, I asked, "What are you doing tonight? Not staying in by yourself, are you?"

"No, I'm seeing some friends at Debbie's. And in case you're interested, she doesn't like Marty's father, either."

"So I gathered." I felt a stab of jealousy. Anna must have spoken to the girl before she telephoned me. "Well, I'm glad you're going out. It'll do you good."

"That's what Debbie said. I don't really feel like it, to be honest, though."

"Nonsense. You deserve it after putting up with that awful man." I hesitated. "Are you doing anything tomorrow?"

"Not so far. Why?"

I felt ridiculously nervous. "If you're not, I wondered if you might like to go out somewhere?"

"It's nice of you to offer, Donald, but I better not. I'm not sure what Marty's father's doing. He might want to meet me again or something."

"Of course. I only wondered. Well, you know where I am if you want to get in touch." I was glad she could not see me. My face was burning like a schoolboy's. After I had put the telephone down I told myself that I was overreacting, that she had not thought anything of either my offer or her refusal. But that did little to ease my embarrassment.

To take my mind off it, I thought about Marty's father, indulging in self-righteous anger against him. His entire attitude, particularly his treatment of Anna, was deplorable. There was simply no call for it. I spent a while contemplating scenarios in which I told Westerman exactly what I thought of him, while Anna stood by as a grateful witness. After half an hour of such juvenile fantasies, I felt much better. Until I remembered the reason he was here in the first place.

I wondered what if any effect he would have on the investigation into Marty's disappearance. Hopefully none, but it was a situation I would rather have avoided. Then I wondered how Zeppo would react to the news.

I decided not to tell him.

ᏕᏇ

Monday lunchtime came and went without sign of Anna. I found it difficult to concentrate on the everyday chores of the gallery. Even when a garish and enthusiastic American came in and bought one of my more expensive pieces for cash, I found myself resenting the intrusion.

I had not spoken to Anna again. On Sunday, despite her refusal of my offer to go out, I had called around to see her. But she was not in. The doorbell rang hollowly, and there was that indefinable quietness about the flat that said it was empty. I left feeling the same way.

It was after two o'clock before she arrived at the gallery, and my relief at seeing her was instantly tempered with anxiety for what might have occurred.

"Sorry I'm late. It took longer than I expected."

"That's all right. Did you have any luck with the embassy?"

She took her coat off and hung it up. Her motions were slow and deliberate, as though she were very tired. When she turned to face me again, I noticed she had faint black smudges under her eyes. I wondered how long they had been there. "Sort of," she said. "Well, not even sort of. Yes, we did." She gave an apologetic smile. "Sorry, I'm not quite with it today."

"What happened?"

She took a deep breath and sat down. "The embassy have finally agreed to get involved. Marty's father did all the talking. I just sat there like a jellyfish. He told them that he'd spent time and money to come over here, so the least they could do was take it as seriously as he did. He went on about how it was completely out of character for Marty to do something like this and said he could supply written references from the university and half a dozen other sources to back him up, if need be. Anyway, to cut a long story short, they finally agreed to give us their backing when we went to the police, if we needed it. So that was where we went next. Marty's father demanded to see the detective inspector instead of the sergeant I'd spoken to last time and got all high and mighty with them. It was a bit embarrassing, really. But it worked, I suppose, so that's the main thing. Marty's now been moved onto a 'high priority' category. That means that instead of just having him on file, now the police will actively start looking for him."

"How will they do that?" I hoped my tension did not show.

"Circulate his description to other divisions, try to trace his movements. Generally make more of an effort, I suppose. I don't know how much good it'll do, but at least they're trying."

She kneaded her eyes with one hand. "I don't know what's the matter with me. I should be relieved that they're actually doing something at last, but I'm not. I know I'm being stupid, but now the police are taking it seriously, it seems to make it more real. As though something *must* have happened to him."

I found it easy to reassure her. From what she had said, the police could search from now to Judgment Day without finding anything. "I think that's probably just reaction," I said. "The fact that the police have started to look for him isn't going to alter where he is or why he went, is it? All it means is that you have a better chance of finding him sooner."

"Oh, I know that, really. It's just . . ." She shrugged. "Well, like you say, it's probably reaction. And Marty's father doesn't help."

"I take it he's no pleasanter?"

"You could say that. And I'm in his bad books more than ever now. I stayed at Debbie's on Saturday night and didn't get back to the flat until Sunday afternoon. He phoned about ten minutes after I'd got back in and said that he'd been trying to get hold of me since the night before. It wasn't anything important, but he made it clear he disapproved of me being out. He didn't actually accuse me of being unfaithful, but he might as well have." She shook her head, exasperated. "I wouldn't mind so much, except it's the first time I've been out since Marty went missing. And I probably wouldn't have gone at all if he hadn't upset me so much."

I was outraged that he could even think such a thing. "He's a despicable little man. Don't let him bother you."

She hesitated. "Actually, he might have done something to upset you as well."

"Me?"

Anna nodded, grimacing. "After we'd been to the police station, he insisted on going to see the detective. I thought he

just wanted to talk to him himself, to find out how far he'd got.
Anyway, Mr. Simpson hadn't found out anything else since the
last time we spoke to him and seemed pleased when I said
that the police were finally getting involved. Then, out of the
blue, Marty's father suddenly said that now they were, we
wouldn't be needing a detective any more. I didn't know what
to say. I was just so surprised. And it was the way he said it.
Not 'I'm sorry' or 'thank you' or anything like that. He just
blurted it out! I didn't want to argue in the detective's office,
so I waited until we were outside before I asked him what he
thought he was doing. He said that Simpson was obviously in-
ept, and that now the police were taking over there was no
point risking amateurs clouding the water and antagonizing
them. So I told him he still shouldn't have done something like
that without discussing it first with me. And you, because
you're paying, after all. But he said there was more at stake
than personal pride, and he wasn't going to waste time on etiquette. After that, I couldn't bear it any longer. I said I'd phone
and left him there. If I'd been with him another minute, I
think I'd have strangled him."

She looked at me, contritely. "I'm sorry about the detective,
Donald. He had no right to do that."

I agreed but was relieved he had. It was one less factor to
worry about. And a considerable expense saved. "Well, I suppose he is Marty's father," I said. "And the police have far more
resources than a private detective anyway."

"I suppose so. It's just his attitude. I was going to be his
daughter-in-law eventually, so you'd think he'd at least make an
effort to break the ice." She stopped. "I said 'was.' Not 'am.' "

"It was only a slip of the tongue."

"It's the first time I've done it, though." She looked on the
verge of tears.

"You've had a trying day. What with the police and the embassy and the detective. It doesn't mean anything."

"No." She shook it off and smiled. "Anyway, talking of Marty's father, I've got a favor to ask."

"Yes?"

"I was stupid enough to ask him over for a meal again. This was before we went to the detective's, I might add. It doesn't promise to be a very joyous occasion, but I wondered if you'd mind coming as well? I know it's asking a lot, so if you'd rather not it doesn't matter."

"Of course I will. I'd love to." Westerman or no Westerman, I was pleased that she had asked.

"Oh, thanks. I was hoping you would. It would have been pretty grim with just the two of us."

"Aren't you inviting anyone else?"

"No, I don't think so. The fewer people I inflict him on, the better. Not that I want to inflict him on you," she said quickly. "But I thought I might not seem so bad if he sees I mix with respectable pillars of society like you. And he might mellow a bit with someone his own age."

The last comment was unfortunate, but I refused to let it bother me. Anna had still invited me rather than anyone else, age notwithstanding. Flattered, I remembered my protective fantasies of the weekend.

I dared Westerman to bully her while I was there.

Chapter

16

I had already reached the conclusion that Westerman was congenitally obnoxious, and his behavior during the meal at Anna's did nothing to change my mind. I would have expected at least a softening, if not an actual cessation, of his hostility for that night at least. But from the moment he arrived it was clear that there would be no such thing.

"You met Donald briefly on Saturday," Anna said, taking his coat. "He owns the gallery I work at."

Once again he shook my hand without enthusiasm, responding to my greeting with a short nod. Anna's smile was already beginning to look like hard work.

"Would you like a drink?" she asked him.

"No thank you."

"There's mineral water or fruit juice, if you want something nonalcoholic. Or I can make you a cup of tea or coffee?"

"No thank you."

There was an awkward silence. "Well, I'd better see to dinner," Anna said, giving me an apologetic glance. She went into the kitchen, leaving the two of us alone.

"We might as well sit down," I said, pleasantly. I lowered myself onto the sofa. Westerman sat stiffly opposite me. I wondered if he ever relaxed. He showed no indication of doing so now. Neither of us spoke. I felt it was his turn to attempt conversation and waited for him to say something. However, he showed no inclination of saying anything ever again. As the silence grew, so did my annoyance, and I was tempted to play him at his own game. If not for Anna, I would have. But she was depending on me to help her through a difficult evening, and I would hardly be doing that if I behaved as badly as Marty's father. For her sake I had to be sociable.

Etiquette, about which Westerman clearly cared little, demanded I make some reference to his son. "I was glad to hear that the police are finally doing something to find Marty."

"It's high time someone did."

His criticism seemed too broad spectrumed for my liking. "Yes, Anna had a devil of a job trying to convince anyone to help. That's why we had to resort to hiring a private detective."

"I met him. I thought he was amateurish. Now the police are taking a hand there's no point him getting in their way."

There was no trace of apology or gratitude in his voice, and he had the irritating habit of not looking at me when he spoke. His remarks were addressed to a blank space in front of him. "Well, it saves me further expense, I suppose. I received his bill yesterday. Amateurish or not, he wasn't cheap."

"Then I guess you'll be glad you don't have to hire him any more. Although whether your police will be any more effective, I wouldn't like to say."

The way he said "your police" implied that shared nationality meant shared liability. My dislike of the man was growing by the second.

"How long are you planning to stay?" I asked, trying to change the subject.

"I have to be back in ten days. I'm supposed to be running a business, as Marty's well aware. I don't have time for distractions like this. But under the circumstances there didn't seem to be much choice."

So his resentment extended to his missing son. If he was concerned about him as well, he was making a good job of hiding it. I made another attempt to be civil. "I know you're a businessman, but I'm afraid I don't know anything more specific than that. What field are you in?"

"Bathroom accessories."

"Is that retail or wholesale?"

"Both."

"Well, I hope the American economy is in a better state than ours. We're in something of a recession over here at present."

"So I hear."

"Is business quite good?"

"It's better when I can stay and run it."

I abandoned any further efforts to draw him out and instead tried to establish at least the pretense of common ground.

"Yes, I know what you mean. I'm a businessman myself." I smiled depreciatingly. "Well, if you can call running a gallery business. I'm an art dealer."

"I know."

He clearly had no intention of helping me with the conversation. And I had nothing left to offer except insults. I held them in check and made one last attempt. Hopefully in a subject even he would not snub.

"I think Anna's taken all this quite well. It must have been very hard on her."

"It's been very hard on a lot of people. Including Marty's mother and myself."

"Yes, I imagine it must be. How is Mrs. Westerman taking it?"

Westerman looked briefly at me before returning his gaze to whatever it was that was occupying it. "As well as can be expected. Neither of us wanted him to come here in the first place. American universities were good enough for his brother and sister, I don't see why they weren't for him. And now I've had to come and chase after him because he's had a fight with his girlfriend."

This was the first mention of Marty's siblings. It was also the first indication of his father's feelings about his disappearance.

"Is that why you think he left?"

"I can't think of any other reason. According to his tutors, his work at the university was going well. He had no financial problems. He was always emotionally stable in the past. So why else would he walk out?"

I felt obliged to object. "I don't know, obviously, but Anna says they hadn't argued at all."

His mouth twisted slightly. It could have been a smile. "So she claims."

I knew I was arguing against my own interests, but I could not let that pass. "I hardly think Anna would lie about something like that."

He permitted himself another brief glance at me. "So you think it was just a coincidence that this happened just before he came back to America with an English girl he'd only known for a matter of months? I'm afraid I find that hard to believe."

"From what I saw of them, they seemed very happy together."

"Then why did he leave?"

Of course I had no answer to that. I should have been pleased that Westerman had so readily accepted the obvious explanation, but his implied slur on Anna infuriated me. Neither of us spoke again until Anna came in and announced that dinner was ready.

It was a dismal affair. Anna did her best to keep a conversation running, and out of consideration for her I tried as well. But Westerman steadfastly refused to be drawn into it. I began to wonder why he had come at all. He ate mechanically and sparingly, speaking only when a direct question was asked of him and even then answering in monosyllables whenever possible. Eventually, Anna had nothing left to say, and I could think of nothing to help her. The meal continued in complete silence, broken only by the scrape and tinkle of cutlery. Only Marty's father seemed indifferent to it, as though such awkwardness were his natural environment. If he was always so ill mannered, I could well imagine it was.

"Coffee?" Anna asked, after dessert was over. Westerman had been the last to finish eating, unconcernedly taking his time while Anna and I sat and waited for him. I expected and hoped he would refuse. There seemed little point in him staying.

He dabbed his lips with the napkin. "I take it black, without sugar."

"I'll help you clear the table," I said to Anna.

Once the kitchen door had closed she leaned against the wall and puffed out her cheeks. "God. I'm really sorry about this. If I'd any idea it was going to be this bad, I wouldn't have asked you."

"Nonsense. No one should have to suffer that man by themselves for an entire evening."

"It's not your problem, though. You shouldn't have to put up with it."

"Neither should you. I knew what he was like when I accepted." I tried to make light of it. "Besides, it's an experience I wouldn't have missed. It's not every day you can have dinner with the most unpleasant man in the world."

"He's not much fun, is he?"

"I'm afraid not." We grinned at each other like conspirators.

"It's times like this when I wish I kept rat poison. Do you think he'd notice if I put some in his coffee?"

"He might not, but everyone else would think it was a distinct improvement."

We began giggling, trying to smother it so the sound would not be heard in the next room. Suddenly the door opened. Westerman stared at us coldly.

"Am I interrupting something?"

Anna's laughter died immediately. But she could not keep from smiling as she wiped tears from her eyes. "No, not at all. I'm sorry, we were just . . ."

"I was telling her about something that happened at the gallery," I explained, rescuing her.

Marty's father looked from one of us to the other, then at neither as he spoke. "I came in to tell you not to bother with the coffee on my account. It's late. If you'll call a cab for me, I'll leave you to enjoy your anecdotes in peace."

Anna went through the motions of persuasion. "Are you sure you won't stay for a cup?"

"No, thank you." He turned and went back into the lounge. We followed him. He stood in the center of the room while Anna ordered a cab.

"By the way," he said, when she had hung up, "I spoke to the university today. I told them they could let someone else use Marty's room. They offered to save it for him, but I told them not to bother. I couldn't see why they should when he hadn't even had the decency to tell them he was leaving."

Anna looked appalled. "You can't do that!"

"I already have."

"But what about all his books? And his research? All his files, his notes and everything are there! What's going to happen to them?"

Westerman was untouched by Anna's consternation. "Frankly, I don't care. If Marty comes back soon he can claim them. Or you can collect them, if you want to. Failing that, unless some sympathetic tutor decides to store them for him, I guess they'll be thrown out. That's what I advised, at least."

"You'd got no right to do that!" Anna had gone red.

"I'd got every right. I'm his father. If Marty's going to be irresponsible, then like it or not it's up to me to sort out his affairs as I see fit."

"But there's three years' worth of work there! More!"

"If it was so important he shouldn't have left it. And since he did, he can hardly expect other people to look after it until he decides to come back. If I was the head of his department I'd burn all of it right now. But I suppose they're too liberal minded to do anything like that."

"I can't believe you're serious!" Anna almost shouted. "He's your son, for God's sake! How can you be so bloody callous? Marty's gone missing, and you want to burn his work? What sort of a father are you?"

"The sort who has to cross the Atlantic to straighten out the mess his son left behind when he decided to run away."

"Run away?" Anna seemed about to attack him. "Marty's

missing, can't you understand that? He's not a . . . a spoilt little kid who's hiding in the wardrobe! He's disappeared! No one knows where he is or what's happened to him, and you're acting like he's done it to spite you!"

I had never seen Anna so angry. Never believed she could be. Westerman, on the other hand, appeared perfectly calm. "I might not know where he is now, but the reason he went is pretty obvious."

"Now just a—" I began, but Anna could not have heard me.

"What's that supposed to mean?" she demanded.

"It means I don't think we have to look any further than this room."

"You mean he left because of me?"

"I can't see any other reason. And after this display that seems more than enough."

Anna stared at him. When she spoke her voice was low and throaty with emotion. "How dare you! How *dare* you! What right have you got to come here and say that? Who the hell do you think you are?"

"I'm his father, that's—"

"Then why don't you start acting like it?" she snapped. "Show some bloody concern for a change! You act like you're not even interested in what's happened to him! All you seem bothered about is the 'inconvenience' he's caused and getting back to your . . . your stupid little company! And you've got the nerve to stand there and tell me it was my fault Marty left? Christ, how would *you* know? You're one of the reasons he came here in the first place. If anyone drove Marty away it was you, years ago!"

There was silence. The area around Westerman's nose was white. "I think I'll wait outside for the taxi."

Anna was trembling. Her flush had died, leaving her face pale. "I'm sorry. I shouldn't have said that."

"If you would be so kind as to fetch my coat."

Without another word, Anna went to get it. Westerman and I stood without looking at each other. Anna came back and handed it to him.

"Thank you. I'll see myself out."

I thought Anna was going to say something else, but she remained silent. Westerman went into the kitchen. We heard the front door open and close.

"Oh, shit!" Anna said. She looked about to burst into tears. "Excuse me." She almost ran out of the lounge. I heard her lock herself in the bathroom.

After a while I poured myself a brandy and sat down to wait.

It was some time later when she came back. Her face had been scrubbed clean of makeup. Her eyes looked red. She sat down, giving me a weak smile.

"Well. That wasn't exactly a rip-roaring success, was it?"

I went to pour her a drink. "That was hardly your fault. That man has to be one of the most obnoxious people I have ever met."

She bit her lip, fretfully. "I shouldn't have said that to him, though. About Marty."

"I don't see why you should feel bad about it. The man showed no concern for your feelings."

"I know, but . . . well, I just wish I hadn't. Things are bad enough between him and Marty without me making it worse like that."

"I still think he asked for it. He was the one being unfair. All you did was defend yourself."

She didn't answer. She rested her head back on the chair, looking tired. "I'd better get in touch with the university tomorrow. I don't want them throwing anything out."

"I'm sure they won't do that. Certainly not just on his say-so. I dare say whoever he spoke to is capable of seeing for himself what sort of a man he is."

"I hope so. I think I'll still give them a call, though." Her face contorted. "How could he *do* something like that?"

"Perhaps it's his way of punishing Marty for the 'inconvenience.' "

"The inconvenience," she echoed. "God, I wish that's all it was." Abruptly, she stood up. "Well, I better clean everything up. Thanks for coming, Donald. I'm sorry it was such a rotten evening."

"At least the food was good."

She smiled politely but did not respond to the compliment. It was obvious she wanted to be alone. I offered to help with the washing up out of courtesy but was not surprised when she refused. I said good night and left.

Despite Anna's views on the subject, in my opinion the evening had been by no means all bad. As much as I despised Westerman, I was still realistic enough to realize that his prejudice was perhaps the best thing that could have happened. Particularly if he communicated it to the police. He was over for another ten days. Provided nothing untoward was discovered during that time, I could not see the investigation carrying on for long afterward. Cautiously, I allowed myself the luxury of optimism once again.

It was therefore all the more disconcerting when the police found their first lead.

Chapter

17

It was only a few days after the meal with Marty's father that the two policemen came into the gallery. One was in uniform, the other in plain clothes. Both Anna and I immediately stopped what we were doing.

"Miss Palmer?" the one in plain clothes asked. He was the taller of the two, a heavyset, military-looking man with a thick mustache several shades paler than his hair.

Anna had tensed. "Yes?"

"I'm Detective Inspector Lindsey, this is Sergeant Stone. Could we have a word with you, please?"

All the color had drained from Anna's face. I doubt I can have looked very much better. I had my own fears. "Why? What about?"

"Is there somewhere we can talk in private?" The policeman glanced at me. I felt a nauseous touch of paranoia.

"It's all right, you can talk to me here," Anna said, interpreting the look. "This is about Marty, isn't it?"

"It might be better in private."

"There's the office," I said, but Anna shook her head.

"No, it's all right, I'd rather you stayed." I was too anxious to feel flattered, by no means certain I wanted to hear what he had to say. Anna turned back to the policeman. She was holding herself rigid. "Have you found him?" Her voice was deliberately calm.

The policeman looked away from me. From that point on, I ceased to exist for him. "No, we've not found him yet. But we do have a possible lead." He paused. I could smell the sour, rotten smell of cigarettes on his breath. "This may be a little upsetting for you, but I've got to ask if your boyfriend has any homosexual tendencies that you're aware of?"

Anna now looked more confused than frightened. "Homosexual tendencies? No. Not at all. Why?"

The policeman ignored her question. "Has he ever given you cause to suspect that he may be homosexual?"

"No, of course not! Why?"

Suddenly, I saw the connection. Blood rushed to my head as I struggled to keep the realization from my face.

"We've received an identification from someone who claims to have seen your boyfriend in a gay club in Soho," the policeman went on. I told myself it could not be the same club where Marty had met Zeppo. Surely no one would remember him from a single visit. But the thought did little to reassure me. I became aware that the sergeant was looking at me. I tried to ignore him.

"Recently?" There was a note of hope in Anna's voice.

"Before he disappeared. We don't have a definite date. But we've reason to believe he went there several times."

Some of the tension drained out of Anna. She seemed suddenly disappointed. "Which one was it? The Pink Flamingo?"

Both policeman looked at her in surprise. "You know about it?" the senior one asked.

"Yes. Marty went there quite a few times. He went to one or two others, as well, but I can't remember what they're called."

He stared at her. "I thought you said he hadn't any homosexual tendencies?"

"He hasn't. He didn't just go to gay clubs. He went to other types as well. It was part of his research."

"Research?" The very flatness of his tone conveyed his incredulity.

"That's right. He's taking a Ph.D. in anthropology. He's writing a paper on behavioral patterns in different types of nightclubs. How it's affected by money, sexuality. That sort of thing." She sounded as though she were reciting it by rote. It was similar enough to what Marty had told Zeppo to convince me she was.

The two policemen exchanged a look. "So your boyfriend told you he went to gay clubs as part of his studies?"

The color was back in Anna's face now. More than was normal. "He didn't just 'tell' me. That's why he went. Marty's not gay, if that's what you're trying to make out."

"We're not trying to make anything out, Miss. We just want to establish his reason for going. Did you ever go to any of these gay clubs with him?"

"No."

"Why not?"

"Because I'm a girl. If Marty went with me, we'd attract attention. It would be obvious we were a couple. Marty wanted to blend into the background so he could just . . . you know, observe without bothering anyone."

"How far did he actually go in order to blend in?"

"I've told you, he used to sit and watch. That's all."

"But you never actually went with him."

"No. Look, what's the point of all this? I want to know where Marty is now, not weeks ago!"

The policeman nodded, placatingly. "So do we, Miss. I know this isn't very pleasant for you. It's not for us, either, but it's the first lead we've had, and we've got to see if it's worth following up or not. I've got to ask you these questions, if only so we can discount it, you understand?" He waited for Anna's terse assent before continuing. "Now, how often did he go to these clubs?"

Anna shrugged, sullenly. "I don't know. A few times. Not often."

"Once a week? Twice a week?"

"Less than that. I've told you, it wasn't often."

"Once a month, then?"

"Perhaps. Something like that."

"Did he go on any particular nights? I mean, was it always on a Friday, or a Saturday? Or at a certain time of the month?"

"No, it varied. He went on different nights so he could compare them."

"And did he ever mention anyone he had met?"

My heart jumped at the question. "He didn't go to 'meet' anyone!" Anna snapped. "He went purely as an observer. How many more times do I have to say it?"

"He never mentioned anyone in particular, then? No names?"

"No."

"So he just used to sit in a corner and mind his own business? What if someone came up to him?"

Anna's color had concentrated into two points of red on her cheeks. "Well, I suppose he spoke to some people, obviously. But he never used to go out of his way to talk to anyone. He only spoke to them if they came up to him first. Look, I know what you're thinking, but it wasn't like that!"

"Did he ever tell you what he talked about?"

"Yes, sometimes. It was always to do with his work."

"But he never told you who he used to speak to?"

"I've told you, it wasn't anyone in particular! He used to go and just . . . just *look*, that's all. And he's not been for weeks now anyway! If you don't believe me, ask the university! They know all about it!"

"I'm sure they do. Did he ever stay out all night?"

"No, of course not!"

"Late, then?"

"No! I mean, sometimes it would be two o'clock or something, but that's all."

"Have you any idea why he was interested in this particular field?"

Anna hesitated, searching for a concrete fact to repudiate the policeman's insinuations. "He's an anthropologist! That's the sort of thing they do. He thought it was a . . . a worthwhile field of study, that's all. The same as the other aspects of his thesis. This was only a part of it, you know."

"Have you any homosexual friends?"

"No."

"Did he keep notes about his visits to these clubs? A diary, perhaps?"

"He doesn't keep a diary, but he makes notes about the clubs he visits," Anna said. I felt my heart lurch again. That had never occurred to me.

"Are all his notes at the university"

"Most of them, yes. Some of them are at the flat."

"Would it be all right if we had a look at them?"

I could see Anna did not like the idea. I found myself wildly hoping she would refuse. "I suppose so," she said reluctantly. "But if you're hoping to find anything incriminating, you're wasting your time."

"We're not looking for anything incriminating, Miss. We only want to find out where he is, the same as you." His tone was condescending.

"Well, trying to make out he's gay isn't going to do any good. I don't know why he went, but it wasn't because of that. I live with him, for God's sake, don't you think I'd know if he was?"

"I'm sure you would. But we've got to examine every possibility, haven't we? It could be, for instance, that someone he met at one of these clubs knows where he is now."

"You mean he might have run off with another man," Anna said flatly.

"I don't mean anything. At this stage I'm just keeping an open mind."

"Is that what you call it?"

"Look, Miss—"

"If that's all, you'll have to excuse me. I've work to do." She turned her back and walked away. I heard her footsteps going upstairs.

The policemen looked at each other. The sergeant shrugged with his eyebrows. The inspector turned to me. "Can you tell

Miss Palmer we'll be in touch about her boyfriend's notes? We'd like to look at them as soon as possible."

I nodded, trying to gather myself. I did not trust my voice. But I could not leave it at that. "Do you think this could have some bearing on his disappearance?" I asked.

Upset by Anna walking out, he tried to intimidate me. He stared for a moment without speaking. "I really don't know, sir. Have you any ideas on the subject?"

"Me? Oh, no, not at all. Well, except that Marty didn't strike me as being gay."

"Well then, perhaps he's not. We'll just have to see, won't we, sir? Thank you for your time." His tone was so exaggeratedly polite it bordered on parody.

"How did you find out about the nightclubs? Is it standard procedure?"

"Well, it is and it isn't," he said. "Mr. Westerman's description was included with a bunch of missing teenage boys by accident. The gay community's like a magnet for missing teenage boys. Amazing how many of them end up there. As it turned out, your Mr. Westerman was the only one our source recognized." He smiled coldly. It seemed designed to try and intimidate more. "So you see, not all police cock-ups are bad ones, are they?"

On their way out, the sergeant stopped and studied a painting. "My wife would love that." It was the first time he had spoken. "How much is it?" I told him. He looked at it again. "Jesus Christ."

They left.

◌◌

I knew now I could not put off telling Zeppo any longer. I telephoned him that evening. For once he answered almost straight away. He seemed in an irritatingly good mood.

"Well, well. If it isn't the poor man's Tate. What can I do for you? Don't tell me you've done something else stupid. Have you?"

"No, I haven't. But I think we'd better talk."

"Why? Is Anna begging for it already?"

"Just come over as soon as you can. I'm at home."

He became more serious. "What's wrong?"

"Probably nothing, but you still ought to hear about it."

"Hear about what? What's happened?"

"I'll tell you when you get here."

I hung up before he could say anything else. I knew that was the fastest way of getting him over. I took the receiver off the hook as an afterthought. I did not relish the prospect of facing him with the news, but I could not trust it to the telephone.

He wasted no time in coming. "So what's happened?" he demanded, before I had even closed the door. I took a deep breath.

"The police came to the gallery today. It seems that someone has identified Marty from one of the gay clubs."

Zeppo closed his eyes and put his head back. "Shit! Oh, *shit*!" He slapped his hand against the wall.

"It's not as bad as all that—"

"Like hell it's not! Where did they see him?"

"Don't worry, it wasn't the same club you went to. It was another one."

"You're sure?"

"They said it was the Pink Flamingo. The one he went to regularly. That's the only reason he was recognized. And even that was only by accident." Zeppo's hand was still on the wall. He was staring up at the ceiling. I went on quickly. "There's no reason for them to link him to you. In fact, this could turn out for the best. From what the police were asking Anna, they seemed to think that Marty was homosexual and that he might have run away with another man."

Zeppo stopped gazing at the ceiling and looked at me. "Are you really that stupid? Turn out for the best? Do you know what's going to happen now? Eh? They're going to go around every gay club in London to see if anyone else remembers him. And what happens when they get to the club I met him in? Suppose someone there remembers seeing him with me?"

"That's not very likely. It's not as if Marty was the sort to stand out in a crowd."

"*No, but I fucking am!*" He pushed himself off the wall at me. Spittle flecked my face. "What do we do if they flash his photograph, and some queer says, 'Oh yes, I remember him, he was with this big, dark-haired hunk'? What the fuck do we do then?"

I tried to sound unconcerned. "Why should we do anything? If the worst comes to the worst, *if* they ask questions at that particular club, and *if* someone happens to remember a face from one night weeks ago, even then all the police will have to go on will be that he was at a table with a tall, dark-haired man. Of which there are hundreds. You didn't see anyone there you knew, did you?"

"No, but—"

"So let's not get too hysterical, shall we? I know it's a shock. It was for me at first. But then, once I had time to calm down and think about it, I realized that there was no reason for it to be. How long were you in there with Marty? For an hour? If that? I know you think you're something special, Zeppo, but really, do you think you're so good that even your companion will be remembered weeks after the event? If they even manage to find anyone who was there that night and saw you?"

His cheeks muscles worked. "Perhaps not." He sounded grudging. I pushed my advantage.

"Besides which, what is there to possibly link him with you? How many people know about . . . well, about your earlier activities? As far as most people are concerned, you're the epitome of masculinity. So why should anyone link you with a gay club in Soho?"

"What about Anna? If the police get my description, she'll know it's me."

"Of course she won't! Zeppo, as far as the police are concerned, Marty has run away. Voluntarily. They're not worried about him. They won't be issuing an all-points bulletin on the six o'clock news with a Photofit picture of you. All it will be, if it's anything at all, will be a description. Of someone everyone will assume is a homosexual. And since Anna doesn't think of you like that, she won't make the connection. Think about it. There is nothing, absolutely nothing, to link you with someone who met Marty in a gay nightclub. No motive, no reason. Nothing."

He was calmer now. "You better be right."

"I am." In fact, I had rationalized it so well that for a moment I felt as confident as I sounded. Then I remembered Marty's notes, and the sudden wash of fear instantly undermined my new confidence. In that second I knew I was not going to tell Zeppo about them.

But whatever I felt, it could not have shown in my face. At any rate, Zeppo seemed completely reassured. "In that case I think I'll let you give me a drink now I'm here," he said. He began walking toward the lounge. Suddenly I could not stand the thought of him being there a second longer.

"No. I'd like you to go now."

He turned and looked at me in surprise. "What?"

"I said I'd like you to go."

An astonished smile spread across his face. "Getting a little tetchy, aren't we, Donald? What the fuck's eating you?"

"Nothing's eating me. I just want you to leave, that's all."

"What about your duties as a host? You insist I come here, then five minutes later you want me to go again. That's not very hospitable, is it?"

"I'm not in a very hospitable mood."

"Then you shouldn't have asked me over, should you?" I could see he was beginning to enjoy himself. That only irritated me more.

"I asked you over because I had something to tell you. Now I have, there's no reason for you to stay."

"Donald, you mean you dragged me all this way just for that, and now you want me to leave without even having a drink? You could have told me on the telephone and saved me the journey." He held up his hand. "Sorry—I forgot. The phones are all bugged, aren't they? You don't like the CIA listening in."

"For someone who was having a panic attack a moment ago,

you've suddenly become very blasé. And no, I don't like using the telephone for something like this. I have no desire to end up in prison because a housewife in Tooting Beck happened to get a crossed line."

"You're getting very agitated all of a sudden."

"Perhaps that's because I've had enough of your attitude. I'm tired of having to put up with your tantrums. I didn't force you to get involved. You chose to of your own accord, for money, not as a favor to me, and I've had enough of you holding me responsible whenever anything doesn't go quite according to plan! We knew there would have to be some kind of investigation, and it's me who has to bear the brunt of that, not you. So I can well do without having to contend with a . . . a homicidal model threatening violence every time there's the slightest hiccup!"

Zeppo had listened with his head slightly tilted to one side. "Does this mean you don't love me any more?"

"It means I would like you to leave!"

"Okay, Donald. If that's the way you feel about it." He went to the front door, an amused expression on his face. He opened it and turned to me.

"By the way," he said. "Your flies are undone."

I simply stared at him. Smiling, he went out. I looked down. They were.

Chapter

18

There was no way I could stay at home for the rest of that evening. I had to get out. More specifically, I had to go to Anna's. The thought of what might be contained in Marty's notes, the possibility that he might have made some reference to Zeppo in them, made it impossible for me to idly sit in and wait. Only minutes after Zeppo had left, I was in my car and driving to her flat.

She was not expecting me. But she had been angry and upset after the policemen's visit, which gave me an excuse to see how she was. I had no idea if she would even be home, but I was willing to risk a wasted journey. Anything was better than sitting alone, running through permutations of discovery.

There was a light on in her window. I felt relieved, then anxious. I told myself it was too soon for her to know anything, but the possibility was enough to make my heart thud as I climbed the steps to her flat. I tried to prepare myself, rehearsing how best to react, and rang the doorbell. I waited as footsteps came toward the door. Then Anna opened it.

I saw at once that something was wrong. Her face was set, closed as stone. She did not even seem surprised to see me.

"Hello," I said, blustering past my doubts. "I thought I'd call and see how you were."

"I'm all right, thanks." Her voice was carefully guarded. She stood back. "Come in. Marty's father's here."

She held my eyes with hers as she spoke, and I immediately understood the reason for her mood. A weight was lifted from me.

"Shall I go?" I asked, almost whispering.

"No, it's all right. I don't think he's staying much longer." She made no attempt to lower her voice. I raised my eyebrows, questioningly. Her lips tightened, and she gave a short, disgusted shake of her head as she turned away.

I closed the door and followed her into the lounge. Westerman was standing in the center of the room with his coat on. His mouth was even more pinched than usual. The open end of their quarrel gaped obviously.

"I'm sorry, I didn't mean to barge in," I said to him. "I had no idea you were here."

"Mr. Westerman just called around to let me know he's going back to America tomorrow," Anna said. Westerman's lips pinched a little more.

I looked at him inquiringly. "Really? I thought you were going to stay another week?"

Anna cut in before he could answer. "He was. But now he's spoken to the police, he's decided to leave early."

He shot her a quick, furious look, before addressing himself to some indeterminate point between us. "I can't see any point in wasting any more time. As far as I'm concerned, I know all I need to. Or want to."

"Mr. Westerman wasn't happy to hear that Marty's been to gay nightclubs." Anna was speaking to me but never took her eyes off him. He turned and looked directly at her.

"I doubt any father would be pleased to learn his son's a homosexual."

"Oh, for God's sake!" Anna erupted, "I've already *told* you! He went as part of his research, that's all!"

"Research!" Westerman snorted. "There's only one reason people go to places like that. And if he prefers the company of perverts to decent people he can stay with them and rot as far as I'm concerned."

Anna was struggling to control herself. "Listen. For the last time, Marty's not homosexual. I don't know where he is or what's happened to him, but I know it's nothing to do with that. If you don't believe me, ask the university."

"What for? From what I've heard about British intellectuals they're all moral degenerates and pederasts themselves."

Anna shook her head, violently. "I can't believe I'm hearing this! Marty's *missing*! Does it matter what he did or who he mixed with?"

Westerman looked at her with an expression of triumph. "Obviously not to you, but I'm glad to say where I come from people still have some moral values."

"Moral values?" Anna said, incredulous. "How can *you* talk about morals when you're prepared to abandon him like this? What's moral about that?"

"A damn sight more than mixing with deviants! I've made an effort to accept the things he's done in the past, but this . . . !" He shook his head, mutely outraged.

"What 'things' has he done in the past?" Anna demanded. "You mean like studying anthropology instead of selling toilet bowls? Like coming here instead of going to an American university? How can you be so bloody narrow minded? Marty's your son, for God's sake! You can't just give up on him! He's your *son*!" She repeated the fact as though Westerman had overlooked it. He gave a brittle shake of his head.

"Not any more." He made as if to leave. Anna moved in front of him.

"You can't just go! If you pack up and go home, the police are going to give up as well."

Westerman shrugged. "Quite possibly. In fact, I intend to contact the police and embassy and let them know the reason I'm leaving."

"Why?" Anna cried. "Can't you at least let them make up their own minds?"

"I'm sure they will. But if Marty's going to disgrace himself, I want to make it quite clear I don't condone it."

"*Disgrace* himself?" Anna began, but Westerman was already moving to the door. I felt I had to say something.

"I must say I think you're being completely unreasonable!"

He did not even look at me. "It's none of your business. And I've no intention of discussing my actions with an aging dilettante."

I was still spluttering as he walked past me into the kitchen. Anna went after him.

"I'd like to say it's been a pleasure meeting you," she said. "But I'd be lying, and one hypocrite in a room's enough." She opened the front door and stared at him coolly. "Goodbye, Mr. Westerman."

Westerman hesitated and seemed on the point of saying something else. Then he turned and left without another word.

Anna shut the door, not quite slamming it. She came back into the lounge. Neither of us spoke. She stood beside the table, staring into space. I realized I was shaking.

"Of all the . . . the insufferable . . . *swine!*" It was a woefully inadequate response, but anger and humiliation had robbed me of a more potent vocabulary. I avoided looking at her.

Anna said nothing. Her silence began to make me feel uncomfortable. I risked a glance. Her eyes were shiny with tears, but she held herself perfectly still. I searched for something to say but once again found nothing.

"The bastard!" The words came without warning. Her face was twitching with the effort of holding back from crying, out of anger as much as anything else. "The coldhearted, fucking *bastard!*"

I was shocked at her language. She realized I was staring at her and quickly shook her head. "I'm sorry, Donald, but . . . *Christ*, how can he? His own *son!* Doesn't he care?"

"Apparently not."

"How can he be so . . . so *sanctimonious* about it? He's so bloody self-righteous! Doesn't he realize what he sounds like? And the way he insulted you. There was no excuse for that. Yet he still acted as though *we'd* done something wrong!"

I still felt I had to say something to reestablish myself. "The man's clearly unbalanced. I'm not sure who he hates the most, the English or homosexuals."

Anna showed no sign of hearing me. "Why has he got to make such a big issue out of going? If it upsets him that much, why doesn't he just go? Why has he got to make a point of telling the police his reasons? It was hard enough convincing them to take Marty's disappearance seriously in the first place. If they think his own father's convinced he's run off because he's gay, they won't even try any more."

"I wouldn't worry about him influencing them. I'm sure they're capable of seeing Marty's father for what he is." I was sure of no such thing. Which made it all the easier to say.

Anna made no comment. Then she smiled tiredly across at me. "I bet you love coming here, don't you? Never a dull moment."

"I do seem to pick my moments to call, don't I?" I said, and with sudden vertigo remembered the reason for my visit. Anger at Westerman had driven it out of my mind. My tension returned.

"I don't know about you, but I feel like a drink," Anna said. "What would you like?"

I clutched at the offer. "A brandy, if you have one. If not, whisky will be fine."

I waited while she poured the drinks and handed me a glass. I cleared my throat. "Have the police called for Marty's notes yet?"

"No, not yet." She sat down and rubbed her eyes. "I don't know what they expect to find anyway. Love letters between him and another man or something? If they do, they'll be disappointed. There's nothing like that in them."

It sounded more like an assertion than an opinion. I forced myself to wait until I had taken a drink before I asked, "Have you had a look yourself?"

"Only at the file he left here, not the ones at the university."

"And there was nothing in it?"

"No, but I never expected there to be. Just notes, like you'd expect."

I cleared my throat again. "Is the one here recent?"

She nodded. "It's got the notes he was working on when he disappeared. I know because he always dates everything, and the last date is the day before I came back from Amsterdam."

I tried to quell my sudden excitement. "So they don't give any clues?"

"No, nothing. I never thought they would. I don't know why he left, but it certainly wasn't anything to do with him going to gay clubs. He hadn't been for weeks anyway. And if he'd been planning to go while I was away, he would have told me." She shrugged. "I don't suppose that'll make any difference to the police, though. It's a nice, handy little explanation for them. Particularly when his own father lets them know what he thinks."

I said something vaguely reassuring, but I cannot remember what. I was no longer paying attention. All I could think was that Marty had been as good as his word. Unless there was some record of his meeting with Zeppo in his notes at the university, which was unlikely, he had kept it a secret. The only danger that remained was if someone remembered seeing them at the nightclub. That was a possibility, but somehow I could not make myself feel too concerned about it. I sensed that the crisis point had been reached and passed, and suddenly the tension ebbed out of me. Without warning, I yawned.

"I'm sorry," I said through it. "Excuse me."

"You must be tired."

"I am, rather. It's been a long day." One of the longest I had known, actually. Now it was over, reaction had left me exhausted. Yawning again, I made my excuses and left. It was all I could do to stay awake long enough to drive home. I considered calling Zeppo to tell him the good news about Marty's father but decided that could wait. It would serve him right to sweat a little. By half past nine I was in bed.

It was the best night's sleep I had had in weeks.

～

Westerman left the next morning, as he had said he would. Anna tried telephoning him at his hotel, presumably in the desperate hope of making him change his mind. But he had already checked out.

She contacted the police. Again, as promised, Marty's father had notified them that he was leaving, and when Anna pressed they admitted he had also made his views on the situation clear. They assured her that the investigation would be unaffected, but she was not convinced.

"I suppose they'll still keep it open or on file or whatever they do," she said. "But I can't see them worrying about it too much. As far as they're concerned now, Marty's just another gay who's come out of the closet and left his girlfriend."

I made reassuring noises, but of course she was right. What had been halfhearted to begin with now seemed almost certain to become even more perfunctory.

Once again, there was a sort of lull. If the police were doing anything, it failed to produce any further news. Then, a week after Westerman had left, Anna was late again. I had come to recognize that as almost invariably meaning something had happened, and a small twist of anxiety began to eat at my confidence. It flared when I saw her face as she walked in.

"Is everything all right?" I asked.

She did not look at me. "Marty's bank statement came this morning." She began to speak; stopped, as though the words hurt her. "Nothing's been taken out of his account since before he disappeared."

She stood there without moving, head hung slightly, still with her coat on and and her bag slung over one shoulder. She did not seem to know what to do with herself.

I tried to think of the correct thing to say. "Does he have another account anywhere?"

She shook her head.

"Well, perhaps he drew enough money out to last him for a while."

Anna still did not look at me. I had the impression these were all points she had already considered and dismissed. "The last withdrawal was for a hundred pounds. He couldn't still be living on that."

I wished I had saved the checkbook and credit cards. Zeppo could have used them in supermarkets, or anywhere else anonymous and busy, to give the impression that Marty was still in circulation. But it was too late now. And it would have been a further risk.

"Have you told the police?"

"I phoned them before I came here. They said the same as you, that he might have another account. When I told them he hadn't, they said he might have one I didn't know about. But I know he hasn't. All his money's in that one."

"Did you tell them that?"

She nodded. "They said he could have got a job somewhere by now, and that if he didn't want anyone to know where he was, he wouldn't risk writing checks on his old account anyway." She looked lost and helpless. "They didn't seem to think it was anything worth worrying about."

"They were probably only trying to reassure you."

She looked at me miserably. "I don't want reassuring. I'm not stupid. I just want to know that someone apart from me wants to find him."

I knew what she wanted me to do and shied away from it. I thought I was safely past that sort of involvement. Then I looked at her face and knew there was no avoiding it.

"Would you like me to talk to the police?" I asked. "I don't know if it'll do any good, but I'll try if you want me to."

Her expression became instantly grateful. "Would you mind? After what Marty's father said to them, I know they won't take much notice of me. But they might listen to you."

There was no reason why they should, but I smiled. "I can only try, can't I?"

Anna waited downstairs while I telephoned from the office. I asked for the detective inspector who had been to the gallery: the telephone gave a series of clicks, then I was connected.

"Inspector Lindsey."

"My name's Donald Ramsey. You came to my gallery last week to speak to my assistant, Anna Palmer, about her missing boyfriend. Marty Westerman. An American."

"Yes?" Waiting for me to get to the point. I hurried on.

"She received a bank statement this morning from her boyfriend's account, and it appears that the last withdrawal was made several days before he disappeared. Since then nothing's been taken out. Obviously, Miss Palmer is quite upset."

"Just a second." Something was put over the receiver, muffling it. I waited. It was taken off. "Yes, I'm sorry. Go on."

A little disconcerted, I searched for my thread. "As I was saying, Miss Palmer's upset about this because she thinks it might mean that . . ." The words caught. "Well, she's worried that it means something's happened to him."

"She's already let us know about this, hasn't she?" His voice was slow and deliberate. There was an ironic, almost mocking quality to it.

"She telephoned you this morning. I don't think it was you she spoke to, though."

"So how can I help you?" He might as well have asked, "So what do you want me to do about it?"

"Well, basically, I would like to know what you intend to do with the information."

"Was the situation not explained to Miss Palmer?"

I refused to let him intimidate me. "From what she's said, I don't think whoever she spoke to was particularly helpful. She's very worried, obviously, and wants to know that everything possible is being done to locate her boyfriend."

"It is. I thought we'd already made that plain to her. On several occasions."

Indignation made me forget myself. "Then perhaps you can tell me what you intend to do now you know he's been missing all this time with apparently no money?"

"What exactly is your relationship to either Mr. Westerman or his girlfriend?"

"I'm Miss Palmer's employer. A friend. Of them both," I added, lamely.

"You aren't a relative, then?"

"No."

I heard him sigh. I could almost smell his tobacco breath. "Mr. Ramsey, let me explain our position. Every day we receive literally dozens of calls from people who have someone missing. Some are more urgent than others. This morning, for example, I've just been speaking to a mother whose five-year-old daughter has been missing for thirty-six hours. The little girl is a diabetic. The mother has only just reported her missing because she's been out all this time and thought her daughter was 'at a friend's.' Which means that we now have a five-year-old girl who is God knows where, who is probably in urgent need of medication and who has already been missing for over a day and a half. *That* worries us. A fully grown adult who leaves home with a suitcase, clothes, checkbook and passport does not. It might be very distressing for his girlfriend, but it does not merit us pressing the panic button. Particularly not when this person's own father tells us he's satisfied his son has left of his own free will and for his own good reasons."

He paused. "Now we hear that this person has not touched his bank account since he left home. Well, that may or may not be a cause for concern. There can be any number of different explanations for it. He might be living with someone who is paying all his bills, for instance. He might have found a job and not wanted to use his old account for fear of being traced by his girlfriend, whom he has walked out on. He might be wandering around with amnesia, not even sure what a checkbook's for. Or he might be lying dead somewhere, as a result of an accident, a mugging or perhaps even a jealous boyfriend.

"It could be any of those or any one of a dozen other reasons. And to be perfectly honest, it doesn't make any difference. That is not being callous. That is simply stating the simple truth. We have already done everything we reasonably can. If anyone fitting his description turns up, alive or, regretfully, otherwise, at any hospital, train station or wherever, we will know about it within a matter of hours. If he leaves the country, we will know about it almost immediately. I am told his visa does not expire for several more months, so he has every legal right to be here, but even if he hadn't, we could do no more to locate him than we have already. Short of organizing a nationwide manhunt, which, bank account notwithstanding, is not justified, there is nothing else we can do. I am very sorry for his girlfriend. I am very sorry for all the other girlfriends, boyfriends, wives, husbands, parents and sundry other family members who also have loved ones missing. Of which, as we speak, in this division alone there are several hundred. Many of which have been on file for considerably longer than Miss Palmer's boyfriend. And of which, at this current moment in time, I am most concerned about a little girl with an ignorant mother and diabetes."

I heard him breathing. "Now. Does that explain the situation clearly enough for you?"

It did. Clearly enough not to mind his condescending and faintly contemptuous manner. "Yes, I think so. Thank you. I'm sorry to have bothered you."

He relented a little. "Tell Miss Palmer that we're doing everything we can. If we hear anything at all, we'll let her know."

"I will." I said goodbye and hung up. I waited a moment before going downstairs, letting my euphoria bleed off before I faced Anna. I no longer had any doubt that Marty's fate would remain lost to history. The way ahead was finally clear.

Now it was only a matter of time.

For Anna, the final nail in Marty's coffin was not long in coming. His bank statement, and the subsequent indifference of the police, hit her hard, and I had put down her increasing quietness to that. I had lost track of time and did not realize the significance of the date until the morning she spilled coffee on my lap.

I was on the telephone when she arrived at the gallery and so did not immediately notice the state she was in. I mimed drinking and pointed toward the filter machine; I had set it going, but the telephone had rung before I could pour my customary cup of black coffee. Only half listening to my caller, I watched abstractedly as Anna's cotton skirt, a bonus of the increasingly warmer weather, swung against her as she walked.

She disappeared into the kitchen area. I could hear her moving about, and then there was a clatter of dropped crockery. But I heard nothing actually break, and a moment later Anna reemerged and came toward me with a cup and saucer. I nodded thanks to her, concentrating now on my telephone conversation, and as I reached out to take it, she suddenly fumbled and tipped the whole thing onto my lap.

I dropped the telephone and leaped up as the scalding coffee spilled onto my legs.

"Quick, get a cloth!" I shouted, shaking the front of my

trousers, struggling to keep the steaming fabric off my skin. Anna didn't move. "Hurry!" I snapped. And stopped. Her face had crumpled. Silent sobs were jerking at her shoulders, and as I looked on, tears began to stream down her face.

"I'm sorry." Her voice was almost inaudible. "I'm sorry."

"It's all right, it doesn't matter." I straightened, wincing as the still-hot cloth stuck to my thighs.

"I'm sorry." It seemed all she could say. Her arms twitched at her sides, as though she did not know what to do with them.

"No harm done. It could have been worse." In fact it could, quite easily. I had been resting an open journal on my lap, and much of the coffee had landed on that.

But my reassurance did no good. Anna still stood and sobbed. I hurriedly retrieved the receiver and told the confused caller I would call back. Then I turned to Anna, hovering uncertainly. Over the past few weeks I had seen her close to tears on several occasions. But nothing like this. She was inconsolable. "What is it? What's the matter?" I asked. She showed no sign of having heard. "Anna, please, tell me what's wrong."

Her body heaved and shook. "*He's dead.*"

The words sent a shock through me. "Who's dead?" It was a stupid question. She could only mean one person.

"Muh . . . Marty."

I felt numb. "How . . . Have the police found him?"

It took her a moment to get the words out. I waited, agonized. "Nuh . . . no, but he is. I nuh . . . know he is!"

Relief made me dizzy. For an awful moment, I had thought he must have been discovered. But if he had, she would have said so. What she'd said was based on conviction, not facts. "Of course he isn't. Don't say such a thing."

She smeared her eyes with the side of her hand, like a small child. Her sobs tugged at her. "He is. He's dead, I *know* he is!"

I moved forward, hesitantly. Her emotion unnerved me. "You don't know that, Anna."

"I duh . . . do." She hugged herself. "We should have gone to Am . . . America today."

Then I understood. "Oh, Anna, I'm so sorry. I didn't realize."

"If he was st . . . still alive, I wuh . . . would have heard from him by now."

I searched for the right thing to say. "He might have forgotten the date."

"Nuh . . . no, he wuh . . . wouldn't. I kept thinking we'd still guh . . . go, somehow, that he'd cuh . . . come back before this, but now I know he nuh . . . never will. The puh . . . plane left an hour ago, and I nuh . . . knew then . . . I knew . . ."

No more words came. The sobs took her over completely. I tentatively put my hand on her arm, and she surged forward, burying her face in my shoulder. I hesitated and then held her. Her breath was hot and damp through my shirt, her tears scalding. I stroked her back, feeling the warmth of her flesh through the thin fabric. The heat and weight of her body was against me. Her breasts pressed to my chest. I closed my eyes. The sound of the door chime made me open them: a couple stood in the gallery, staring at us.

"We're closed." I said. "Could you call back later?" They left, not altogether happily. I did not care. I felt proud to have Anna in my arms.

But as she continued to sob with no sign of stopping, I began to grow concerned. As minutes passed with no change, I had to accept that the situation was beyond me. I had no idea how to comfort her. Much as I wanted to keep her to myself, I realized I needed help.

The only person I could think of to call was Debbie, the girl I had met at Anna's flat. I could get no sense from Anna when I asked for her friend's telephone number and finally led her to a chair and sat her down while I went through her bag. The girl's number was in a small address book, which, fortunately, Anna had listed by Christian names. I kept my voice low as I called Debbie at work and quickly explained the situation. My earlier jealousy had disappeared completely. I felt only relief when she immediately said she would come.

Anna flung herself on the other girl as soon as she arrived. I stood back, embarrassed, as Debbie began to cry almost as copiously herself. I drove them to Anna's flat and saw them inside, then left as soon as I decently could. I was not needed. And such naked displays made me uncomfortable.

I drove away feeling tense and exhausted. I began to head back to the gallery automatically, but halfway it suddenly occurred to me that I had no desire at all to spend the rest of the day there. It would still be too fraught with the memory of the morning's events. I felt I needed a break, time to air myself and breathe after the emotional bloodletting.

At one time my idea of recreation would have been to lose myself for an hour or two in one of the major galleries. Now, however, I felt little attraction at the thought of staring at more paintings. I racked my brain for an alternative, but I was too set in my ways to be inventive. Then I saw a poster by the side of the road, and in a second my mind was made up. With a spontaneity I had not felt in years, I set off for London zoo.

I had not been to a zoo since I was a child, and the thought of live exhibits instead of inanimate ones seemed inordinately appealing. Feeling only slightly embarrassed, I paid my entrance fee and went inside.

It was midweek, and despite it being a sunny day, the zoo was pleasantly quiet. I wandered between the cages and enclosures, remembering the pungent, swampy odors from my childhood. The somnambulant, muscular danger of the reptiles kept me engrossed for almost half an hour, but the big cats I found disappointing. Out of the context of their natural habitat, the slothful, bored-looking beasts had lost their animation and their dignity. They made poor watching.

I moved on. A group of schoolchildren were clustered in front of the zebra enclosure, raucously jostling for a look into the pen. I strolled over to see what had excited them. One of the zebras was sniffing at a mare's hindquarters. Protruding from between its rear legs was an amazingly long and startlingly purple erection. Quite uninhibited by my presence, the children gleefully nudged each other and shrieked as the zebra attempted to mount the mare. I walked away quickly, glad when the crude comments and laughter of the young audience was left behind.

Bypassing the primate section, I stopped in the cafe for a cup of tea and, succumbing to childish hedonism, an ice cream. I took an outside table and basked in the pleasantly warm sunshine. I did not notice the man at the next table until he spoke.

"Nice day, isn't it?"

I looked across, unsure it was me he was talking to. He was middle aged, with thinning, sandy hair. "Yes, very." I was not in the mood for conversation and hoped he would not persist. But he did.

"I love coming here. Great atmosphere, isn't it?" I smiled and nodded. "I haven't seen you here before, though. Do you come a lot?"

"No. This is the first time in years."

He beamed as though that confirmed something. "Ah." He played with his cup. "I come here all the time. I don't like the idea of anything being caged, though, I must admit. I much prefer things to be able to be out in the open. But it's not always possible, is it?"

He was waiting for an answer. "No, I suppose not."

He looked pleased, shifting slightly in his chair to face me. "You know what I mean, then?"

It seemed a strange question. "Yes, I think so."

"Oh good. Good." He seemed suddenly self-conscious. He glanced at his watch. Then, with studied casualness he said, "Would you like to have a drink back at my flat?"

It was a second or two before I realized I was being propositioned. I felt my face instantly begin to color up. "No. Thank you."

"It's not very far."

"No. Really. I must be going." I still had half a cup of tea and some ice cream left. Leaving them, I pushed my chair away and quickly stood up. My thighs caught the edge of the table and rocked it, rattling the dishes and slopping tea into the saucer. I still could not get out and had to push the chair further back. It scraped agonizingly loudly on the floor and clattered as I hooked my foot on one of its legs and almost tripped. I cast a brief glance at the sandy-haired man as I hurried away. His face was averted, but the back of his neck had gone a bright red. It probably matched my own.

I left the zoo without looking at any more of the exhibits. I ate out and arrived home a little after eight o'clock. For once the thought of spending a night in did not seem daunting.

I made myself a drink and telephoned Anna's flat. Debbie answered. "She's in bed," she said, when I asked how Anna was. "I had to call for a doctor not long after you left. I couldn't do anything with her. I mean, I've seen her upset before but never anything like that. It was frightening."

I felt a sly satisfaction that she also had had to call for help. "Is she any better now?"

"Well, the doctor gave her a sedative, and that quietened her down a bit. She's sleeping now, thank God. That's probably the best thing for her. I'm going to stay tonight. I don't think it's a good idea to leave her on her own. I mean, I'm not saying she'll *do* anything, but someone should be here in case she gets hysterical again."

"What about tomorrow?" I felt panic at the thought of having to cope with Anna like that on my own.

"I've got the morning off, but I've really got to go to work in the afternoon. But I phoned her parents, and her mother's going to come over at dinnertime. I'm glad, because Anna really needs someone looking after her until she gets over this. I mean, all the pressure she's been under lately, she was bound to crack sooner or later. I've seen it coming. She's been bottling it up for weeks, and I suppose yesterday must just have been too much for her. You know, knowing that was when they should have gone to the States. It's like that was her cut-off point, or something. I've tried to tell her it doesn't mean anything, but she won't listen. She's convinced now that Marty must be dead, and it's not as if you can say much to reassure her, is it? I mean, what *can* you say? It doesn't look very good, does it?"

I was not going to be drawn into that. "How long is Anna's mother staying?"

"Oh, she's not staying. She's going to take Anna home with her."

"Home?" I echoed.

"To Cheltenham."

That was something I had not expected. "For how long?"

"I don't know. Until she gets her head together, I suppose." Something in my voice must not have sounded quite right. "You don't mind, do you? Her taking time off, I mean?"

"Good Lord, no. Of course not. As you say, she needs someone to look after her." It was easier to sound blasé than to feel it. The thought of a separation of possibly weeks left me with a hollow feeling in my stomach. I told myself that I had to allow for some period of adjustment, and that a complete change of scene might make Anna recover all the more quickly. But that did little to make me feel any happier.

The prospect of life without Anna, even for a short time, was awful to contemplate.

❧

I went to see her before she left the next morning. Debbie answered the door. "How is she?" I asked, keeping my voice low.

"She seems better. Not hysterical like yesterday, anyway. Just quiet, like she's in shock or something. Her mother's here."

We went into the lounge. Anna was on the settee. I was shocked by the change in her. She looked paler and more lifeless than ever. She gave me a watery smile that flickered out almost immediately. Her mother was sitting close by. By contrast she seemed to dominate the entire room before she spoke. She was large and buxom, and even her floral print dress shrieked and demanded attention.

"I'm pleased to meet you, Mr. Ramsey," she said when Debbie introduced me. "I've heard a lot about you."

I made the usual self-depreciating sounds. Her hand felt dry and cool, almost leathery. "How are you feeling, Anna?" I asked.

"Okay." Another weak smile.

"Would you like a cup of tea, Mr. Ramsey?" her mother asked. She did not wait for an answer. "Debbie, would it be too much to ask you to put the kettle on? I'm sure we could all do with a cup before we go."

"I'll do it," Anna said, starting to get up. Her mother put a hand on her arm.

"No, that's all right, darling. I'm sure Debbie won't mind. Will you, dear?"

Debbie clearly did. Letting her face show her objection, she turned to me.

"Would you like a cup, Donald?"

"Please. If it's no trouble."

"Actually, I think I'll have coffee," Anna's mother said. "Wake me up for the drive home. Half a sugar, please."

Stonyfaced, Debbie left the room. Mrs. Palmer smiled at me, the mistress of ceremonies. "I hope we've not taken you from your work. From what I hear, you've been giving up enough of your time as it is."

"No, not really."

"I'm sure you're just saying that." She turned her domineering attention to her daughter. "Anna, darling, while Debbie's putting the kettle on, why don't you finish packing? Then we can all sit down together."

"There isn't much left to do."

"No, I know, dear. But once it's done, it's done, isn't it? Then we're ready to leave whenever we feel like it."

Without further argument, Anna mechanically rose and left the room. Her mother waited until the door had closed and then turned back to me. "I'd like to thank you for what you've done for Anna. From what she and Debbie have told me, you've been a great help."

"There's not really been very much I could do."

"Nonsense. You've supported her, that's something. And then there was the detective. Why Anna didn't come to her father and me, I don't know. She's such an independent girl. But if you tell me how much it was, I'll write you a check. There's no reason why you should have to pay for it."

"That's not necessary."

"Of course it is! You've done quite enough for Anna as it is. Now you must tell me how much it was."

It was easy to see why Anna had not wanted to involve her parents earlier. It would have been a constant battle not to be swamped. "No, it's quite all right. Really."

"I insist."

"So do I. It was the least I could do." I smiled, but my tone was firm. I was not going to let this woman railroad me.

"Oh." She seemed nonplussed at being refused. "Well, I suppose if you're adamant, there's nothing I can do about it. Thank you. That's very decent of you." She sighed. I sensed a change of tack. "It's quite a mess, isn't it?"

"I'm afraid so."

She lowered her voice as a concession to privacy. "What do you think about it all, Mr. Ramsey?"

"I really don't know. I'm not sure what to think, to be honest."

"No, it is rather worrying, isn't it? I must say, when Anna first called and said Marty had vanished, I thought it was a lot about nothing. Well, no, that sounds callous. I don't mean it was nothing to *Anna*, but I thought he had simply left her. And to be perfectly honest, although I wouldn't say this to her, I wasn't particularly sorry. I wasn't happy about her going to America in the first place. It was so *rushed*. Meeting someone one minute, living with them the next. And then planning to move abroad with them. Perhaps I'm old-fashioned, but it all seemed a bit premature to me. Do you know what I mean?"

I inclined my head noncommittally. She took it as agreement. "I said from the start that it wouldn't last. Not to Anna, of course. I knew better than that. But it struck me as being . . . well, a bit unrealistic, shall we say? So when I heard he'd gone, I thought, 'Oh well, it's probably for the best. Better now than later.' "

I could not have agreed more. But loyalty to Anna prevented me from saying so.

"But now it's gone on for this long without hearing anything," she continued, "it does rather make you wonder exactly what's happened to him, doesn't it? He'd have to be very cruel not to get in touch with Anna at all, and he never struck me as being like that. Then again, I must admit I hardly knew him. They kept themselves to themselves." She paused. I waited for the next question. "What did you make of him, Mr. Ramsey, if you don't mind my asking? You probably knew him better than I did."

I answered carefully. "I only knew him through Anna, so I can't claim any deep insight. But he never struck me like that, either."

She sighed again. I thought I detected a shade of disappointment. "No, that's what I thought. But as you say, you only knew him through Anna. And when all's said and done, even she had only known him for a matter of months. Less than a year, anyway. I might be being cynical, but I don't think that's really long enough to know everything about someone, no matter how much you think you do."

I looked thoughtful but said nothing. "Do you think he might have left her for someone else?" she asked, after a moment.

"I don't know. Anna doesn't seem to think so, and I suppose she should know better than anyone."

She looked at me rather archly. "Well. That depends." She leaned closer. When she spoke again, her voice was hushed, as though she were in church. "I gather the police think he might have been homosexual."

I noticed how she used the past tense. "I don't think they've actually said that in so many words," I said, "but . . ." I shrugged. She nodded as though I had confirmed her suspicions.

"I must say, that was something that had never occurred to me. But it does make you think, doesn't it? It opens up all sorts of possibilities."

I did not comment. This was obviously not good enough for her. She pressed further. "Do you think that might . . . well, might have anything to do with what's happened?"

"I really wouldn't like to say."

"No, of course not." She hesitated. "But what do you think? Do you think he might have been that way inclined?"

I thought back to when I had encouraged Zeppo to that same point of view. "I'm sure Anna would have realized if he was."

Now there was no mistaking her disappointment. "Not necessarily. It's not the sort of thing one advertises, is it? A friend of mine was married for twenty years and never knew her husband was a transvestite until she found him in her clothes one day."

She seemed almost as much of a homophobe as Marty's father. "I don't think there was ever any suggestion that Marty wore Anna's clothes," I said.

"No, I'm sure there wasn't. But he *did* go to those nightclubs, didn't he? And Anna only had his word for what happened." She gave me a meaningful look. "It does seem a bit peculiar, don't you think?"

It appeared I had met someone whose antipathy to Marty matched my own. But I did not want to compromise myself by agreeing with her. My loyalties lay with her daughter, and I was not sorry when Debbie saved me from answering by returning with the tea. And Mrs. Palmer's coffee. With half a sugar.

Anna was summoned from the bedroom—by Debbie—at her mother's command. Mrs. Palmer commandeered the conversation, and I was happy to let her. The occasional comment from either Debbie or myself was enough to keep her commentary running. Anna said nothing. She did not appear to be listening.

Finally, putting her mug down—I noticed Debbie had given her a chipped one—Anna's mother announced that it was time to go. My tea was unfinished and so was Debbie's. Anna's remained untouched.

I had managed to avoid thinking about Anna leaving until

then. Suddenly, I felt the pit drop out of my stomach.

"Are you sure you wouldn't like to stay for lunch?" I asked.

"No, thank you all the same. I don't want to hit the rush hour."

"You'll have plenty of time. And I think you'll find the rush hour lasts all day."

Mrs. Palmer would not be put off. "We'd still better be making tracks. The sooner we go, the sooner we'll get there."

With this homily, she began preparations for their departure. These consisted of instructing Anna to fetch her suitcase from the bedroom and Debbie to take the mugs back into the kitchen. "Give them a quick rinse while you're there, will you, dear?" she asked. I was permitted to remain while she busied herself poring deeply into her handbag and renewing her lipstick and powder.

We left the flat. I carried Anna's suitcase downstairs and packed it in the boot of her mother's Volvo. Debbie hugged her and gave her a kiss: I stood back, uncertainly. Anna came and put her arms around me. She was on the verge of crying again. "Thanks, Donald. I don't know what I'd have done without you."

I patted her back. She let go and climbed into the car. I waved as they pulled away, and then they were gone.

Debbie snorted angrily. "God, I pity poor Anna, having her for a mother. I mean, what did her last slave die of?"

I did not answer. I was too choked to speak.

Chapter

20

Anna was away for much longer than the two or three weeks I had hoped. It was almost two months before I saw her again. During the third week, when I was beginning to hope she would soon be back, her mother telephoned to say they were taking her to Tunisia for a month. Predictably, she did not ask if I minded Anna having the time off; she presented it as a *fait accompli*. I consoled myself by nurturing a sense of injustice. But that was immediately forgotten when Anna herself called a few days later. It was good to hear her voice again, and I reassured her that I did not mind her going in the least. Cheered by talking to her, at that moment in time I meant it. Anna, on the other hand, seemed unexcited by the prospect. She sounded as though nothing mattered to her very much one way or the other.

Without Anna to look at and occupy me, I fell into a mechanical, listless routine. Life would begin again when she returned. Until then, I was merely treading water. I hired a temporary assistant from an agency, but the sight of another girl in the gallery only made Anna's absence more marked. I coped by switching myself off as much as possible, functioning on a surface level only: a state of semipermanent limbo. It worked so well that when the girl eventually left, I could remember neither her name nor what she looked like.

I contacted Zeppo only occasionally during that period. He was his usual sardonic self, hiding behind sarcastic comments any relief he felt at the petering out of the police investigation. But even he failed to reach me. His barbs slid off almost unnoticed, which I realized later was probably the best reaction I could have had to them. The last time I spoke to him I said I would let him know when Anna got back and hung up. I think he was beginning to say something when I put the receiver down.

My state of apathy was unassailable. Or so I believed. On the morning I received my first postcard from Anna—bland and perfunctory—I was also contacted by someone else. Someone much less welcome.

It was when I was trying to explain the basics of my cataloging system to the temporary assistant. The girl's repeated inability to grasp it was beginning to rub at my patience. I lacked the energy to be angry, but I felt a tired, irritable frustration at her continual stupidity. When the telephone rang it seemed a further, needless distraction.

"Look, just don't do anything until I get back," I told the girl as I went to answer it. "Hello, The Gallery?"

"Mr. Ramsey? Margaret Thornby, here."

This time I had no difficulty placing either the voice or the name. I felt a weary resignation.

"How are you?" she asked. "Well, I hope?" I assured her I was. "Just phoning to let you know I'm coming into the center again later this week, and I thought if you weren't too busy we could perhaps meet up sometime."

I made a polite expression of interest and asked what day it would be. "Thursday," she said. "Is that convenient for you?"

"Is that this Thursday?" I asked. "The nineteenth?"

She gave a laugh. "Well, it's this Thursday, but don't ask me what the date is, because I haven't a clue. I'm awful on things like that. I've got a diary somewhere, though, if you want me to check."

"No, that's all right. There's no need. I'm afraid if it's this Thursday I won't be able to make it anyway. I'm out of town all

morning, and I've a meeting scheduled in the afternoon." The
excuses came easily, fabricated without effort from my lassi-
tude. I waited for the expressions of regret, already looking past
them to the goodbyes and the mild relief I would feel on hanging up.

"Oh, have you? Well, never mind. What about Thursday
evening, then?"

"Thursday evening?" The question pierced through my
complacency.

"Yes. If you're not doing anything. I'm going to be staying at
my daughter's overnight, and the friends I normally see are
both on holiday, so if you're not busy we could make it the
evening instead." Again, she gave a laugh. "It'll save my daughter having to think of something to entertain her mum."

I scrambled for an excuse. But the sudden departure from
what I had expected was too sharp: I could not make the adjustment in time. "Mr. Ramsey, are you still there?"

"Yes, yes. I'm sorry, I was just . . . I thought someone had
come in." I searched for inspiration. None came. My mind was
blank. "Yes, Thursday evening's fine," I heard myself say.

"Oh good. What time suits you?"

"Whenever." Numb, I let her fix a time and arrange a suitable place to meet. When she had finished, I put the phone
down. The feeling of relief I had looked forward to had been
replaced by a dull sense of entrapment. I went back to where
I had left the girl. She had followed my instructions to the let-
ter and done absolutely nothing. She looked at me, waiting
mutely for instructions.

"Take an early lunch," I said.

The threat of Thursday night cast a pall over the interven-
ing days. Whenever I tried to rationalize it away, I would think
of what Anna had said, and it would immediately darken. I
could see no innocent reason for the woman's persistence, nor
could I think of a way to avoid it. As horrific as the prospect of
spending an evening alone with her was, I could not bring myself to confront her with excuses.

I awoke on Thursday morning with a leaden sense of oppression. Its weight lay heavily in my stomach as I went into the gallery and tried to get through the rest of the day. The ordeal waited for me at the end of it like an impassable block. I could not see beyond it. My entire future was reduced to that single evening.

Anna seemed far away.

The hours passed quickly. I closed the gallery, showered and changed and tried to tell myself it would, if nothing else, soon be over. The Thornby woman had suggested a restaurant with a small bar in it. I went there early. Not, needless to say, out of eagerness but because I needed a drink before I faced her. I ordered a gin and tonic, sat down and looked around. I was relieved that the restaurant was not a particularly intimate one. I looked at my watch. I had nearly twenty minutes before she was due. Time enough for another drink, if I wanted one. Feeling the closest to being relaxed I had all day, I took my first sip and, over the top of the glass, saw the door open and Margaret Thornby walk in.

My stomach curdled. All enjoyment of the drink vanished. In the moment before she saw me, I swallowed half of it, regardless. Then I had been seen.

She smiled and began to walk over. I forced an answering smile onto my face. A waiter intercepted her and made some polite inquiry, and she murmured something in reply, motioning toward me. I stood up as she approached the table.

"I'm sorry I'm late," she said, sitting down. "Have you been waiting long?"

"No, I've only just arrived." I wondered what she was talking about. She was more than fifteen minutes early.

"Oh, that's all right, then. To be honest, I forgot if we'd said seven or half past. I tried phoning you a while ago, but you'd obviously set off, so I thought, 'Oh God, it must have been seven,' and dashed around like a mad thing to get here on time." She looked at her watch. "I'm only seven minutes late, so that's not too bad, is it?"

I did not bother correcting her mistake. "There was no need to rush yourself."

"Well, I don't like being late for people." She laughed. "As you probably remember." I smiled, again not knowing what she was talking about. Then I realized she must be referring to when we had bumped cars. She had been hurrying to meet her son. She looked at my glass. "That's a good idea. I think I'll have one myself before we eat."

I remembered my manners. "Of course. What would you like?"

"What are you drinking?"

"Gin and tonic."

"That sounds nice. I'll have the same, please."

I tried to hide my unease as I ordered the drink. It seemed ominous that she had chosen the same as me. "Cheers," she said, raising her glass. I did likewise, regretting that I had not had the foresight to order myself another. Now I would either have to appear gluttonous or nurse an almost empty glass until she had finished hers.

"Oh, that's welcome," she said, setting her drink down. "I feel I've earned that. Today's just been one fiasco after another. One of the main reasons I had for coming into the City today was to look at a supposedly authentic set of Queen Anne chairs. This woman phoned me at the beginning of the week and said her aunt had died, and was I interested in buying them? I said of course, because those sort of things don't crop up every day, do they? I would have liked to have gone to have a look at them earlier this week, but she said they'd got to bury her aunt first. Only decent, I suppose, but I daresay old aunty wouldn't have minded anymore."

I smiled.

"Anyway, I got over there this morning, and guess what? Blow me if the damn things weren't only reproductions! And not even very good ones at that!" She spread her hands, inviting me to join in her amazement. I did my best.

"Well, I tried to break it to this woman and her husband gently, but they started getting very offish with me," she went on. "Well, she did at least. He didn't say very much at all, just stood behind her like a limp lettuce. It was clear who wore the trousers in that house, if you know what I mean. So finally I said, 'Now just a second. I'm very sorry that your aunt didn't know the difference between Queen Anne chairs and a Formica stool from Woolworth's'—well, I didn't quite put it like that, but I felt like it—'but that's hardly my fault. You're quite welcome to get as many opinions as you like, but they'll all tell you the same thing.' "

She pointed at the ashtray on the table. " 'Those chairs weren't built any earlier than the nineteen fifties,' I said. 'And if Queen Anne had anything to do with them, she must have lived a damn sight longer than the history books tell us!' "

She laughed. " 'That shut her up. 'Well, what shall we do with them, then?' she asked. As if it was *my* responsibility! 'Put 'em on the bonfire!' I said, and left them to it!"

I realized some contribution from me was expected at this point. Smiling my approval, I murmured, "Quite right." It was enough. She paused only long enough to take another drink before going on.

"And then, as if that wasn't enough, I was supposed to be meeting my daughter this afternoon—have I told you she's an art student? Well, she is. Anyway, she's got a degree show coming up soon, so I said I'd buy her something to wear for it. You know what students are like, never any money, so I thought I'd help her out a bit. Anyway, I was supposed to be meeting her at two o'clock—she couldn't make lunch, which was why I wondered if you were free—and so I waited at this little wine bar place she'd suggested. Ten past two. No sign of Susan. Half past two. Still no sign of Susan. Well, when it got to quarter to three, I thought, 'Well, something's wrong here,' and tried to contact her. So I phoned the art college and finally spoke to someone who said she'd already left. I didn't know what to do then, so I gave it another half hour and decided I'd better call around to her digs. She's not on the phone, you see, so I couldn't ring her. So I trailed around there—she lives in Tooting, by the way—and of course there was no Susan there either. Well, there I was, standing on the pavement, just beginning to wonder what I was going to do, when one of her flatmates turned up. Stuart, he's called. Smashing young man. I hadn't met him before, but he let me in and made me a cup of tea and told me that Susan had gone to the pictures!"

She raised her eyes ceilingward. "Well, I wasn't too pleased, I can tell you. Luckily, I'd managed to calm down a bit by the time she finally turned up. 'What are you doing here, Mum?' she asks, and before I can say anything, Stuart says, 'I told your mum you'd been to the pictures. To see that Warhol film.' Well, I don't know if she had or not, but it took her a second or two to say, 'Oh . . . yes, that's right!' so you can draw your own conclusion." She chuckled, shaking her head. "I think these youngsters think we must have been born old. Not that I was bothered where she'd been, I only wanted to know why the hell she'd left me hanging about all afternoon. So I said, 'I thought we were going to buy you a new dress or whatever?' " She held out one hand, turned palm up. "Of course, she'd forgotten all about it."

She chuckled again. "Anyway, we got it all sorted out in the end. Then, of course, she wanted to take me out tonight. 'No,' I said, 'I'm sorry, but you've had your chance. I'm afraid some other lucky person's got that pleasure.' " I felt my face begin to burn and hid it by taking a drink from my almost empty glass. She did likewise from hers. She set it down again, smiling fondly.

"Kids. Who'd have them?" She looked across at me. I was acutely conscious of being the object of her attention. "Do you have any?"

It was the first time anyone had ever asked me that question. "Me? Oh no. No."

"Very wise. Pain in the neck half of the time. As I said to my daughter today, 'If I had my time again, I'd stick to cats. More fun and less trouble.' "

I realized this was a joke and dutifully laughed with her. A waiter appeared and told us our table was ready. Glad for the reprieve, no matter how short, I let him lead us into the restaurant proper.

The table was set in a corner. I saw this with dismay and

looked around for a less secluded one. There were several, but I could think of no reason to ask to move. We sat down, and my embarrassment was compounded when the waiter lit the candle in the center of the table. There seemed to be a conspiracy to create a romantic mood. I wondered how I could have thought that the restaurant was not intimate. Now it seemed all too much so. I felt like announcing to everyone in the room that we were not a couple.

The waiter handed us each a menu. "Now, before we go any further, I want to make it clear that this is my treat," she said. "No arguments."

Preoccupied, I had not been about to make one. I realized I should at least go through the motions. "No, I'll get this." I made an effort to be gallant. "It's the least I can do after letting you down this afternoon."

She held her hand up. "No, I shan't hear of it. I invited you, so this is on me."

"No, really—"

"I tell you what, you can get it the next time."

My smile froze. The words settled uncomfortably into my stomach, precluding any thoughts of hunger. *Next time.* I felt a clammy sense of claustrophobia. I managed to mumble some sort of acquiescence and pretended to study the menu, staring at the calligraphed lines without reading them.

When the waiter returned, I ordered the first thing my eye focused upon. I had no appetite. I agreed readily to my hostess's choice of wine and prayed it would not be long in coming. I badly needed a drink. I felt rigidly self-conscious, my tongue lying in my mouth like a wooden club. Fortunately, I was given little opportunity to exercise it anyway.

She prattled on through the meal, requiring only the occasional word from me to sustain her monologue. I was given an unstructured mishmash of her views, her family and whatever else happened to occur to her while she was speaking.

I also learned that she did not have a husband.

"George—that's my husband—always used to say that any man who didn't play golf had to have a serious character defect.

That was his excuse, anyway, whenever I used to go on at him for spending all his spare time at the club. 'Margaret, you should be thankful,' he'd say. 'Some men have mistresses, some men are alcoholics, some men are gamblers. All you've got to contend with is a white ball and a few acres of grass.' "

She laughed. "He was right, of course. When I was widowed for real, I found out that being a golf widow isn't half so bad."

I realized that this was one of the points where I was expected to say something. Reluctantly, I asked, "When was that?"

"When was I widowed? Oh, over two years ago. Don't worry, I'm over it now. There's no danger of me blubbing or getting maudlin or anything. Bit of a blow at the time, of course. Car crash. Right out of the blue. But life goes on, doesn't it? I'd got the business to keep me occupied, and it wasn't as if the kids were young and needed looking after. Mind you," she laughed, "at times like this afternoon, I sometimes wonder."

As she spoke, she leaned across and briefly touched my arm. It took a vast effort of will not to move away. "But listen to me, I've not stopped talking yet," she went on. "I must be boring you silly. You must tell me to shut up if you feel like it."

"No, that's quite all right."

"Anyway, what about you? I've been so busy gabbing I've not given you a chance to say anything about yourself. You're still quite a man of mystery. I know what sort of car you drive, but that's about all. Are you married?"

The suddenness of the question burned my face. Her head was tilted inquisitively. "No. No, I'm afraid not." I felt myself being backed into a corner.

She gave a little nod. "No, I didn't think you were. No ring," she explained, nodding at my finger. "And you didn't seem the type."

She smiled, looking at me very directly. I had no idea what the married type looked like and did not care. I busied myself taking another drink.

"Rather a nice wine," I said.

"Yes, it's not bad, is it? Although I must admit I don't know the first thing about wines. I'll drink any old plonk so long as it's not like vinegar. I've not got a very discerning palate. I know what I like, but that's about it."

That last sentence seemed imbued with all sorts of unpleasant connotations. I realized I was sitting tensely and made an effort to relax. Perhaps some of my awkwardness communicated itself, because there was a lull in the conversation, the first of the evening. Our plates were empty; there was nothing else to occupy us. The silence grew. I searched for something to say but came up with nothing. I was on the verge of making another comment about the wine when she spoke.

"So. How did you get into the art business?"

Glad to leave the awful quiet behind, I gave her a condensed version of my early life. She listened attentively, and I shut my mind to everything except my narrative. At least it was a safe subject.

"I'd no idea you were once a starving artist yourself," she said. "I expect you still paint for your own pleasure, don't you?"

"No, I'm afraid not."

"Not even occasionally? Don't you miss it?"

I had never really considered it before. "No, not really."

She seemed surprised. "Was it a conscious decision? I mean, when you were disillusioned about being an artist, did you think, 'Right, that's it,' and pack your brushes away?"

"Not exactly." I thought back. "I just lost interest. I was technically proficient, but that was all. There always seemed to be something missing, I'm not sure what. Someone once commented that I painted with 'a cold hand.' " I paused, embarrassed and angry at letting myself be drawn out. "Eventually I just stopped."

"Oh. How sad." She dismissed it with a smile. "Well, I expect you don't have much time anyway, these days. Still, if you have any of your old paintings, I'd love to see them. Perhaps they're better than you remember. You never know, you might feel inspired to take it up again."

I felt a jolt of panic at the hinted intimacy. "I don't have any. I threw them all out years ago." It was the truth.

"You threw everything away? Oh, what a shame. I bet you regret it now, though, don't you?"

I had never thought about it. But now I was glad I no longer had any work to show her. I gave a noncommittal shrug, feeling my tension return stronger than ever. The waiter appeared and removed our plates.

"Well, I don't know about you, but I'm going to have a dessert," she said. My heart sank. She studied the sweet menu. "I think I'll try the pavlova. I know it's loaded with calories, but I don't care. How about you?"

I had no appetite, but it seemed easier to have something than not. It would give me something to do. "Yes, the pavlova sounds fine."

"You should see some of my daughter's work," she said, as the waiter brought the dessert. "Not the stuff she's doing now so much, although her tutors seem impressed enough with that, but some of her earlier pieces. Of course, I can't claim to be any expert, but I think it's pretty damn good." She gave an apologetic laugh, and suddenly her hand had reached out to touch me again. It lay heavily on my arm, implicitly connecting us. "I bet I sound just like any other proud mother, don't I? Oh well, it can't be helped. I suppose I am."

The hand was taken away. She went back to her pavlova. "Still, if I do say so myself, she has a definite talent. You'll have to meet her sometime, so you can make up your own mind."

I gripped my spoon. The feeling of claustrophobia was stifling. She went on, blithely tying me to her.

"Damien, on the other hand, can't draw for toffee. Absolutely hopeless. In fact, I'm not sure what he wants to do with his life. I don't think he does, either. I love him dearly, but I do wish he'd hurry up and settle down to something. Or with someone, even. He's the eldest, and I've said to him if he doesn't hurry up and produce grandchildren soon, I'm going to be too old to enjoy them. Only kidding, of course. He's got the travel bug, and he's got to get that out of his system before he does anything else. Mind you, if nothing else, he has got some amazing slides of the places he's been. I know other people's photographs are normally boring, but some of these are absolutely breathtaking! In fact, you must come over sometime while he's still here and have a look at them." She smiled. "You could even risk my attempt at a curry, if you like. That's my latest thing, since he's got back from India. What's the matter?"

She was staring at me with concern. As she had been talking, I had felt myself growing tauter and tauter. I realized I was still rigidly clutching the spoon. "Are you all right?" she asked, and leaned forward to touch me again, and this time I could not help it. I jerked my arm away.

She was left with her hand stretched out over the table. Her face was wide eyed with surprise. The moment seemed suspended with an awful clarity. I noticed she had a small, white smear of cream on her top lip. I tried to say something.

"I . . ." Nothing else came. My throat felt constricted. At last, her hand sank down and was withdrawn back to her side of the table. "I'm not . . . I don't . . ."

"What? What is it?"

She stared at me with shocked incomprehension. I tried again to form the words. "I'm . . . I'm not . . . I think you've got the wrong impression."

She blinked. "Wrong impression?"

I could not look at her. "This . . . Meeting again. I don't think it's a good idea." She did not say anything. I fixed my eyes on the tablecloth. The wreckages of the pavlovas confronted me. "I don't . . . I don't want a . . . a relationship."

I forced myself to look at her. Now her expression was almost one of horror. "Good God," she said.

"I'm sorry . . ."

"Good God." Her hand went to her mouth. She closed her eyes.

"I don't want to be rude . . ."

Her head was turned slightly away. "Whatever gave you the impression that I . . . that I expected anything like that?"

Something about the way she said it gave me a premonition of disaster.

"The telephone calls . . . All the invitations . . ." My voice trailed off. What had seemed obvious now suddenly seemed much less so. She slowly set her spoon down on the edge of her plate. She looked down at it as she spoke.

"Mr. Ramsey . . . I enjoy meeting people. I always have, but now I make a point of doing it. I was married for thirty years, and when my husband died it left a gap. I fill it the best way I can. I don't believe in putting any more pressure on my children than I have to. They have their own lives to lead, and so I try to make mine as busy as possible."

She looked up at me. Her mouth was trembling. The smudge of cream was still on her lip. "I know I talk too much, and that sometimes puts people off. And I know I'm too pushy sometimes, and that puts people off, too. But I'm not looking for anyone to take my husband's place, so you're quite safe. If you misunderstood that, I'm sorry. I can't see that I've really done anything to give you the impression that I was being anything more than friendly, but obviously I must have. Even so, I don't think you had to make your . . . your reluctance quite so obvious."

She suddenly reached for her handbag and swiftly took out her wallet. She set several ten-pound notes on the table. "I said I'd pay, and I will." She stood up. Her chin was quivering. "To be honest, Mr. Ramsey, I thought you were gay anyway. So you needn't have worried after all."

She walked quickly out of the restaurant. I looked around. One or two people had glanced up as she left, but no one was near enough to have heard what had been said. I sat where I was. For the time being, I was incapable of moving. I groped for my equilibrium, thought of Anna and found it. The woman was unimportant. She did not count. Absently, I wiped my arm with a napkin where she had touched me. After a while a waiter appeared and asked if I had finished. I let him take the plates and her money. There was a substantial amount left over, but I left that as a tip.

I went home.

Chapter

21

That was the last I saw of the Thornby woman. I half expected
her to try and sue me over the car accident now, possibly pro-
ducing some newly found "witness," or a delayed injury. But
nothing of the sort happened. The claim continued to go
through without a hitch.

More than anything, I felt relieved that at least she would
not be pestering me again. The memory of the awful night was
still painful, but only when I thought about it. Consequently, I
avoided doing that. Soon the incident was shelved safely away,
causing only the faintest twinge if something happened to remind me. And then I heard news that wiped even this from my
mind.

Anna was coming home.

I received another postcard, saying that she would be back
at work the following Monday. The message was brief, but the
tone seemed much brighter than the first. Like clicking a
switch, I came to life again.

The next few days were both a pleasure and a torment.
Knowing that Anna would soon be back made even the most
mundane act enjoyable, but at the same time the wait was unbearable. By the weekend, I had worked myself up to such a
pitch that I felt ill.

On the Monday morning I went to the gallery early. I bought

a bunch of flowers for Anna and tried to occupy myself by making sure that everything was neat and tidy for her arrival. When I had finished there was still a half hour left to fill. I sat down and watched the clock. The two-month wait was approaching its final minutes, time passing more slowly with each one.

Then, just before nine o'clock, I heard the *ching* of the bell as the door opened, and suddenly Anna was there.

"I'm back!" she said, grinning.

"Anna!" I could think of nothing to say. "You look wonderful!"

She did. There was no sign of the pale, lifeless girl I had said goodbye to. Her skin glowed with a warm, golden tan, and her hair, tied loosely back, shone bronze from the sun. She looked fit and healthy and more beautiful than I had ever seen her.

"Thank you. A month in the sun does wonders." She kissed my cheek. My flesh felt seared. I breathed her familiar fragrance, complemented by the underlying smell of suntanned skin. "Have you managed to cope without me?"

"Limped along with the help of a somewhat retarded temp. How was Tunisia?"

"Hot. And pretty boring after the first two weeks."

"It certainly doesn't seem to have done you any harm." I could not stop smiling. "It's good to see you. Oh, and I bought you these." I produced the flowers, a little self-consciously.

"Donald, they're lovely! Thank you!" She laughed. "I'm the one who's been away. It's supposed to be me who brings you a present. Speaking of which . . ." She rummaged in her bag and came out with a tissue-wrapped object. "I've brought you a bottle of the local plonk. It's awful, but you've got to bring souvenirs back, haven't you? And I got you this as well."

She handed me a small parcel. "I found it by accident," she said as I unwrapped it. "We got lost one day and ended up driving through this tiny little village in the middle of nowhere. An old man was making them."

The paper came off. Inside was a hand-carved wooden

statue of a woman. It was crudely but skillfully done, and while it was not particularly to my taste, I had to admit it was still quite a beautiful little thing.

"They were all different, but she was my favorite," Anna said. "I hope you like it. It'll be difficult changing it if you don't."

"It's lovely. Thank you." Even if it had been the most taste-less piece of junk, I would probably have felt the same way. It was a gift from Anna and therefore priceless.

"It's for being so considerate. You know." She seemed em-barrassed. So was I. But touched.

"You didn't have to bring me anything. But thank you any-way. I'll give it pride of place. And thank you for the plonk as well. I was going to suggest opening it this afternoon, but if it's as bad as you say, perhaps that wouldn't be such a good idea."

"Not if you value your stomach lining."

"In that case I'll save it for someone I dislike." Zeppo, per-haps. I hesitated, awkwardly. "How are you feeling now?" I felt I had to ask.

She nodded reassuringly. "I'm okay. Mum and Dad were right about getting away. It was what I needed. I'm all right now." She smiled at me to confirm it, and suddenly her eyes were filling up. She gave a shaky laugh and wiped them. "Well, almost. Sorry."

"No need to be."

"I was determined I wasn't going to do that, too." She gave them a final wipe.

"You don't have to apologize."

"I don't want you to think I'm going to burst into tears at the drop of a hat, that's all. I'm over that now."

"It's all right, really."

"I'm just a bit edgy after going back to the flat last night. Everything was just the same, and I thought . . ." Her eyes filled up again. "Oh, bugger."

I offered her a handkerchief, but she shook her head. "No, I'm all right now, thanks. It's just getting used to being back, that's all. It's a bit harder than I thought."

"You shouldn't expect too much of yourself. You can't rush these things."

"No, I know. It wasn't so bad while I was away, but now I'm back everything's . . . everything's still here, you know? Nothing's changed." She took a deep, uneven breath. "It'll be better when I've cleared away the rest of Marty's things. It was a bit too much like walking into a shrine last night, with everything of his still there. It was as though he was going to walk in any second." She shrugged. "I know that's not going to happen, though. I know I'll probably never even find out what happened to him, but that's something I'm going to have to learn to live with. And the sooner I do, the better."

She gave me a rueful smile. "That's the theory, at least. It seems easier said than done, doesn't it?"

"I think you're doing remarkably well."

"It doesn't feel like it." She straightened, sniffing away the last of the tears. "Anyway, now I've got that out of my system, how about a cup of coffee?" She smiled, more convincingly now. "I promise not to spill it on you this time."

That was the last time Anna broke down in front of me. Over the next few days I occasionally had the impression that her cheerfulness was only a facade. But it was in my interest as much as hers for me to let it go undented. I let a week pass to give her time to settle in and get used to being back.

Then I called Zeppo.

⟲

I planned to reintroduce him gradually, over a period of weeks. Zeppo, however, had other ideas. Even so, their first meeting went smoothly enough. It was at the same restaurant where we had "accidentally" met him before, and he behaved perfectly. I noticed with satisfaction that Anna seemed genuinely pleased to see him.

"You look great," Zeppo said to her. "Where was it? Tunisia?"

"That's right. And you look as if you've been away yourself. Don't tell me you got that color here."

Zeppo was indeed looking very tanned and fit. The two of them went well together. I was suddenly conscious of my own flaccid pallor.

"No, I've been doing a shoot in the Caribbean," he said. "Two weeks on Dominica. It was hell."

"I can imagine."

I said nothing. Although I had not seen Zeppo since the night I had thrown him out of my house, I had spoken to him several times during Anna's absence. If he had been to the Caribbean recently, he had taken his telephone with him.

"So. How are you now?" He put a slight inflection of concern into his voice to let Anna know what he meant. Anna acknowledged it with a smile and a nod.

"Okay, thanks."

I was surprised at his tact. And more than a little relieved. When I had spoken to him the night before, I had warned him that Anna was still not over what had happened. He had been less than understanding.

"Don't worry. Once she gets my hand in her pants she'll feel much better," he had said.

I knew he was only baiting me, but I still did not entirely trust him. I did not want him pushing Anna too quickly, either when I was there or, even worse, when I was not. But that afternoon he gave me no cause to complain. He behaved perfectly and made no overtures toward her that I was aware of. He stayed for the half hour we had agreed and then, with a glance at his watch, made his excuses.

"Call into the gallery now you're back," I told him.

"I might drop in later this week," he said and left.

Later that week turned out to be the next day, as we had arranged. I made a show of pleased surprise when he stopped by for a coffee, hiding my annoyance that he was an hour late. But when he appeared the following day as well, my surprise was as genuine as Anna's.

"Is there any particular reason for this ad lib? Or are you just enthusiastic?" I asked, when Anna went to deal with a client.

"A bit of both. The girl I was supposed to be seeing tonight's gone and broken her arm, the silly bitch. So I thought I'd kill two birds with one stone and take Anna out instead." Zeppo smiled at me, slyly. "With a bit of luck this could be the big night. A quick drink, a nightclub, then back to my place and fuck her brains out."

For once his deliberate crudeness slipped by me almost un-noticed. I tried to conceal my sudden panic. "Don't you think it's a little premature?"

He smirked. "I think that's the last thing you've got to worry about."

"But she's only been back a week. And she's still not over Marty yet."

"So this'll take her mind off it. After the first ten minutes she won't even be able to remember his name." He frowned. "Why are you looking like that? Come on, Donald, this is what you've wanted, isn't it?"

"I still think it's too soon."

"Is it hell. A bit of tender loving care is exactly what she needs. A sympathetic ear. A shoulder to cry on." He grinned. "A nice, stiff cock."

I felt my mouth compress. I shook my head. "No."

"No? What do you mean, 'No'?"

"I mean exactly that. I would have thought it was simple enough for you to understand."

Zeppo stared at me. "Well, you'll have to excuse me for be-ing stupid, but I'm afraid it's not. Ridiculous as it seems, I was under the impression that you wanted me to get her into bed. So why start dragging your heels now?"

"I'm not. I simply don't see any point in spoiling things by rushing. When we've spent so much time over this so far, I don't think waiting another week or two is going to make any difference."

He was still looking at me. "You're being shifty, Donald. Is there something I should know? Because if there is, you'd better tell me."

I tried not to seem evasive. "Of course there isn't. I just think we should give her a little more time to find her feet, that's all."

"Not much point when I'm going to sweep her off them, is there?" His witticism seemed to please him. He gave an exaggerated sigh and shrugged. "But you're the boss. Your will is my command. I will not fuck Anna tonight. Happy now?"

Relieved, at least. "Yes, thank you."

"Am I still permitted to actually take her out? Or is that forbidden as well?"

I took a deep breath and plunged. "Actually, I'd rather you didn't."

It took the wind out of his sails. But only for a moment. "Oh, for fuck's sake, Donald! What's the matter with you?"

"Nothing's the matter with me. I just—"

"Just what? Do you want to carry on with this or not? Because if you don't, say now, because I'm not pissing around indefinitely!"

"No one's asked you to. I'm merely saying that I don't want you seeing Anna alone at night yet."

"Why not, for Christ's sake? She's a big girl! She's over eighteen! Are you frightened I'm going to drag her into an alley and rape her or something?"

"Would you mind keeping your voice down?" I hissed. "She's only downstairs. And yes, the thought had crossed my mind."

He sagged back in his chair. "I don't believe this. Do you really think I'm that desperate? You can't be serious!"

"I'm afraid I am. Perhaps you won't actually drag her into an alley, but I'm well aware that one thing can lead to another. Particularly at night, after a few drinks. And I've not gone to all this trouble and expense just to have you walk in one morning and tell me it 'accidentally' happened the night before. I've already told you I want to know before the event, not afterward."

Zeppo laughed incredulously. "What would you like, an announcement in *The Times?*"

"No, just to know when it's going to happen."

I waited. If Zeppo pressed further, I would have to tell him the rest. And I was not ready for that just yet. But I was saved by his own malicious brand of humor. He smiled, sadistically superior.

"*It?* What do you mean by 'it,' Donald?"

"You know very well what I mean."

"I'm not sure I do. You've got to learn to be more specific. By 'it' do you mean when I fuck Anna? Is that what you're trying to say?"

"I'm not trying to say anything. And I'm not going to play juvenile games. You know what I'm talking about."

He was grinning. I could feel my face beginning to burn. "Why don't you say 'fuck' if that's what you mean? Or 'shag.' Or 'screw,' if you'd rather. Of course, if you wanted to be old-fashioned you could always just say 'make love.' Not that love has much to do with it very often. But even that's better than 'it,' don't you think?" His grin was broadening. "Come on, Donald, be a devil. Say what you mean. They're only words."

"I've already said all I intend to."

He chuckled. "You really are a prissy bastard, aren't you? All right, Donald, if it'll make you happy, I won't take Anna out after six o'clock without a chaperone."

He looked condescendingly pleased with himself. But for once I did not mind. His baiting had not upset me half as much as he believed. It had distracted him from what could have been a much more uncomfortable line of questioning, and for that I was grateful.

"If you're so keen to start seeing her at night, I suggest the three of us could go out somewhere," I said. Still mellow, Zeppo shrugged.

"Now why was I expecting that? Okay, Donald, if you want to be a gooseberry, that's up to you. Just name the day."

"Thursday's convenient for me. I don't think Anna's doing anything then. Is that all right for you?"

"I'll make a date in my diary. What sort of scintillating evening do you have in mind? How about a nice, racy strip joint? Or would you rather just go clubbing?"

I ignored him. "The Ballet Rambert's in the West End this week. I think I should still be able to get tickets. You do like Prokofiev, don't you?"

"Love him to bits. I can't wait." Zeppo raised his eyes skyward. "The ballet! Jesus wept!"

⌖

After that, I knew I could not put off telling him the rest for much longer. Yet I still avoided it. It was not just cowardice. Now the denouement was almost here, I was no longer in any hurry. The anticipation was almost pleasurable enough in itself. I wanted to savor it for as long as possible. And so I dallied, postponing the inevitable and miserly eking out the last days of Zeppo's ignorance.

The three of us now began to go out more often. Usually it was only for a drink straight after work—Anna seemed glad to put off going home—but occasionally we would go to the theater, or a restaurant, and spend the whole evening together. For me these were the best of times, golden hued and perfect. I could even, letting myself believe his act, forget my dislike for Zeppo.

Only once was there a sour note. We were in a pub one evening, when someone came up to the table.

"Anna! What are you doing here?"

I looked up at the young man who had spoken. Anna beamed at him.

"Oh, hi, Dave. I might have known I'd find you in here. Liquid dinner again, is it?"

"You've no need to talk. I bet that's not lemonade you're drinking."

Anna grinned. "That's different. I'm here with my boss, so it's allowed. This is Donald." I smiled hello. "And Zeppo." She made no attempt to qualify who Zeppo was.

"Are you still okay for tomorrow night?" the newcomer asked. Anna nodded.

"Eight o'clock. I'll be there."

He grinned. "Great. I'll see you then." He nodded toward a group at the other side of the pub. "I'd better get back. It's my round."

He smiled once more at Zeppo and me, then left. I sat stiff backed. I had no idea who he was, but his easy familiarity with Anna hinted at all sort of intimacies. And she was seeing him the next night. I felt hugely, hotly jealous.

"Friend of yours?" asked Zeppo

"Well, he's the boyfriend of a friend of mine," Anna said. "He's really nice, but he drinks like a fish. Caroline—that's his girlfriend—is cooking a meal tomorrow night, and it's a dead cert he'll be out of his head before it's over. I don't know how she puts up with it."

Reassured, I made an effort to be magnanimous. "He seemed pleasant enough."

"Oh, he is. He still will be when he's falling over in about two hours' time. That's the only reason he gets away with it."

Zeppo began to tell us about someone he knew who had a drinking problem—Zeppo always seemed to have a story for every occasion—but I only pretended to listen.

My moment of insecurity had passed, but I remained shaken. The reminder that Anna still had a social life I knew nothing about was a painful one. I told myself that it was un-realistic to expect otherwise, that so long as it did not interfere with our relationship, it did not really matter. But the jealousy lingered. I did not want her seeing anyone except us. I wanted to possess her exclusively.

However, my resentment of her other friends, known and unknown, was short lived. It could not survive without fuel, and Anna gave me none. I no longer felt that I was merely her employer. Over the next few weeks, the three of us went out together more often than ever. I could almost pretend that this happy balance was permanent, and although at the back of my mind I knew it had to end sometime, that there would come a point when I would be an unwanted third party, I came to see this as something that was always reserved for some remote future. The present, where I played an equal part, seemed immutable.

The first inkling that I had become superfluous came one evening after we had been to the theater. It had been no different from any of the other times we had gone out together since Anna's return. I had detected no change in her attitude, to either Zeppo or myself. It was a warm night, and we had gone on to a pub with a small courtyard so we could sit outside. Zeppo was engaged in another of his anecdotes, but I was not really paying attention.

Then Anna laughed.

It was the first time I had heard her laugh, really laugh, since Marty's disappearance, and I was not blind to the fact that it was Zeppo who had caused it. Neither was he. As he made a further quip, Anna, still laughing, reached out and touched his bare arm. It was completely spontaneous, innocent but at the same time intimate, and Zeppo's eyes briefly flicked over to me. Then his attention was on Anna again. As he continued with his story, he put his hand on her forearm. There was nothing innocent or spontaneous about his action, but Anna did not seem to notice. Or mind.

Suddenly, I was aware that I was on the outside. For a few seconds I might as well not have been there, and I felt a sour feeling in my gut at my exclusion. The moment passed quickly—Anna was too considerate to neglect me for long—but the feeling remained. And now, aware of it for the first time, I noticed that the way she looked at and responded to Zeppo was subtly different from the way she looked at and responded to me. I could fool myself no longer. The time of procrastination was over.

If I had still been in any doubt, it was wiped out only minutes later. The residue of her laughter still about her, Anna excused herself and went to the toilet. Zeppo waited until she was out of earshot before leaning closer.

"Donald, old son, why don't you fuck off home and let the two of us get on with it?"

My mouth went dry. I took a drink, stalling. "I think it would look rather suspicious if I left now."

"Balls. It'll just look like you're being romantic. She'll be grateful to you for it." He grinned. "Almost as much as she will to me."

I searched desperately for excuses. This was neither the time nor the place to have this conversation. "No. Not tonight."

"Oh, for Christ's sake, Donald, come on! I've been holding back so far because you said it was too early. Well, now it's not. If I don't do something soon the poor cow'll be rubbing herself against the table leg!"

"You're disgusting!"

"And you're an old fart. Look, do you want me to fuck her or don't you? If you don't, let me know now, because I'm sick of pissing around. If you do, then tonight's as good a time as any. You wanted to know in advance, I'm telling you. So which is it to be?"

"I'm not going to be forced into—"

"Nobody's forcing you to do anything. If you don't want to leave now, fine. Stay. But I'm still going to take her back to my flat afterward. Okay?"

His attitude angered me. "No," I said, emphatically.

Zeppo balled his fists. "Jesus Christ! What is the *matter* with you? All right, why? Why not? Give me one good reason!"

I looked around to make sure no one was listening. "I'm not prepared to discuss it now."

"Well, too fucking bad, because you're going to! I've had enough of your little games. Either tell me why I shouldn't screw her tonight, or I will anyway!"

"Don't you dare!" I had actually begun to shake. Right then I wished I had never set eyes on him.

"Why not? We're both consenting adults. Anna's a big girl, she can make her own mind up. So how are you going to stop us?"

I was almost choking. "I'm warning you, if you do I won't give you a penny!"

He was grinning now, infuriatingly sure of himself. "So what? At this rate I'll be dead of old age before I get anything anyway. Besides, she might be so good I won't be bothered about being paid."

Abruptly, his entire demeanor changed. The sneering face became solicitous. "Are you sure you don't want a doctor?" he asked.

I was thrown completely off balance. And then Anna appeared beside me. "What's the matter?"

Zeppo was looking at me with a worried expression. "Donald's got chest pains."

"No, I've . . . I'm fine," I stammered, struggling to come to grips with the new situation.

"Are they bad?" Anna looked and sounded concerned.

"No, really . . ."

"You're a bit flushed," Zeppo said. The foul-mouthed, threatening creature of only moments ago had vanished. "Do you feel out of breath at all?"

"No, I'm fine," I said, trying to sound normal and immediately sounding breathless.

"Do you want me to call a doctor?" Anna asked.

"I'm all right, really." I forced a smile. "It was probably indigestion. It's gone now."

"Perhaps we'd better go," Zeppo said to Anna, and I suddenly realized what he was trying to do.

"No!" I insisted. "There's no need. I feel fine. Really."

Anna still looked worried. "I think we should go. It's getting late anyway."

Despite my objections, I could do nothing to dissuade her. We left the bar, and Zeppo hailed a taxi. Before I could stop him, he had given my address to the driver.

"We should drop Anna off first," I said, desperately.

"I'd rather see you home," she said. "I can be dropped off later."

"But you live nearer."

"I think we'd both feel happier seeing you home first." There was nothing in Zeppo's voice to suggest the glee I knew he would be feeling. "The sooner you get to bed, the better. You'll probably feel better after a good night's sleep."

There was nothing I could do. Helpless, I sat silently, aware of the occasional concerned glances from Anna. Quite probably I did not look at all well. By that time I did not feel it.

The taxi stopped outside my house, and I reached for my wallet. But Zeppo put his hand on mine, preventing me from taking out any money. "Don't worry about paying," he said. "This one's on me."

He leaned over and opened the door for me to get out. I could think of no reasonable excuse not to. His face was deadpan as Anna wished me good night and made me promise to call the doctor if the chest pains returned. I stood on the street as the door was slammed and the taxi pulled away. Anna waved through the rear window. So did Zeppo. Then they turned a corner and disappeared.

Almost beside myself with anger and panic, I let myself in and poured a drink. I forced myself to give the taxi enough time to drop Anna off and take Zeppo home and then telephoned him. My hand shook as it held the receiver. The phone rang hollowly in my ear, but no one answered. I almost called Anna then. But I could not openly ask if Zeppo was with her, and I could think of no other excuse to call.

I made myself wait five minutes and then tried Zeppo's number again. Then I waited another five. And another. I had lost count of the number of times I tried, and then there was a *click* as the receiver was picked up at the other end.

"Zeppo?" My heart jumped and began to race. But the voice at the other end was not the one I expected.

"Hello?" It was an old woman's, thin and querulous. Anticlimax made me feel leaden.

"I'm sorry, Wrong number."

"Who?"

"I've dialed the wrong number. I'm sorry to have bothered you." I was about to put the receiver down, but she spoke again.

"Who are you?" Her voice was raised and feeble. I spoke a little louder.

"I said I've got the wrong number. I'm sorry."

"Who did you want?"

"Someone called Zeppo. I must have misdialed."

"Steptoe?"

I closed my eyes. "No. It doesn't matter. I'm sorry if I disturbed you."

"There's nobody here called Steptoe."

"No, I know. My mistake."

"What?"

"I said I know!"

"Why'd you call me, then?"

"It was a mistake. I'm sorry. Goodbye."

Her voice was becoming louder and more irritable. "Do you know what time it is?"

I hung up. Exasperated, I called Zeppo again, making sure to dial the right number. When the phone was answered almost immediately, I expected to hear the old woman's voice. But this time it was him.

My first overriding emotion was relief. But that was quickly lost in a surge of anger. "How *dare* you do that to me!" I shouted. "How *dare* you!"

"Hello, Donald. You're not miffed about something, are you?"

I could almost see his smirk. "This time you've gone too far! How *dare* you?"

"You've said that twice already."

"Where's Anna?"

"She's in the bedroom. Just a second, I'll call her."

Before I could say anything, I heard him shout, "Anna, get dressed, it's Donald. He wants a word with you."

I was paralyzed. I tried to make myself hang up, but nothing happened. I felt hot panic as I waited for Anna's voice.

"Just kidding," Zeppo's said instead. "Bet that had you shitting yourself, didn't it?"

My legs would suddenly not support me. I sat down, trembling.

"Donald? You still there?"

"Yes." My voice sounded weak. I tried to clutch at my anger for support. "I don't find your sense of humor very amusing."

"Better than not having one." He laughed. "Oh, come on, Donald, you asked for it. It serves you right."

I did not know which of his moods I disliked the most, sullen, aggressive or playful. "Where is Anna?" I asked, a faint anxiety still lurking at the back of my mind.

"Safe and sound at home. We stopped off for a drink at a pub, and then I escorted her to her door. All very proper, don't worry. I didn't even give her a good-night kiss."

Reaction was beginning to set in. I lacked the energy to argue. "I trust you enjoyed your little joke?"

"Yes, I did, actually. But just think of it as a warning. Next time I won't be joking. I'm tired of being messed around. I don't like being treated like hired help, and if it happens again I won't just leave Anna on her doorstep. So either tell me what you're playing at, or you can shove your money and your pictures, and I'll fuck her anyway. What's it to be?"

I rubbed my eyes. I felt very tired. Suddenly, I could not wait to get him off the line. "I'll meet you after I close tomorrow. At your flat."

"What's wrong with now?"

"Tomorrow," I repeated. "I'll tell you then."

Chapter

22

"There's a Mr. Dryden on the line for you."

Anna waited expectantly, but although I had heard the words they failed to register. I shook myself. "I'm sorry, Anna. What did you say?"

"There's a Mr. Dryden on the phone. Shall I tell him you're busy?"

"No. No, that's all right, I'll speak to him." I was in the back room of the gallery, ostensibly to finish cleaning a tobacco-stained oil. But the materials lay almost unused at my feet, the canvas as dirty as before, except for one corner where the colors shone through more brightly. I had managed that much before my mind wandered.

"Are you all right?" Anna asked. She had been solicitous all day, concerned after my "chest pains" of the previous night. But I had been too preoccupied to feel touched. I smiled reassuringly.

"Fine! Just daydreaming." That was almost the truth. The meeting with Zeppo that evening was preying on my mind, but there was another reason for my distraction.

I had had the dream again.

Once again I was in the same room as before, watching my mother brush her hair. But this time there was nothing comforting in the sight. The feeling of contentment and security had gone. Instead, as I lay on the sofa and watched her hair gleam in the firelight, I was filled with apprehension. Each crackle of the fire, each brushstroke, seemed pregnant with impending catastrophe. I knew that something terrible was about to happen but had no idea what. I could only lie there, my anxiety growing with each moment, waiting for the unknown disaster to arrive.

This time when the doorbell rang in the dream I did not wake up. I saw my mother put down her brush and come toward me. The white silk of her robe glowed in the half-light as she studied me for a moment before walking from the room. There was a pause. I heard the door being opened and listened in dread to the murmur of voices. My mother's and one other. A man's. A stranger's.

Then my mother laughed, and my fear became panic. I knew with awful certainty that the moment had arrived, and with utter terror I heard her say, "It's all right. He's asleep."

I woke. I was sweating. I stared around my room, heart bumping, until I realized where I was. Gradually, I calmed down. But I could not go back to sleep. I lay and stared at the ceiling, watching it lighten with the approaching dawn. I could not understand why the dream had been so disturbing. It was not as though it had been a nightmare. It was just a dream, after all. There was nothing in it to justify such a strong reaction.

But telling myself that had done little good. Even daylight had failed to lift the mood of foreboding the dream had instilled. I almost had another accident on the way into the gallery, and since arriving I had been unable to concentrate on anything for more than a few minutes.

Now, with Anna watching me, I began to walk to the telephone in the gallery before I realized what I was doing and stopped.

"I'll take it in the office."

I went upstairs and closed the door. I picked up the telephone. "Thank you, Anna." There was a click as she replaced the other receiver. "Donald Ramsey speaking."

"Hello, Donald. It's Charles Dryden here." The voice was

plummy and rather smug. "I thought I'd let you know that I've come by one or two new pieces you might be interested in."

At one time that would have been enough to make my stomach knot with excitement. Dryden was a specialist dealer in erotica. I had dealt with him several times in the past, although I did not particularly like the man. He had no feel for the pieces that passed through his hands. To him they were simply objects to be bought and sold, appreciated in direct proportion to their market value. But he had his uses. I had come by several beautiful pieces through him. And, indirectly, I had him to thank—or blame—for my present situation. It had been in the back room of his shop that I came across the examples of Zeppo's less public modeling work.

Now, however, my customary excitement was diluted to a mild curiosity. "Oh yes?"

"Two Rowlandson prints. And a Fuseli." The way he said this last implied a silent fanfare.

"A Fuseli? Authenticated?"

"Of course." He sounded slightly indignant. Despite his merchantlike motives, he still had professional pride. "No doubt about it. I'd put it as one of his later courtesan drawings. It's from the same collection as the Rowlandsons. They've all got unimpeachable provenances. But the Fuseli is quite exceptional. Absolutely exquisite."

I distrusted this last piece of information, since Dryden's aestheticism was purely monetary in nature. But he was rarely mistaken about the authenticity of his pieces, and a Fuseli, exquisite or not, was a find indeed. Any serious collector would be desperate to possess it. Not long ago so would I. Now I found myself completely unmoved.

"I appreciate your letting me know, but I think I'll have to pass on them," I said.

"Oh." Dryden's surprise was obvious. "They are all excellent pieces. Particularly the Fuseli. I'm sure that would be very much to your taste."

"Quite possibly, but I'm afraid I'll still have to say no."

"Well, of course that's up to you. But I think you'll regret it.

Perhaps you'd like to see them before you make up your mind . . . ?"

"I don't think that's necessary. I'm really not interested in buying just now."

There was a subtle change in his tone. "In that case, perhaps you might be interested in selling? I know you have a sizeable collection yourself. If you're considering letting go of one or two pieces, I'm sure we could come to some arrangement."

With shock, I realized he thought my reasons were financial. My dislike for him grew. "I've no intention of either buying or selling. I simply don't want to add to my collection at the moment."

He picked up the coldness in my voice. Now I was no longer a prospective client, he responded to it. "That's your choice, Mr. Ramsey. I'm certain I don't need to tell you what an opportunity you're missing. But I'm sure you have your reasons. If you change your mind—about anything—you know where to find me."

"Thank you. I don't think I will." I hung up before he could, furious that he should have the nerve to try to patronize me. The man was nothing more than a common trader. I had no doubt that Dryden had already made, or was planning to make, similar telephone calls to other possible buyers, hoping to play them off against each other in a blind auction. I was glad that I had robbed him of at least one potential bidder. But as I began to calm down, I began to think about what he had said and wonder if he had not had a point. Although I had no financial need, perhaps I should consider selling some of my pieces. They no longer held any fascination for me, and there is no point in keeping anything once the passion for it has gone.

Then I remembered my meeting that evening with Zeppo, and suddenly my collection and Dryden and his wares seemed unimportant. Even the unsettling influence of the dream finally faded into the background in the face of this much more real crisis. This was the watershed. Everything depended on Zeppo's reaction to what I told him.

Shaking off the last wisps of my earlier abstraction, I focused my energies on preparing myself for the coming confrontation, imagining almost every permutation of Zeppo's possible reactions to what I had to say and preparing my arguments in advance. There was one, however, that I shied away from considering too closely. Refusal.

Even so, fear of it was very much with me later that afternoon as I said good night to Anna, closed the gallery and drove to Zeppo's flat.

He answered the door with a sardonic grin on his face. "Nice of you to drop by." I had nothing to say. I followed him inside silently. "Drink?"

"A brandy, if you have it."

"Oh, I think I might just be able to rustle one up." He went over to a black table that held a vast collection of bottles. From what I could see, they were all costly and famous brands. But not necessarily the best. His knowledge of quality seemed to depend largely on name and price, and I reflected that his modeling career must pay better than I expected. The room too was expensively, if rather gauchely, decorated. But I was not really concerned with that just then. He handed me a drink and sprawled on the huge black leather settee opposite. He smiled condescendingly.

"So. Confession time."

I looked into my glass. "It's hardly a matter of confession. More making sure we understand each other."

"Donald, you can call it whatever the fuck you like so long as you tell me what you're playing at."

"I'm not 'playing' at anything."

"Well, you certainly seem to have been making up new rules as we go along. So come on, let's have it. What's been going on in that devious little head of yours?"

"You're making this sound much more Machiavellian than it is. I've not been plotting anything, I assure you."

"What is it, then? Second thoughts?"

"No, not at all. Far from it."

"So what's wrong? Either you still want me to get Anna into bed or you don't. Which is it?"

I could not look at him. "Yes. I do."

"Then why all this pissing about?" There was an impatient edge to his voice. I could feel him staring at me. There was no avoiding it now.

"Because . . ." I stopped. The words refused to come.

"Yes? Because?" Zeppo prompted. "I'm waiting, Donald."

I wondered if he already knew. It would be like him to torment me.

"Because I want to watch," I said.

When there was no immediate response, I looked up. He was staring at me dumbly. I felt a small flicker of satisfaction. Obviously he had not guessed after all.

"You want to *watch*?" he echoed.

"Yes."

His poise reasserted itself. The smile came back: he relaxed into the sofa. "Fine. I'm sure Anna won't mind. We'll just put a chair by the bed for you. Would you like some popcorn as well?"

"I'm serious."

"So am I. Is there anything else you'd like while we're at it? Any more surprises you've got lined up for me?"

"No."

"Oh, good."

"I don't find your facetiousness amusing."

He snorted. "Well, what did you expect? Congratulations? Jesus!" He looked sharply over at me. "You do just want to watch, don't you? You're not thinking about joining in as well?"

"Of course not!"

"Don't look so appalled, Donald. You're hardly in a position to start with the moral outrage routine." He gave an incredulous laugh. "All your prudishness when I've talked about fucking her, and it turns out you're nothing but a dirty old man who gets his kicks by watching someone else shaft the girl he fancies."

"It's not like that."

"Oh, no, of course it isn't. What is it, then? Scientific interest?"

"I'm paying you. I don't have to explain my motives as well."

"Donald!" His tone was teasing. "You want to share a beautiful moment with me and you won't even tell me why? Shame on you!"

I could feel my face burning. "You already know why. This . . . this is the nearest I can get to . . . to possessing Anna myself. I don't think it's too much to ask."

"Oh, don't you?" Zeppo gazed at me, a half smile on his face. "And don't you think Anna herself might have something to say about it? Or do you seriously think she won't mind you having a ringside seat?"

I looked into my glass. "Anna doesn't have to know anything about it."

Zeppo's smile grew. "Ahh, I get it now. You want your own private peep show! You sly old voyeur, you!"

"Do you have to demean everything?"

"What is there to demean? Having someone's boyfriend bumped off so you can hide in a closet and slobber while she's serviced by a paid stud is hardly a noble enterprise, is it?"

"I don't think your moral record entitles you to criticize anyone."

"Who's criticizing? All it boils down to is that you want to get your rocks off, and if this is how you like doing it, then that's up to you. I'm just pointing out that you've got nothing to be pious about."

"I didn't expect you to understand."

"Oh, I understand all right. Probably better than you do." His smirk was infuriating.

"Whether you do or you don't doesn't concern me. All I want to know is if you'll cooperate."

The leather hissed and creaked as he lounged farther back on the sofa. "What if I don't?"

"Aren't you forgetting the little matter of certain photographs?"

"Fuck 'em. You daren't use them now. So as I say, what if I say no?"

I kept my face deadpan. "Then I'll find someone else."

"You think you can?"

"It would be inconvenient, but I don't see why not."

"And what about what you owe me so far?"

"I expect a settlement could be made. But since you wouldn't have done what I originally employed you for, it probably wouldn't be very large."

"And what about Marty?"

"I'd take that into consideration. But that was a side issue, not the main one."

Grinning, Zeppo shook his head. "Donald, you're unbelievable. A prick, but unbelievable. All right, it's no skin off my nose. If you want to watch an artist at work, who am I to spoil your fun?"

His tone was indulgent, an adult conceding a favor to a child, but I did not care. I took a drink of brandy to steady myself and hide my relief.

"There's still the little problem of Anna, though, isn't there?" he went on. "How do you propose working it so she doesn't realize she's on *Grandstand*? Unless you've changed your mind about drugging her?"

"No," I said, firmly. "Nothing like that."

"Why? She wouldn't mind what we did then. You could even have a go yourself afterward, if you wanted."

"That is a disgusting suggestion!"

He laughed. "I thought you'd like it. Don't worry, I'm only kidding. I don't think I could face the thought of a threesome with you. But I still think doping her might not be a bad idea. It'd make things much easier."

"No. That's out of the question." I had not gone through all this just to see Anna in a drug-induced stupor.

Zeppo shrugged. "Okay. It was only an idea. But while we're on the subject . . ." There was a small lacquered wooden box on the low coffee table. He opened it and took out a mirror and a quantity of white powder. I watched as he divided the powder into two thin lines on the surface of the mirror and, with a smile at me, sniffed them sharply, one into each nostril.

"Wow." He blinked several times, still inhaling. "That's hit the spot. Want some?"

"No, thank you."

"Suit yourself." He repacked the box and closed it. He wiped his eyes. "You were saying. Drugs are out."

"I take it that little display was supposed to upset me?"

"Now why would I want to do that? I just felt like a little snort, that's all. Helps me put my thinking head on. If you ever want a little something yourself, by the way, let me know. I'm competitively priced."

Despite myself, I was shocked. "You mean you sell the stuff? You're a dealer?"

He smiled, enjoying himself. "We're both dealers, Donald. Supply and demand. Don't worry, though. I only dabble. I've not got around to selling it to schoolkids yet. Just one or two friends."

I wondered how much more there was about him I did not know. I tried not to let him see how shaken I was, but he must have guessed from my expression. He laughed.

"Come on, Donald. You know me. I'll do anything. It all helps to keep the wolves from the door, doesn't it? Pay for those little luxuries." He held up the lacquered box and waggled it. "And this little luxury isn't cheap, believe me."

I made an effort to compose myself. "Whatever you do with the rest of your time doesn't concern me. We were talking about Anna."

"Yes, that's right, we were, weren't we? You want to watch me fuck her, but you disapprove of using drugs on moral grounds. That's about right, isn't it?" He had the same bright-eyed look about him I had seen before. Now I knew why. I said nothing. "So, since drugs are out, how do you suggest we do it?"

I shut my mind to everything else and applied myself to the problem at hand. I had had weeks to think about it. "Can I see the rest of your flat?" I asked.

❧

After he had shown me around and I had explained my idea, we sat down again to discuss the finer details. For the moment, our differences were forgotten. Finally, Zeppo nodded.

"Fair enough. I'll pass that. But it'll take a day or two to sort it out."

"That doesn't matter. We should have plenty of time before the weekend. Provided Anna proves as amenable as you think." The thought brought with it a cold jolt.

"Don't worry. She is." His confidence was complete.

"Can you think of anything we haven't considered?"

Zeppo pursed his lips. "No," he said after a second. "So what happens now?"

I felt the first heady touch of euphoria. The last doubts and fears had gone.

"You can ask us both to dinner," I said.

Chapter

23

The shadows were lengthening and the day had lost much of its earlier heat when I turned onto the street where Zeppo lived. I pulled into the first available parking space, edging in between a Citroën and a motorcycle.

"I think his flat is a bit farther up," Anna said.

"Is it? What number are we at?"

"Twenty-two. He lives at fifty-eight, doesn't he?"

"Yes, you're right. I wasn't thinking." But by that time I had turned the engine off. "Ah, well. At least we've found a space."

We left the car and walked the rest of the way to Zeppo's flat. It was only a short distance but enough to make my car difficult to pick out, I saw as we climbed the steps. I rang the doorbell. After a moment Zeppo opened the door, smiling.

"Come in." He smelled crisply of cologne. I stood back and let Anna enter first. She wore a sleeveless white blouse that just hung to the waistband of her loose white skirt. When she moved, a thin brown strip of flesh was sometimes visible. Her tan had faded a little since she had returned from holiday, but the past week had been cloudless and hot, and she had clearly been in the sun that afternoon. Her skin was golden and glowing, and her hair gleamed with copper highlights.

I followed her inside. A warm aroma of cooking greeted us. Anna sniffed. "Something smells good."

"That's the furniture polish. We're having sandwiches."

I laughed obligingly and hoped Zeppo would hurry up and offer us a drink. I needed something to help me relax. Both Anna and Zeppo appeared perfectly at ease, but that was hardly surprising. Seduction was no novelty for Zeppo, and Anna was as yet unaware that this evening would be different from any other. I, on the other hand, was a bag of nerves.

With the end actually in sight, it had been harder than ever to patiently wait for the last few days to pass. Zeppo had called into the gallery the morning after our meeting and invited us both to dinner on Saturday. I had held my breath until Anna accepted, but the shock came from Zeppo, not her.

"It's a bit of a farewell celebration, actually," he had said. "I'm going to Brazil on Monday."

That was news to me. "You lucky devil!" Anna said. "How long for?"

"Only two or three weeks. I'm modeling beachwear again. I wanted to do it in Blackpool, but they insisted on shooting in Rio, so what can you do?"

I had not known what to make of this at all. I confronted him alone later. "Why didn't you tell me you were going away?" I demanded.

"Because I didn't decide to until this morning."

"You mean there is no modeling job?"

"Donald, you can be amazingly dense sometimes. That's right, there is no modeling job. I was telling porkies."

"Why? Why complicate things?"

"Why does it complicate things? If anything, it'll make it easier. Give Saturday evening the poignancy of leaving. Parting is such sweet sorrow and all that crap. Besides which, it'll get me out of the way afterward. Stop her from pestering me."

"And what if something goes wrong? What if you don't manage to . . . to . . ."

"To fuck her?" He grinned. "Don't worry, I will. Don't be such an old woman, Donald."

"I'm not being anything, except prudent. I don't want to have to wait another three weeks, that's all. Not now."

"You won't, I've told you."

A sudden thought struck me. It had never occurred to me before, and I was horrified to think I had overlooked something so simple. "What if Anna *can't*, though?"

"What do you mean, 'can't'?"

I had the feeling he knew perfectly well what I meant. I struggled for a delicate way of phrasing it. "I mean what if it's . . . if it's her time of the month?"

Zeppo cocked his head, smirking. "If you're talking about her having a period, don't worry. She won't be."

"How can you be sure?"

"Because it's Saturday."

He said it as though that explained everything. I hesitated, unwilling to show my ignorance. But I had to ask. "What has that to do with it?"

"Come on, Donald. Even you must know that girls don't have periods at weekends."

He said it so seriously that for a moment I was unsure. It was not a subject I had ever had cause to acquaint myself with. Zeppo laughed delightedly.

"Oh, for fuck's sake, Donald, I knew you were naive, but I didn't think even you were that gullible!"

I stood there, stiffly embarrassed, until he had finished laughing at me. "I repeat, how can you be sure?"

Zeppo wiped his eyes, still grinning. "Because I saw she had a packet of tampons in her handbag ages ago and made a note of the date. Unless she's in the habit of carrying them around with her all the time, we're well in the clear. And even if we weren't, it wouldn't necessarily matter. I tell you what, I'll get you a sex-education pamphlet. You can read it before this Saturday—so you know what's going on."

His ridicule had stung but been quickly forgotten in the face of my growing excitement. The scene I had imagined ever since I had seen Anna naked in the mirror would soon be a reality. All I had to do was wait a few more days.

Now, however, the waiting was nearly over, and the thought of what was going to happen in a matter of hours made me feel giddy. And, after the first drink, garrulous.

"You know, Zeppo, if anyone had told me you were a cook I wouldn't have believed them, but that smells very good indeed. What is it?"

"Gambas a la plancha," he said from the kitchen, from where sizzling sounds were emanating. "Or prawns fried with garlic, if you prefer. Followed by paella."

I smiled over at Anna. "I take it we're in for a Spanish evening, then. Actually, I was thinking about paella just the other day and wishing I knew a good Spanish restaurant in London so I could have it more often. It never tastes the same when you cook it at home." I realized my gaffe and immediately became flustered. "Well, it never does when I try it, that is. I'm sure that yours is much more authentic, Zeppo. It certainly smells delicious. You'll have to give me the recipe for it before you go on holiday. But you're not going on holiday, are you, I was forgetting. I meant to work. Brazil."

"Anna, could you just stir these while I take the bread through?" Zeppo asked.

"Yes, sure." She went into the kitchen, leaving me sweating and confused in the lounge. Zeppo came out carrying a basket of cut French bread.

"More wine, Donald?" he asked, and as he leaned to take my glass, hissed, "For fuck's sake stop gabbling!"

He went back into the kitchen, and when Anna came out I excused myself and went to the bathroom. I splashed water onto my face and drank a little from the tap. Then I sat on the edge of the bath and took deep breaths until I felt composed enough to face them again.

Zeppo was just bringing in the prawns. I sat down at the table, the three of us forming a triangle, and occupied myself with a piece of bread. I had no appetite, and my only lasting impression of the food is that it was hot. I burned my mouth on the first forkful and ate without taste or pleasure. But Anna was loud in her praise, so I joined in, taking care not to sound too effusive.

Luckily, that was no longer a problem. From being unable to

shut up, I suddenly found myself with nothing to say. I smiled and laughed and otherwise responded to the conversation but contributed little to it. It was a struggle not to constantly keep looking at my watch, and as the minutes passed the urge became stronger and I grew even more silent.

But neither Anna nor Zeppo seemed to notice. They had enough to say without help from me, and each listened raptly whenever the other was talking. Even I could not help but be aware of the frisson between them, and that part of me that was not anxiously watching the time felt a glow of paternal pride at being responsible for bringing them together.

Then the telephone rang. I jumped, jolted out of my trance, and spilled wine on my hand.

"Excuse me," said Zeppo and went to answer it. I dabbed at the wine, thankful that Anna did not appear to have noticed. She was watching Zeppo.

I forced myself not to stare as I heard him say, "Hello? Yes, that's right. Okay . . . Yes, he is. Just a second." He turned to me. "It's for you, Donald. Somebody called Roger Chamberlain."

I did my best to look surprised as I went and took the receiver from him. "Hello?" I said. The dial tone hummed steadily in my ear. "No, of course I don't mind. How on earth did you know where to find me?" I paused. The tone continued. "Oh, so I did. No, that's okay. Is everything all right?" I glanced over at the table. Anna and Zeppo were studiously trying to mind their own business. "Oh, no! You haven't! That's awful! What have they taken?" Again, I paused. "And have they left a mess?" I sighed loudly. "That's terrible. I don't know what to say." In fact, I really was running out of ideas. The dial tone was an unimaginative prompter. "Yes . . . yes . . . no . . . No, of course not. Yes, I'm sure. About an hour, okay? Yes, I'll see you soon."

I hung up and went back to the table. "Bad news?" asked Zeppo.

I sat down. "Yes, it was, rather. That was a friend of mine. He's just got back from holiday and found he's been burgled. It sounds like they've left his house in an awful mess and taken almost everything that's not nailed down. He's in a terrible state."

"Has he called the police?" Anna seemed suitably convinced.

"Yes. They've already been, but they weren't very helpful, apparently. He wants me to go over. He had quite a nice little collection of watercolors, and most of those are missing, but what's upset him even more is that whoever did it defaced the ones they've left. He wondered if I'd go over and see if they can be salvaged. You don't mind, do you, Zeppo?"

"No, of course not."

"Do you have to go straight away?" Anna asked. "Couldn't it wait until tomorrow?"

"Well, I suppose it could, but I think he would like someone to talk to. He lives by himself, and it must have been quite a shock for him." I hoped Anna would not question me too closely, but I was flattered that she wanted me to stay.

"How can anyone do anything like that?" she said. "It's bad enough stealing something, but spoiling what's left . . ." She shook her head.

"Sickening," agreed Zeppo. "Can you stay for dessert, or do you have to go now?"

I looked at my watch. The hands and numerals formed a cipher that meant nothing to me. Now that the moment had come, the time was unimportant. "I think I'd better. I told him I'd be there in an hour, and he lives quite a way away." I had a sudden moment of panic, my mind a blank, as I waited for Anna to ask exactly where he lived. But she did not.

"I just hope the police catch them," she said. "Have they left any fingerprints?"

"He didn't say." I stood up, forestalling further inquiry. "I'd better go. Thanks for the meal, Zeppo. I'm sorry to have to dash like this."

He stood up. "That's okay. I'll see you to the door."

Anna began to get up as well. "No, don't bother," I said quickly. "You stay where you are. I'm disturbing everyone enough." I bent and kissed her cheek. Her skin felt hot and taut. "Have a nice evening."

She said goodbye, and I followed Zeppo into the hallway. "Proper little Olivier, aren't we?" he muttered. Then, raising his voice, he opened the front door a crack and said, "'Bye, Donald. I hope your friend gets his things back."

"So do I. Sorry to have to go like this."

"Don't worry about it. I'll talk to you later. 'Bye."

"Goodbye."

Zeppo put his finger to his lips and firmly closed the door. I followed him back down the hall, careful not to make a noise. Before we came to the lounge, another door stood open. I went inside and Zeppo quickly pulled it shut behind me.

I put my ear against it. "What a shame," I heard Zeppo say, and then his voice was cut off as he closed the lounge door. I listened for a moment longer but could make out nothing but indistinct murmurs.

I relaxed for the first time that evening. I looked around the room. It was dim, a fabric blind covering the single window. A chair waited by the wall. Next to it was a low table on which stood a glass, a jug of water and a bottle of brandy. There was also a small penlight and an object I did not at first recognize. I moved nearer and saw it was a wide-necked cardboard bottle, the sort used by hospital patients to relieve themselves. I was impressed by Zeppo's foresight. That was something I had not considered. But then I saw the note underneath it. "You can use this for whatever you want. The tissues are on the dressing table." When I realized what he meant I put the bottle down again, angrily.

I sat in the chair and examined the wall in front of me. There was a hole in it, several inches deep and large enough to accommodate my head when I leaned forward. It exposed a thin skin of plaster and wooden laths, and in this another, smaller hole had been made. It looked like a miniature letterbox. I peered through it but could make out little in the failing light. Satisfied that everything was as it should be, I sat back in the chair and poured myself a small brandy.

So far, except for my earlier bout of nerves, it had all gone as planned. The telephone call had come as Zeppo had promised. He had ordered an alarm call from the operator for some point during the evening but refused to tell me when. "You'll only be counting down if I do. It'll seem more natural if you don't know when to expect it." It had also been his idea to use a fictitious rather than real friend. "If you're going to lie, make sure you can't be found out," he had said. I had bowed to his experience.

I looked at my watch, straining to read its face. Only a few minutes had passed, but the room was already noticeably darker. The window gave out onto the rear garden, where no streetlight would brighten it. Restless, I crossed over to the door and listened again. Anna and Zeppo's voices were just audible, but I could make out nothing of what they were saying. I hesitated and then opened the door an inch.

Immediately, I felt a sudden surge of déjà vu. Unbalanced, I tried to shake it, but the feeling remained. For a moment I felt on the verge of identifying it. Then the sensation had passed. Disregarding it, I concentrated on listening to the voices in the other room.

". . . of mine. But he came home while they were still in the house," I heard Zeppo say.

"Oh, no!"

"Yeah, but Alex lives in a world of his own and went straight to the kitchen to make a cup of coffee. So, like an idiot, he sat there sipping his Nescafé, while the rest of his house was looted!"

I heard Anna laugh. "You're joking!"

"No, honestly. I saw him the next day. Apparently, he sat there for half an hour, and it was only when he went to the loo and saw that the front door was open that he began to wonder what was happening. And even then it wasn't until he noticed his TV had gone that he realized he'd been burgled."

"Didn't he hear anything?"

"Oh, yeah. He said he'd heard all these bumps and thuds but didn't think anything of it. Just thought it was the house creaking! I told him he should either get a burglar alarm or move to a quieter house."

They both laughed. Anna said something I could not catch, and I heard a chair scrape back. I tensed, ready to close the door, but then Zeppo's voice came again, fainter than before. He was in the kitchen. I opened the door another crack, trying to make out what he was saying.

". . . stupid. I knew I'd forgotten something." I heard what sounded like the refrigerator door opening.

"What is it?" Anna asked. "Nothing vital, I hope?"

"That depends if you call champagne vital or not." Zeppo's voice grew louder as he spoke. "Personally, I think it is. It completely slipped my mind. I got carried away with the cooking. I thought we could celebrate my new job. Even if it is just for a few weeks."

There was a muffled pop. "Whoa," Zeppo said. There was a pause. "Mmm, that's gorgeous," said Anna. "Poor Donald's missed out."

"Ah, well. We can always save him a glass. Anyway, I'd better see to that paella. It's probably stuck to the bottom of the pan by now."

"Can I help?" I could not hear Zeppo's answer, but presumably it was affirmative, because a moment later there was the sound of another chair being pushed back, and then both their voices became indistinct. I listened for a while longer, but apart from the occasional laughter, I could make nothing out. I closed the door and went back to my brandy.

I gave them time to return to the lounge and then took up my position by the door again. Muted noises were still coming from the kitchen. Then a dish clattered, and I heard Zeppo suddenly exclaim, "Ow! That's hot!"

"Put it under the cold tap." Anna's voice was more distinct now.

"No, it's okay. I'll be a martyr. If I pass out, call an ambulance."

"You're very brave."

"Don't laugh. It's worse than it looks."

"It'd have to be, I can't see anything."

"I've got a low tolerance to pain." A pause. "Is that enough for now?"

"Yes, that's plenty, thanks. It looks wonderful."

"Fresh from the tin."

"If that's from a tin, tell me where you buy them from." She gave an appreciative moan. "God, this is delicious!"

"Thank you. But you can't make it yourself like it is in restaurants, can you?"

They laughed, and I felt my face burn, knowing it was at my expense. My neck and back were aching, and I straightened, rubbing them. Careful not to make a noise, I carried the chair to the door and positioned it close to the gap. I sat down and leaned forward.

There was a hypnotic fascination in being able to eavesdrop on them. Innocent and banal as their conversation was, there was an illicit delight in being able to listen from the safety of my hiding place. Both my room and the hallway were in darkness now, and a thin band of light showed around the edge of the lounge door. I gazed at it, entranced. On the other side, Anna and Zeppo were intent on each other. I was a secret, third party to this moment of their private lives, and I gave myself up to the fantasy that neither of them were aware of my presence. I experienced a thrill of sheer, sensual pleasure and for a few heady seconds had the wild impulse to take off my clothes and listen to them naked. But of course I did no such thing. I only stared, hypnotized, at the rectangular outline of light, engrossed in the voices that came from it.

Plates were cleared, and then Anna gave a low groan. "Oh, God, is that as gooey as it looks?"

"Even more so."

"You're evil. I'll have to diet for a month after this."

"I doubt it. You're not exactly fat, are you?"

"You haven't seen me in a bikini."

"No, but it sounds intriguing."

"Uh-uh. I'd hate to disappoint you."

"I don't think there's any danger of that."

I imagined Anna blushing in the ensuing silence. "More champagne?" Zeppo asked.

"I'd love some. Oh. Is that all there is left? We can't have drunk a whole bottle!"

"Unless there's someone under the table we must have. But don't worry. There's another in the fridge."

"Another! You have been splashing out."

"Well, I thought there'd be three of us."

"Don't open it just for me. I'm tipsy already."

"So am I. We can keep each other company. Anyway, if we don't drink it now it'll go off."

Anna laughed, low and throaty. There was another pop, louder this time.

"Look out, it's a live one!"

Beyond the bright outline, I pictured the champagne being poured, rising then settling in the glasses. I could almost taste it, feel intoxicated with them.

"Can I ask you a personal question?"

There was a minute's hesitation before Zeppo answered. "I should think so." A shadow of wariness was in his voice.

"Is Zeppo your real name?"

Another hesitation. "No. No, my parents weren't that cruel. My surname's Marks, with a kay, so people started calling me Zeppo. As in the Marx brothers. It sort of stuck."

I heard Anna giggle. "It could be worse. At least it's not Groucho, Harpo or Chico."

"Yeah, I get called after the boring one nobody remembers. Perhaps people are trying to tell me something."

"You're hardly boring."

"Thank you."

Neither spoke for a while. Then Anna asked, "So what is your real name?"

Zeppo hesitated again. "Oh, you don't want to know that."

"Oh, I do. Come on, it can't be that bad." Anna's diction was slightly slurred. There was a muttered answer from Zeppo, too low for me to hear. I had no doubt that was what he intended. But Anna had no such compunction. She burst out laughing.

"*Crispin?*" she exclaimed. "No! You're joking!"

"No."

"I'm sorry, I shouldn't laugh. I just can't imagine you as a Crispin!"

"Neither can I," he said, drily. "My parents were religious. They named me after a saint. Of shoemakers, would you believe? The patron saint of cobblers."

Anna was convulsed. "Oh, I'm sorry," she gasped at last. "Does anyone actually call you Crispin?"

"No, thank God. I try not to broadcast it."

"Don't worry. Your secret's safe with me. Does Donald know?"

"Probably."

"What about your parents? Do they still call you that?"

"They don't call me anything. They're dead."

I could feel the effect his words had on Anna. "I'm sorry. I didn't know." The laughter had suddenly gone from her voice.

"It's okay. No need to apologize. It happened a long time ago anyway. I was only a kid."

He seemed to be deliberately inviting questions. I wondered what he thought he was doing. "How old were you?" asked Anna.

"Thirteen. It was a car accident. I went to live with an aunt afterward. I don't think she liked kids. She certainly didn't like me. I left as soon as I was old enough."

"Do you have any brothers or sisters?"

"No, there's just me. I used to wish I had some when I was younger. I was pretty lonely for a while. But I don't suppose I have to tell you what that's like, do I?"

I listened in disbelief. I wondered if he was doing it to spite me.

"No," Anna said. Her voice was pitched very low.

"Is it still as bad?"

A small laugh. "Bloody awful, actually."

"I know it's different for you, with Marty being missing. But I can still imagine what you're going through. You've just got to give it time."

"Mm. I know. That's what everyone says. But . . . oh well, it doesn't matter."

"No, go on. Please."

There was a brief silence. "Well, I just . . . I just wish I knew what had *happened* to him, that's all!" Her voice rose, close to breaking. "If the police came and told me they'd found him, dead, I could cope with that a lot better than this not knowing. I know some people think he's just run off with someone, and sometimes I catch myself thinking that they might be right, that he might be still alive somewhere. But then that only makes it worse. I *know* he's dead, but I don't know how, or why, or if he suffered, or . . . or *anything*! It's that I can't . . ." Her voice finally broke. "I'm sorry. I'm sorry." I heard a chair being pushed back.

"Hey, it's okay. Come on."

"God!" She sniffed, loudly. "I'm such a silly cow! I'm sorry, I'd better go."

"Don't be silly."

"What a farewell party for you."

"That doesn't matter. I only used it as an excuse to see you again anyway."

She gave a shaky laugh. "I bet you wish you hadn't bothered."

"I'm glad I did."

"Thank you." Her voice was soft; calmer. "I'm all right now. Sorry for being such a crybaby."

"You're not a crybaby."

There was a long pause. "I must look a mess. I'd better clean myself up."

"You look lovely."

Another silence. It seemed to go on and on. Then Anna broke it. "Zeppo, I don't . . ." That was all. I stared at the outline of light. Anna said, "Zeppo . . ." once more, so quietly I barely heard her, and then there was nothing. I waited, wondering what they were doing, hoping Zeppo had not forgotten himself. I was considering creeping out to listen more closely when the lounge door opened.

I leaned back from the crack, not daring to close my own

door. I held my breath as I heard them cross the hallway and go into the room next to mine. Heart pounding, I quietly rose and made my way back to the adjoining wall, guiding myself by touch in the darkness. Hands outstretched, I felt the table and tentatively searched with my fingers for the hole in the brickwork. After a moment I found the smaller hole in the plaster. I stooped and put my eyes to it.

At first I could make nothing out. The room beyond was as dark as my own. Then there was a *click*, and I flinched as a bar of light shone directly into my eyes. Blinking to acclimatize them, I peered through the narrow gap.

I was looking out over an enormous bed, sideways on. An imitation Tiffany lamp now provided a soft glow. Facing me was a huge mirror. It showed the wall behind which I was hidden. A stack of shelves fixed to it held plants, books and a rack of cassettes and CDs. My spy hole was invisible among them. At the foot of the bed were Anna and Zeppo.

She had her back to him. His hands were on her shoulders, stroking. He gently turned her around until she faced him, then lowered his head and softly kissed her mouth. Anna tilted her head to him but otherwise stood passively. He kissed her again, still gentle, a mere brushing of the lips. His hands lightly stroked up and down her back. He began to kiss her more insistently, and when her arms hesitatingly went around him, he lengthened the extent of his caress until he was stroking the uppermost curve of her buttocks. But when she began to respond, he stopped.

"Anna . . . I don't want you to do anything you'll regret." His voice was low, husky. "I don't want to take advantage of you."

"You aren't." And this time she drew his head down to hers, arching herself against him. His hands ran up into her hair, pulling her head backward by it, and then one of them went to the buttons at the back of her blouse.

One by one they came undone, revealing a deepening vee of brown skin under the white fabric. He slid his hands across her bare back, one of them sliding beneath the waistband of her skirt. She tugged his shirt from his trousers and began to unfasten it. Still kissing him, she pulled it off, and as she did he slipped the skirt over her hips and let it drop to the floor. It formed a pool of white around her bare legs. I stared at it. There seemed something familiar about the sight, and again I felt a faint, uncomfortable flare of déjà vu. This time it brought with it an unaccountable flutter of unease. I hastily looked back to Anna and Zeppo, trying to ignore it. I wanted no distractions now.

Anna wore only a pair of brief white pants under the skirt. They seemed dazzling against the tanned darkness of her skin. Zeppo removed her blouse and eased them down, sliding them over the swell of her behind, and then she was naked.

She was even more splendid than I remembered. Her back was to me, and her spine arched in a deep, indented curve to the dark cleft between her buttocks. A whiter strip of skin, an echo of her bikini bottom, cleanly bisected them. Below it her thighs were strong and graceful.

Zeppo's clothes joined Anna's on the floor. She tilted her head back as he kissed her throat, his hands cupping her breasts. She hooked one leg behind his, and then he was lifting her, holding her by the buttocks as she wrapped herself around him. He turned, taking the single step that brought them to the edge of the bed, and as he lowered her onto it, I had my first sight of his body. His tan matched hers, a ruddy brown to her gold but unbroken by any strip of white, testimony to the privacy of a sunlamp. He was taut and sleek, with no fat to soften the marked definition of muscle. His member was erect, surprisingly dark and, it seemed to me, abnormally long. I had a moment's fear that it might prove impractical, and then his body came down onto hers.

She ran her hands across his back as he kissed her chest, and my breath caught when his mouth went to her breasts. His hands squeezed and cupped them as his lips encircled first one small, dark nipple, then the other. Then he was moving lower. More and more of her body was revealed as his own descended. His tongue laved her stomach, paused over her navel, then moved on. Eyes closed, she undulated slightly beneath him, hands twined in his hair. He eased between her legs, sliding down still farther until his lower body was off the bed, and the dark patch of Anna's pubic hair was visible under his mouth.

I watched, dizzily, as Anna moaned and offered herself to him. She opened her legs wider and raised her knees, obscuring all but the top of Zeppo's head. Her hands left his hair and she stretched them above her on the pillow. Eyes closed, her head lolled toward me, an intense, almost pained expression on her face. She matched the almost imperceptible motion of Zeppo's head with short, graceful movements of her hips. They gradually increased in tempo, and a small whimper came from her. Then another. Her head turned from side to side, and she groaned, arching her back so that her ribs were clearly visible under the skin. Her breasts thrust out tautly. She groaned again and suddenly reached down and with both hands pulled Zeppo's head hard against her, grinding herself into him. His hands gripped the tops of her thighs, holding her as she began to buck and thrash about, and then in one smooth motion he pushed himself back up her body, between her legs, and Anna said, "Oh, God," as his hips came up to hers.

For a moment they stayed locked like that. Then their bodies were moving slowly and rhythmically together. Zeppo supported himself on stiff arms, his chest suspended above Anna's breasts, lightly brushing them. Her legs were spread wide, knees raised, her heels digging into the bed as she pushed against him. Her eyes were shut tight, and each time their lower bodies met she gave a low moan. Her face was rapt, but Zeppo's was expressionless as he watched her writhe under him. Her hands raked down his flanks, clutching his buttocks, and as her movements became more insistent, a sensation of heat began to grow in my groin. The two bodies began to smack together more violently. He lowered his head to her breasts, sucking fiercely. She wrapped her legs around his waist, almost doubling herself up under him. He lifted his head to look down at her, his face glazed with sweat and concentration, and increased his tempo still further. She cried out, throwing her head back and tossing it from side to side, and I felt the heat in my belly spreading. She cried out again and clung to his shoulders, and as her mouth contorted in a silent scream, I looked in the mirror opposite and saw a second Anna and Zeppo framed there and almost cried out myself as I was racked by a sudden, hot spasm.

I closed my eyes, lost to it, almost fainting. Then it was ebbing, and as the tension left my limbs I sagged weakly back into the chair, only at the last moment remembering it was still by the door.

I clutched desperately at the nearby table as I staggered backward, almost knocking over the jug of water. I only just managed to retain my balance and froze, heart bumping, waiting for signs that I had been heard. But none came. Shakily, I went back to the wall and peered through the thin band of light.

Anna and Zeppo were still locked together, but now all urgency had gone. Anna lay limply, eyes closed, one hand gently stroking the nape of Zeppo's neck. Her legs slowly slid down his until they rested on the bed once more. He lay between them, supporting himself on his elbows, looking down at her with a clinical detachment that contradicted the sweat coating his body. When Anna lazily opened her eyes and smiled up at him, he smiled back: when she closed them, his smile vanished.

I should have left then. I had assumed Zeppo had reached his climax with Anna, that now they would separate, perhaps talk for a while and eventually sleep. I only wanted to linger until then, to see a rounded ending to what I had brought about. But a moment later, Zeppo again began to slowly move his hips, and it was too late for me to leave. I had to stay and watch.

His face still held its same detached expression as his buttocks began to gently rise and fall with a slightly circular motion. He studied Anna's face and supine body coldly, as though the actions of his lower body had no relationship with the rest of him. At first there was no response from her. She lay passively under him, and except for the hand that lightly stroked the back of his neck, she could have been asleep. Zeppo continued to move in the same unhurried, steady rhythm. For what seemed a long while nothing happened. Then Anna shifted slightly, a luxurious, catlike motion. Giving a low murmur, she began to stir against him.

As if this were the signal he had been waiting for, Zeppo turned his head and looked directly at me. Without breaking or altering his pace at all, he closed one eye in a slow, deliberate wink.

The acknowledgment was like a cold shock. I drew back from the hole and stood in the darkness uncertainly, almost giving way to the impulse to leave. But the urge to look back through the sliver of light overwhelmed it. Instead I fetched the chair from the doorway, sat down and put my eyes to the gap again.

I caught them as they were changing position. Zeppo was sliding his legs under Anna's, his hands behind her back, lifting her. She had her eyes open, smiling at him as they came up into a sitting position, facing each other. They kissed. Then Zeppo lay backward until he was flat on the bed and Anna was upright and astride him. She smiled.

"It's my turn now, is it?"

"I've got to save my strength."

Leaning over him, Anna began to move her hips. Her hair fell forward, curtaining her face. Her breasts swung. Zeppo reached up to fondle them, craning his neck to bring them to his mouth. She pushed him back down onto the bed and bent to kiss his chest. Lifting her hips, she began to edge slowly backward. She slid gradually down the length of his body, her hair trailing across him, obscuring her. She moved until she was kneeling between his legs and her head was above his groin, and there she stopped.

Zeppo's face, which had remained impassive, now held a flicker of animation. His eyes briefly shut, and he put his hands to Anna's head in a gesture almost of benediction. Her hair still concealed what she was doing, but then, with a glance toward me, Zeppo moved it to one side.

The gross, slimy object was in her mouth. Her lips were stretched and distended as they conformed to its shape. Hands and fingers stroked and squeezed. Her cheeks hollowed and bulged as her face descended, engulfing more, then rose until the entire length of it was exposed. Her tongue circled, ran down the shaft to its base, then retraced its path. Her lips pursed to kiss the tip before suddenly covering it once more, slobbering over it like an uncouth child with a stick of rock.

I could feel Zeppo's eyes on me. I looked away from the spectacle and saw that he was looking toward me with a expression of amused contempt. As if he knew I had chosen that moment to look at him, he gave a groan, and with both hands on the back of Anna's head, slowly thrust his hips up at her. More of him slid into her mouth as he arched his back, holding her head in place. She pulled against his grip, waiting until he subsided before descending on him in a series of quick, gulping jerks. He groaned again, louder. But when his head turned toward me, his eyes were still cold and controlled.

Abruptly, he lifted her head from him. Freed from Anna's mouth, the thing slapped wetly back against his stomach. Kneeling up, Zeppo kissed her before urging her into a new position. She swung around until her feet were toward me, and at his coaxing lay back on the bed and opened her legs. I was directly opposite. The curly, almost black hair at the juncture of her thighs was entirely visible, and so too was the pink gash that bisected it. It glistened like an open wound, even more so when Zeppo put his fingers to it and spread it wide, exposing a glutinous hole. Then Zeppo pivoted until his crotch was once more in front of Anna's face, angled her onto her side and put his mouth to the raw oval of flesh.

He kept his head tilted so I could see what he was doing. His tongue lightly circled, then pierced the oval's center with a quick stab. I lifted my gaze to the mirror and saw Anna inverted, her mouth on him as before. I looked away, back to

Zeppo. His tongue and fingers stretched, probed and manip-
ulated. Heads busy between each other's legs, they remained
locked until Zeppo pulled away and knelt upright again. His
face was flushed, and there was a new urgency to his movements as he helped Anna reposition herself on all fours. Kneeling behind her, he moved until they were angled obliquely
away from me. There was nothing now I could not see. With
one hand on her buttock, he guided himself into her with the
other, permitting me to see every detail. Then, gripping her by
the hips, he gave a brief glance in my direction and thrust into
her. Impaled, she responded by throwing back her head, exposing the line of her throat. I stared at it, clutching at its
beauty, but even that disappeared as her head sank down onto
the bed and she whimpered, rocking back on her knees to offer her rump to him more prominently.

They coupled like dogs. Zeppo grunted each time he
slapped against her with the viscous sound of disturbed mud.
His hands gripped and clutched, pulling her back onto him.
She squealed. Their rutting became more frantic. He no longer
glanced toward my hiding place. His mouth hung open slackly,
his grunts growing louder, and it was then I became aware of
the smell. Rank and feral, it came to me faintly, but once noticed it was as pervading as rotting fruit. Suddenly the sense
of déjà vu returned. For an instant my mind was taken to the
dream, and I had a brief vision of another, similar scene—*a
partly open door, peering through the crack of light, looking past
the trail of discarded clothes, past the puddle of white silk on the
carpet to the two naked, grunting figures on the bed, staring beyond the clutching white limbs to the faces*—and then I had jerked
my head away and was blundering from the room, fleeing from
the strip of light and the awful, bestial noises. I reached the
door at the end of the hallway and fumbled with the lock, unable to see in the darkness, but then I was outside and the
noises were gone, and the night was cool and empty and quiet.

I stood on the pavement in front of the house, panting. A
breeze chilled the sweat on my body, making me aware of how
damp my clothes were. When I started to shiver I walked back

to the car. I felt clammy and unclean. My clothes clung to me, sticky and abrasive. Every inch of my skin seemed sensitive to the slightest nuance of texture. The cool upholstery of the car greeted me like a balm, and I sat for a while without turning on the engine.

When I drove away, I went past Zeppo's flat without looking at it.

Chapter

24

I intended to leave the house early the next morning. But I slept late, the result of having lain awake until almost dawn. When I realized what the time was, I panicked. I quickly showered and dressed and went downstairs. The shower was a mistake, but although I had had one the night before, my body still felt soiled and sweaty. Even so, I might have escaped in time had I not lingered for a cup of coffee. I had no appetite for breakfast, but it seemed unnatural to leave the house without anything. I told myself that ten minutes would make no difference and had just taken my first sip when the telephone rang.

I did not answer. I knew who it would be and cursed myself for not leaving sooner. Or at least having the foresight to take the receiver off the hook. I tried to ignore the ringing, hoping it would stop, but the telephone continued to clamor for attention. I picked up the receiver.

"Morning, Donald. Not got you out of bed, have I?" Zeppo said.

"No."

"What's the matter with you?"

"Nothing."

"Doesn't sound like nothing."

I hated the sound of his voice. "What do you want?"

"My, we are tetchy this morning! I thought you'd be full of the joys of spring. Obviously I was wrong."

"I asked what you want."

"Well, a little civility wouldn't go amiss. But if that's too much to ask for, I thought I'd pop over and see you. Have a chat. Exchange notes. Settle up."

"I'm on my way out."

"Oh, I'm sure you can stay in for a while longer. Don't you want to talk about last night?"

"It'll have to wait."

"Donald, if I didn't know better, I'd think you were trying to avoid me. You're not, are you?"

"Of course not."

"Oh good. Then let's say I'll see you in about an hour."

"I've told you, I'm going out."

"Well, now you're not," he said, and hung up.

I was tempted to leave anyway. I had no desire to see or speak to Zeppo, and it would serve him right to have a wasted journey. But I knew I would have to face him sooner or later. I might as well get it over with.

Predictably, he was late. When I let him in he looked even more pleased with himself than usual, if that was possible.

"Who got out of the wrong side of bed this morning?" he asked. I ignored him, leaving him to follow me into the lounge. "Don't say you're not talking to me, Donald?"

I turned to face him. "I would appreciate it if we could settle this quickly. You're late as it is."

"I'll consider my wrists smacked." He went to the drinks table. "Don't mind, do you? You can have one yourself, if you like."

"No thank you."

Despite the fact that I was standing, he sat down, stretching out his legs as he took a drink. "So are you going to tell me what's wrong or not? You've got a face like a toilet pan."

"Nothing's wrong. I've simply got a lot to do, and the sooner you leave, the sooner I can get on with it."

"We really are in a shitty mood, aren't we? If you're pissed off because I'm late, it was because I took Anna home before I came here. Am I excused now, or do you want a note from my mum?"

"You mean Anna was still at your flat when you called me?"

"Put your eyes back in, Donald. She was under the shower. She didn't hear. And I didn't tell her I was coming to see you, so you've got nothing to worry about." He stretched. "Anyway, you should grumble. I was expecting a leisurely morning in bed, but the silly bitch got a sudden attack of the guilts and decided she had to go. I managed to give her a quickie in the shower after I'd called you, but that was all. I think she felt disloyal about enjoying it so much." He grinned. "That didn't seem to bother her too much last night, though, did it? What did you think of the show, by the way?"

I did not answer.

"Come on, talk to me. Was it all right or wasn't it?" I looked away, wishing he were anywhere but with me. He grinned. "Don't tell me you didn't enjoy it? Your big night?" There was mocking concern in his voice.

"You came here to collect the picture. I suggest you do that and then go."

"Where are your manners, Donald? I didn't rush you out of my flat last night, did I? Be sociable. I only want to make sure that everything was okay, that's all. I aim to please. If you've any complaints I want to hear them."

"I haven't."

He was enjoying himself. "I'm afraid I don't believe you. Come on, Donald, tell Uncle Zeppo what's upset you. I can see something has. I'm sensitive like that." He waited. I said nothing. "If you won't tell me what it is, I'll only have to guess."

I hated his games. "Nothing. Everything was fine."

"Ah-ah, Donald. You're telling fibs. Did I forget to do something, is that it? I tried to give you a selection, but I suppose I might have missed something out. If you were expecting something a bit more exotic you should have told me. I don't mind doing requests."

"The sketch is on the table. Take it and get out."

"Donald, Donald, that's no way to treat someone you've just shared a beautiful experience with, is it?" He assumed a look of exaggerated concern. "You're not jealous, are you? Is that what's wrong? You didn't like watching someone else shafting your heart's desire. Is that it?"

"Do we have to go through this charade?"

He grinned. "Yes, I'm afraid we do. You got what you wanted, and since it's pretty obvious you didn't enjoy it, I think it's only fair you tell me why. After all the trouble I went to I deserve to know that much." I remained silent. Zeppo sighed. "Okay, since you won't cooperate, on with the guessing game. Let's see, if you're not jealous, what else could it be?"

"You're enjoying this, aren't you?"

"Only trying to help. If you're not happy, I'm not happy. So why aren't you happy?"

I wanted to dent his smug composure. "Why didn't you tell me your real name was Crispin?"

His grin vanished. "Don't try and be clever, Donald. It doesn't suit you."

"I seem to have touched a nerve."

"Don't flatter yourself."

"Then it won't bother you if I tell everyone what you're really called?"

"I wouldn't try and be a smart arse if I were you. You're in no position to."

"Really? I don't see why not."

He gave a hard little smile. "Because if you piss me off, I'll punch you in the stomach until you piss blood." His smile grew less strained. "But we're getting away from what we were talking about, aren't we? About why you didn't enjoy the performance. Come on, Donald, what was the problem? Wasn't it how you imagined it?" I turned away. "Aha! I think I've touched a nerve there myself, haven't I?"

I told myself not to give him the satisfaction of responding. His face leered at me. "So actually seeing Anna shafted didn't fit your sweaty little idea of how it should be, is that it? The event didn't match the fantasy?" He smirked. "I'm right, aren't I?"

I could not keep quiet any longer. "You did it deliberately, didn't you?"

"Did what deliberately?"

"Debased everything! You deliberately set out to spoil it!"

He seemed genuinely surprised. "Spoil it? What are you talking about? How did I spoil anything?"

I knew I was making a mistake but could not stop. "You made it as obscene as you could! The things you did! All that . . . that *positioning*, so I could see everything!"

"I thought that was what you wanted?"

"Not like that! It was disgusting!"

He smirked. "Personally, I thought it was pretty good. And your precious Anna didn't seem to find it too horrible either."

"You intended to ruin it for me from the start, didn't you?"

Zeppo gave an indifferent shrug. "You wanted to watch me fuck Anna, and you did. It's not my fault if it wasn't how you imagined."

"You didn't have to make it like that!"

"*I* didn't make it like anything. That's what sex is." His voice was heavy with derision. "What the fuck did you expect? Something like one of your pretty pictures?" He snorted. "Well, it's not like that. It's not all set poses in real life. Real people move around. It's all sweaty and noisy and smelly. You should try it sometime."

I turned away. Zeppo laughed. "It's no good looking like that, Donald. It's true. Here. Smell."

He pushed himself out of the chair and thrust his fingers under my nose. I jerked my head back and knocked his hand aside, belatedly realizing it smelled only of soap and cologne. But I remembered the taint that had been in the air the night before, and with that memory came other, even less welcome images. I quickly thrust them away and turned on him.

"You disgust me!"

Zeppo's grin turned sour. "*I* disgust *you*? Christ, that's rich! Who the fuck are *you* to be disgusted by anyone?"

This was exactly the sort of scene I had wanted to avoid. "I can't see any point in continuing with this," I said, but Zeppo was not going to be put off.

"No, I bet you can't," he jeered. "Mr. Goody-fucking-Two-Shoes Ramsey! You fucking hypocrite. How can you still act self-righteous after what you've done? Jesus, you make me sick!"

"The feeling's mutual, I assure you."

"Balls! You're not capable of feeling anything!" His voice was thick with contempt. "You're a fucking eunuch, Donald! You should have stuck to collecting all those nice, hygienic pictures. They're much safer than the real thing. They don't do things you don't want them to. And you can still tell yourself it's art, can't you?" He sneered at me. "You might fool yourself, Donald, but you don't fool me. You're just another sad, dirty old man who gets his kicks looking at pictures of other people doing what he can't. Only you're too much of a coward to admit it."

His words no longer touched me. "I don't recall asking for your opinion," I said calmly.

"I don't recall giving a fuck."

We stared at each other. "If you've finished, I won't keep you. The Cocteau's over there."

He went over to the table and picked it up. "I get the frame as well, do I? I am a lucky boy."

"Not really. It's ugly and rather tasteless. Like the sketch. I imagine it will suit you perfectly."

He smiled, relaxed again. "Now, now, Donald. Sticks and stones. Can I at least have a carrier bag? You forgot to gift wrap it."

"The arrangement was for the picture. Nothing else."

"You really are a petty-minded old bastard, aren't you?" He tucked it under his arm and went into the hallway. I followed him.

"Before you leave, I'd like my check back. It will save me the trouble of canceling it."

He reached into his pocket. "Slipped my mind." He crumpled the check and threw it onto the floor. I opened the door, not out of politeness but for the satisfaction of closing it on him.

"Will you be seeing Anna when you get back?" I asked.

He pretended to frown. "Who?"

"In that case I needn't ask you not to come to the gallery again."

"I can't think of anything I'd like less. Except you." Zeppo went down the steps. "Have a nice life, Donald."

I shut the door.

I did not go into the gallery until the middle of the week. I telephoned Anna with the excuse that I was ill. It was strange speaking to her. She sounded the same as ever, unchanged. I felt as though she were someone I used to know well but who I had now lost touch with.

By Wednesday I knew I could no longer put her off from visiting me and went in. I preferred to face her at work rather than in the intimacy of my home. She was very solicitous. Smotheringly so. It was an effort not to be terse.

"What happened with your friend's collection?" she asked. "The one who was burgled," she added, when I looked blank. It took me a moment to realize what she was talking about.

"Oh . . . it wasn't as bad as he thought," I said, vaguely.

"Have the police found out anything yet?"

"No, not yet."

As soon as I could, I shut myself in the office. Anna seemed to sense my mood and left me alone. But I could not stay there forever. After a while I went back downstairs, forcing a smile as I reassured her that I was all right. She went back to her work, and I cast surreptitious glances at her as she bent over her desk. She had on a thin vest that did little to disguise her breasts. They hung loosely under it, swinging ponderously as she shifted her weight. Her thighs were flattened on the seat, meaty and ungainly. She wore shorts, and I could see the tightness of the cloth at the crotch. I thought of the undignified patch hidden there and looked away.

When she stood up and crossed the room, I watched as the flesh of her moved. Legs, arms, breasts. There seemed a heavy, bovine quality about her that I wondered how I could have missed before. Suddenly, I could see her mother waiting behind the youthful facade, could detect the sagging fleshiness of the woman she would become. She turned and saw me watching her and smiled. Her mouth stretched, and I remembered how it had slobbered over Zeppo. It struck me that it was too large for her face. Her lips were too wide, almost rubbery. I smiled back.

The anxiety I had felt about seeing her again faded. I wondered why I should have been so bothered. She was just a girl. Only her persistent intimacy prevented me from withdrawing into my old, now attractive isolation. It was a nuisance, but I was soon able to respond mechanically, without being touched by it. Even her frequent references to Zeppo left me unmoved. Like her, he belonged to the past. And that was something I chose not to dwell on.

"Have you had a postcard from him yet?" she asked one day.

"No." Then, because I felt obliged to, I added, "Have you?"

She tried to sound casual. "No. I expect he's been too busy. Or it'll arrive after he gets back."

"I expect so."

Later, she asked, "Donald, is everything all right?"

"Of course it is? Why?"

She shrugged. "Oh, I just wondered. You just seem a bit . . . I don't know . . . distant, lately."

"Do I? I'm sorry. I've got a lot on my mind."

"Anything I can help with?"

"No. Thank you." On impulse, I added, "One or two little financial problems. That's all."

She looked worried. "Bad?"

"Well . . . let's see what happens, shall we?" I gave a brisk smile and moved away. I felt a small grain of self-congratulation. I had prepared the ground. Now, if I decided to, I could always take it further. She was only an assistant, after all. There had been others before her. There would be others after.

One day she came up to me with a bright smile on her face. "Guess what? A friend of mine's started work at the Barbican and can get us complimentary tickets for the Russian ballet this Saturday! If you can make it, of course."

I looked disappointed. "This Saturday? Oh, I'd love to, but I've already arranged something."

"Oh. Oh well, never mind." She smiled and shrugged. "It doesn't matter. I just thought you might like to go."

"Another time, perhaps."

෨෬

I waited one more week before I called Charles Dryden.

"Good to hear from you," he said. "Are you buying or selling?"

"Buying," I answered.